RAVENWOOD
Stepson of Mystery

AIRSHIP 27 PRODUCTIONS

Ravenwood Stepson of Mystery Volume 4

The Case of the Helbent Thief © 2020 L.R. Stahlberg
The Rabbi's Scourge ©2020 DeWayne Dowers
Voices in the Darkness ©2020 Michael Black
Kincaid's House of Altered Cats ©2020 Michael F. Housel

An Airship 27 Production
www.airship27.com
www.airship27hangar.com

Interior Illustrations ©2020 Ed Catto
Cover illustrations © 2020 Adam Shaw

Editor: Ron Fortier
Associate Editor:Jaime Ramos
Production and design: Rob Davis
Marketing and promotion: Michael Vance

ISBN: 978-1-946183-79-8

Printed in the United States of America

10 9 8 7 6 5 4 3 2 1

VOL IV
Table of Contents

THE CASE OF THE HELLBENT THIEF

by L.R. Stahlberg

Miriam glanced fretfully at her daughter.

"Are you sure she's…?"

"It was a very mild sedative," Father Ricci assured. "I took care with the dosage."

"I-it's not that I don't trust you. It's just…"

"You don't need to trust me Mrs. Watson," he interjected again. "Trust Him."

Miriam fidgeted with the crucifix around her neck. Theresa Watson began to stir.

"You'd best wait outside." Ricci gently guided the worried mother out. He reached for the rosary coiled on the dresser and pressed it into her hand. "Recite the prayer exactly as we practiced."

"Mommy?" the little girl mumbled from the bed. Bright blue eyes tried to peer through a mass of curly blonde hair as she straightened against the pillow. She lifted her arm to rub the bleariness from her face, blinking in confusion, then fright at the leather straps that bound her wrists to the bed post. "Mommy?" she repeated, panicked.

"I'm here, Tessie," Miriam said reflexively. "It's going to be okay." She reached out, but Father Ricci firmly held her arm.

"Mommy I'm sorry! I'll be good! Don't let him hurt me!"

"Do not listen," Ricci said firmly, physically turning her to keep her focus on him as he ushered her toward the bedroom door. "That is not your child. But we'll get her back. I swear it."

"Mommy!" Tessie shrieked. The genuine fear in the child's voice pulled Miriam's pleading eyes back toward the bed. Tears flowed freely, her face growing more desperate as she pulled in vain against the leather straps wrapped tightly about her forearms.

"Oh my God," Miriam sobbed, pulling away. "Father, please. This was a terrible mistake. Let her go."

"Mrs. Watson, no!" Ricci blocked her path with an arm across her chest and an iron grip on her shoulder. His look of momentary anger melted as their eyes met, and with gritted teeth he yanked the rosary back from her hand and whipped it at the bed with a backhand motion.

Miriam stared in abject horror as the prayer beads and cross seared into her daughter's flesh where they struck.

"Outside," Ricci ordered. When she didn't move, he added in a slightly gentler tone, "Please. You don't need to see this." At last she cut off a sob, closing her eyes against the sight of her wailing daughter, and turned to go.

And the door slammed shut.

Miriam looked at the door in bewildered shock. Father Ricci spun around to face Theresa. The little girl in the bed glared back at him through her tousled golden locks; her eyes were no longer wide with terror, but narrowed in menace.

"Oh you just made a *big* fucking mistake," the child sneered.

Ravenwood approached the front door of the modest east side apartment. He paused before it in the hall, bright green eyes regarding the numbers on either side of the peephole with wary concern. The 'nine' was hanging slightly askew and tiny strips of paint had flaked off it. Just as it had appeared to him in his vision.

The fair skinned, dark haired man had drawn his fair share of odd glances from the moment his convertible pulled in front of the building to the moment he stepped off the elevator. More curious than suspicious, though, given the way he carried himself and manner of dress; a well-tailored gray suit, wing tip shoes, gold watch, black leather driving gloves, and the presence of a walking stick despite the absence of a limp. Neighbors pegged him for an uptown playboy out for a night of fine dining and theater.

Of course, he *was*, or rather had been. Would their looks be more odd, or less, the dapper gentleman wondered, if they knew he was a private detective? Surely more, if they knew the nature of his investigations.

Once upon a time, he might have questioned an unexplained flash of cryptic images in his head and an overwhelming urgency to cut short his evening. But the Stepson of Mystery had long ago learned to never ignore such missives from the spirit world. He was needed. That was all he knew. All he needed to know.

Ravenwood rapped on the door with his silver handled cane. He held fast on the second knock, his attention caught by the muted sounds within. He cupped an ear to the door. At first he thought he heard a girl's voice, though it was difficult to tell. The sobbing pleas of the woman that followed though were unmistakable. As was the threatening tone of the man yelling over them both.

Flecks of gold appeared in Ravenwood's eyes as they narrowed and looked cautiously down the hall. Deciding that the severity of the situation precluded civility, he pulled an engraved key from his pocket and shoved it firmly into the lock. He uttered a terse phrase in Mandarin and turned the key. It didn't budge.

He let a slow breath escape through gritted teeth, feeling the brief wash of anxiety over the child's cries ebb away. He whispered the words again, turned the enchanted brass key, and pushed the door as the lock clicked open.

Ravenwood heard a door slam the instant he entered. He headed for it, and the sound of the muffled shouts beyond. He didn't have far to run. A short foyer opened immediately into a living room. A dining room branched off to the left, ending at an open doorway to a kitchen. To the right, a hallway connected four closed doors. One of them rattled violently.

He reached for the door knob, but snatched his hand back with a yelp. The metal was red hot to the touch, even through his gloves.

The ruckus within reached a fever pitch; wood crashing, glass breaking, the child screaming. Ravenwood took half a step back, practically flattening himself against the opposite wall in preparation to break down the door. In that heartbeat before his charge, he squinted quizzically. His head tilted as the man's voice inside changed cadence.

"Is that," he spoke aloud. "Latin?"

Indeed, it was. And after hearing a few more words, he recognized the Prayer of St. Michael. With that realization, he also recognized the voice canting it, and braced himself for what he now knew lay on the other side.

Ravenwood hurled himself shoulder first at the door. The hinges splintered under his weight and he barreled through.

His eyes flashed for a second from hazel to a radiant amber as they processed the chaotic scene that greeted him. A woman; early thirties, unremarkable, sandy blonde hair, shaking madly, knelt in the corner, her hands clenched in prayer. A Catholic priest; an old friend, chanting, white-knuckling the St. James Bible in one hand, a flask of holy water in the other.

And a demon; possessing the body of a girl no older than nine years, pulling wildly against leather straps. Ravenwood tried not to predict which would tear free first, the bed posts or her arms.

The room was all but destroyed. The only light filtered in through a broken window, since every lamp bulb had burst. Whatever had adorned the walls or rested atop a flat surface now lay shattered on the floor. Everything that could be flung against the wall had been. Even the furniture, save for the bed and the...

"Vincent!" Ravenwood yelled, unceremoniously grabbing the priest by his coat.

He yanked the man backwards, barely out of the path of a dresser drawer flying across the room. It impacted with such force that a crack split the wall to the ceiling. The sturdy oak cabinet toppled after it and crashed to the floor.

"Ooh," the demon cooed in the child's voice. "Get a load of fancy pants. Are we having a party, now?"

"Ravenwood!" Father Ricci exclaimed. "How did you...?"

"Not important," he interjected. "Continue the rite before it regains strength."

"It?" the Hellspawn shouted over Ricci's chanting, looking offended. "Oh I assure you, I'm *all* woman." The little girl lifted her legs as far as the restraints would allow. "Want to see for yourself?"

"Be silent, foul beast," Ravenwood ordered.

"Are you sure? She's ripe."

The detective ignored the disgust welling within him. "You don't fool me," he stated.

"Aww," she pouted. "You play nice with me, I'll place nice with you. Promise."

"You're trying to distract us," Ravenwood explained. She put on a good show of ignoring Ricci's exorcism ritual, but he caught an errant glance of worry. "Your little tantrum took more energy than the child could channel at once. Otherwise you'd still be at it and we'd be dead."

"That's what you think, huh?" she countered.

Shards of glass and splintered wood strewn about the room began to shudder. Ravenwood loosened his tie and rushed toward her. Theresa's eyes widened with glee, but before she could utter another of her vulgar barbs, he clamped a hand over her mouth. In his other hand he held the crystal pendant he'd removed from his neck and now dangled directly over her terrified eyes.

"That's right," he whispered darkly. "Christians aren't the only ones who have symbols to ward off demons." He tightened his grip on her jaw as she tried to struggle. "Ah-ah. See? You can pretend you don't hear the words being spoken behind me all you want, but I know better. It's written all over your aura. They're clawing at you from the inside out. Now shush, child. Listen like a good little girl. He's getting to the good part."

Ravenwood waited until the proper point in the prayer, then backed away. The demon screamed as Father Ricci splashed holy water on her in the sign of the cross. Miriam cried out as her daughter lurched upward off the bed. The air grew inexplicably hot as a reddish glow enveloped Theresa in the darkness, then vaporized as quickly as it had appeared.

Silence settled over the room like a shroud.

The air cooled. Miriam rose to her feet, too afraid to speak, until at last, Tessie stirred.

Ravenwood stepped aside so as not to stand in the way of the joyous reunion. And to retrieve his cane. He returned his pendant to its proper place, then nodded to Father Ricci with a broad smile.

"Well then," he declared cheerily as he went about straightening his tie, collar, and suit cuffs. "That was invigorating. As always, Vincent, a pleasure working with you."

Father Ricci's demeanor held considerably less mirth. He merely gave the investigator a level look and said, "We need to talk."

Ravenwood stayed at Father Ricci's behest. While the latter spoke with young Tessie in the living room, the former acquiesced to helping Miriam clean up the bedroom.

The part of him that was accustomed to calling his butler for such menial work wanted to object. The chivalrous part of him, though, refused to leave the poor woman to lift a solid oak dresser by herself, especially when she revealed herself to be a widow. It was apparently the mysterious death of her husband that prompted her to call the church in the first place.

Thankfully the dresser had toppled onto the bed once the drawers were ripped out, so that it rested at an angle, not all the way to the floor. Still, the occult investigator marveled at the force required to accomplish the feat.

Ravenwood joined the Reverend shortly. Ricci stood as he entered, satisfied that the girl would recover, at least physically. With that, they exchanged farewells and thanks, and departed.

"What troubles you, Vincent?" Ravenwood asked at length.

"Besides the obvious, you mean?" Father Ricci glanced uncomfortably at the doors on either side of the hallway as he continued on in silence. Once they gained a semblance of privacy outside, he finally spoke again.

"Apologies my friend," he said, though still in a hushed tone. "Encounters with the netherworld may be commonplace to one such as yourself, but for me…"

"You have nothing to apologize for," Ravenwood assured the priest as his words trailed off. "No sane man should be expected to speak of such things lightly."

"You do."

Ravenwood opened his mouth to reply, but found himself taken aback by the blunt observation. He tilted his head contemplatively. "Would it help if I groused more? Took up chain smoking? I could practice my brooding." His brow knit as he assumed a more pensive expression.

Vincent laughed. "No, I suppose not."

"There. You see how much smiling helps? Now, are you any less committed to your vows, Father, even knowing the world for what it truly is?"

The priest nodded. "Point taken."

"But that's not all you wanted to talk about."

Ricci shook his head solemnly. He walked a few more paces down the street in silence, collecting his thoughts. "Few of us who are taught the rites of exorcism are ever actually called to perform one. Some may never encounter a legitimate possession in their lives. Even those of us with more... focused training will likely engage a demon once every three or so years. Twice maybe, and rarely within their own diocese."

"This year alone," Ravenwood said, "You've faced four."

"Add to that the *three* other confirmed possessions I've been summoned to in as many months since our last meeting." Ricci stopped walking and turned for emphasis. "That's in addition to Theresa Watson."

"Eight?" Ravenwood asked, both intrigued and disturbed. "All in New York? Why didn't you call me?"

"At first I chalked it up to the state of this city, and of our troubled times. The conditions here make New York a literal devil's playground."

On that, Ravenwood could only agree. "Truthfully, though," he added. "Demons *are* rare. Some of my cases involve immortals or creatures of one bent or another. More often I find myself chasing some idiot who stumbles upon magic and fancies himself a mage. But it may put your mind at ease to know that most turn out to be no more than charlatans."

"Exactly my point. What's worse, past entities have been easy enough to deal with. They never displayed the kind of power this one did."

"In other words, we're no longer talking about random events. There's a pattern. And it's escalating."

"I know," Ricci confirmed with a heavy sigh. "Perhaps I just didn't want to see it. I should have called you sooner."

Ravenwood's distant blue eyes refocused on his friend. "Nonsense," he said, clasping his shoulder. "I'm here now. As I recall, you take thorough notes on your investigations. We'll start there. Let us discover what these victims have in common."

Ricci looked up at him, genuinely but pleasantly surprised. "Thank you. Yes. My files are in my office."

"Lead on." Ravenwood gestured to his car. "I'll follow."

A short drive across the Williamsburg Bridge brought the pair to St. Paul's Cathedral, in Brooklyn. The steeple rose amid the surrounding buildings like a beacon of hope to the beleaguered neighborhood.

Ravenwood took note of a small gathering huddled in the parking lot, most likely turned away by the nearby flophouse when they reached capacity for the night. He eased his sleek, Mercedes convertible in the space next to Ricci's older DeSoto, and the pair approached the church's office entrance.

Unbeknownst to the Reverend, they were joined by a third; someone with them not in body, but literally in spirit. The astral presence had no name, but Ravenwood knew him well, for he was the occult investigator's guardian and mentor.

It was the Nameless One who had revealed the world of the supernatural to Ravenwood and trained him in its ways. When not with him physically, as now, the ancient master could project his mind across any distance when called upon or when needed, always honoring a lifelong vow to protect him from the dangers of this world, and the ones that lurked beyond.

Together, they poured over Father Ricci's copious records on his recent cases.

"'Thorough notes' was a bit of an understatement," Ravenwood said approvingly.

Father Ricci nodded. "Well you said it yourself. In your line of work, how many times have you been roped into a fraud? In truth, we get many more reports than this. We are compelled to look into every one, but performing the rite is arguably *the* most sacred thing we do. We must be absolutely certain it is necessary. That requires... diligence. Too often, the 'possessed' is either faking, or in need of some level of psychological therapy."

"Or of incarceration," Ravenwood commented.

Ricci gave a small shrug in concession. "We're certainly not dealing with a fraud this time, I'm afraid."

"Indeed. It is for these events, even if they be but one in a thousand, that we remain ever on guard." The occult investigator read on in silence. After awhile he added, "I see no apparent pattern right off, but I refuse to accept this many incidents to be coincidental."

"And all in Manhattan. None across either river."

"True, but that in itself is not surprising," Ravenwood explained. "One of the reasons demons possess people, besides camouflage, is that without a physical host from this world, they cannot cross running water."

Ricci arched a curious eyebrow. "Really?"

"Well, there are ways, but they take great energy. More often than not, a full manifestation is a one way trip. In ancient days, they didn't care. But once man caught on to the many and varied ways we can hurt them, Hellborne turned to more subtle methods of incursion."

"That much jibes with our historical accounts."

"The point as it relates to our present is that we could be dealing with a single demon hopping bodies."

"You mean he could be here? Physically here?"

The Nameless One spoke up at that, audible only in Ravenwood's mind. *"Were an Infernal present in our realm in such close proximity, I would have sensed it."*

Ravenwood paused as if mulling over Ricci's question, finally replying aloud, "Without more information I can't say for certain. I doubt you've been banishing the same entity over and over again. It would take too long for it to return."

Despite the idle chit chat, Ravenwood's mind remained focused on the papers before him, and of the points on the map the priest had indicated. "We have victims from all walks of life, all levels of income. Most in Lower Manhattan; Battery Park, Tribeca, South Hudson, Alphabet City. But then there's these two; Murray Hill, and clear on the Upper East Side."

"Our paths crossed on that one, as well. You knew the family if I remember correctly."

"You do," Ravenwood mused. "Joel and Laura Cochran. That poor couple. I mean, they're fine now, but they traveled a hard road. They were just starting to taste success when they moved uptown, only to see their new home robbed. Then of all things, a de..."

Ricci turned suspiciously as the word trailed off.

Suddenly Ravenwood flipped back through a file he had already reviewed. "Were any of the other homes burgled."

Father Ricci blinked. "Uh, yes. The Watsons." He, too, joined in rifling through the files anew. "I remember Miriam saying that Theresa hadn't been the same since the break-in."

The investigator jabbed a finger at another file on the desk. "Here, too. Though the time between the theft and your involvement varies greatly."

"How could I have not seen this?"

Ravenwood's lips pursed in thought for a moment. "In your defense, you were more focused on the victims' present danger. And you admitted yourself, you were in denial. But this doesn't prove anything yet. It's not like home burglary is an uncommon event in this city. I just have a place to start now." He started to gather up the files, then stopped at his own presumption. "May I?" he asked, indicating the casework at large.

"Yes, yes of course. You are probably the *only* person I'd trust with them, though."

"Understood, Vincent. I will guard them with my life."

With that, Ravenwood returned to Manhattan.

It had been a long night for Inspector Horatio Stagg.

Two more open homicides made their way to his desk, one of them a robbery, the other a double. Three bodies and two more as of yet unsolved cases for his Captain to pitch a fit over. Some stupid kid made him run five blocks. A late night sting became an even later night waste of time. This old cop was tired, sore, and wanted nothing more than to get home and bash in his pillow with his face.

But first there was paperwork. Always paperwork.

Stagg shambled up the stairs of the precinct to his desk. Of course the elevator was busted again. "The perfect end to a perfect day," he muttered, then stopped short and cursed. He stood in the hall, staring blankly at the well dressed, dark haired man seated on the bench outside the detectives' bullpen.

"Nope," he amended. "*This* is the perfect end to my day."

"Ah, Inspector Stagg," the man called as he stood up. "I was beginning to think the front desk clerk lied to me about your return."

"Ravenwood," Stagg declared gruffly, and shuffled past him, hoping that uttering the name alone would communicate his disposition and lack of willingness to say more.

Sadly it didn't.

"I've been waiting to see you, my friend."

"Not in the mood," he replied flatly.

"Now is that any way to greet the man who helped you close the Hudson Square murders?"

The Inspector regarded him as one might a rat. "Oh yeah! Had a grand old time writing that one up. Thought the Captain would have me walking a beat again. You're gonna land me in Bellevue one of these days."

All too often, it landed on Stagg to be the one to explain their mutual cases in ways that wouldn't get him laughed off the force or committed to an asylum Despite his continued refusal to believe things he saw with his own eyes, and his outward treatment of the occult investigator, Horatio Stagg had become one of the few men in the NYPD he felt he could trust.

Ravenwood also liked to believe that the brusk treatment was an act, a personal defense mechanism to cope with that which he could not explain, and as a safeguard to his career.

At least that's what he kept telling himself.

"Go home," Stagg said.

"I have a case," Ravenwood objected flatly.

"Don't hand me that," Stagg groaned with a dismissive wave. "I don't have time for your hocus pocus bullhockey."

"Actually, I was hired to look into a rash of burglaries," Ravenwood half-lied.

The Inspector just looked at him skeptically.

Ravenwood sighed. He reached into his suit coat and procured a card from his wallet. "Because of all the times I've worked with the police, the city made me get this blasted license. I'm an official P.I. now. Doesn't that grant me some benefit of the doubt?"

"Uh," Stagg chortled. "No."

"Then what good does it do me?"

"It means I'm less obligated to arrest you when you show up at my crime scenes uninvited."

Ravenwood closed his eyes and took a calming breath as the Inspector went about feeding a blank sheet into his typewriter. "Horatio, please," he said in a gentler tone. "I was asked to look into a string of unsolved home invasions. At least, I believe they are connected. They're likely in separate files. These are legitimate crimes."

Stagg thrummed his fingers on the keyboard. Without looking up he grumbled, "Give me the names and addresses."

Ravenwood handed him a piece of paper. Stagg crooked an eyebrow at it. "Only one of these looks familiar. Wait. Are you kidding me? You got one on 77th and one on 14th. That's your idea of a string? You know there's twenty precincts in this borough, right?"

"You can't make calls?"

The Inspector slowly dragged his palm over his face.

Ravenwood glanced around at the mostly empty office, then leaned down and lowered his voice to a conspiratorial tone. "The last time you visited the penthouse, I couldn't help but notice you eying a particular bottle of 1922 Scotch in my liquor cabinet."

Stagg made a show of returning his attention to the typewriter.

"Then what good does it do me?"

After clicking a few keys, he looked up sharply. "Fine," he barked. "I'll have them pulled." He thrummed the keyboard again a few times and resumed typing. He filled in two blanks on the carbon backed form, then looked up again. Ravenwood was still standing there with an expectant look.

"What? *Now*?"

"It's single malt," Ravenwood reminded him.

The cop shot out of his chair with an annoyed grunt. "Okay! Okay. Let's go. Who needs sleep? I can show you the one case we caught. Over here."

"The rest tomorrow then?"

Stagg stopped in his tracks and leveled an icy glare. After getting no reaction for a full beat, he sighed. "I'll call around. But soonest they can be here is end of the shift tomorrow. If you're lucky."

"Just tell me where to go and I can pick them up myself. No need to waste the city's manpower more than necessary."

Inspector Stagg regarded Ravenwood as if for the first time. "Look at you, Mr. Civic Minded," he said, pretending to sound impressed. "Your first client as a *real* private dick and you're taking it so seriously."

The truth, Ravenwood thought, was considerably more dire. If the demonic possessions were deliberate, and increasing in frequency, then time was of the essence. But he decided to keep that detail to himself, lest the Inspector change his mind.

Two blocks away, Clarence Goldberg stumbled out of a tavern door toward a nearby phone booth. He clumsily stuffed himself inside and began to make a call, but a hand thrust itself out of nowhere and pressed down on the cradle in mid-dial.

"Hey," Clarence wailed. "What's your problem, buster. I wush here firs'. Jus' gotta call my wife for a ride home. God damn bartender won..."

Clarence froze as he turned and caught full view of the other man's face. The headlights of a passing car swept over his eyes. For an instant, he could have sworn they reflected with a crimson glow. His pupils were the wrong shape, vertical and narrow like some kind of animal. Veins as black as coal snaked away from them, bulging just under the surface of his skin.

Then just as quickly, he looked like any other random bum.

"I'll just be a minute," said the ragged stranger.

"N-no hurry," Clarence stammered, and extricated himself from the narrow booth. The man allowed Clarence to pass, but held his frightened gaze with an intense stare until he'd scurried all the way back inside the bar.

He slid into the phone booth, dropped a coin in the slot and dialed. The line connected. Without waiting for a greeting from the other end, he said, "You were right. He's talking to the cops. Been in there a long time."

The man winced at the harsh response, but forced himself to relax. "Yeah, no kidding. But he said we had to expect this. No, we *got* to tell him… I know! Worry about that when we have to. What do you want to do now?"

He nodded, breathed a terse confirmation, then hung up and shuffled off into the night.

After reviewing the case file and making Stagg promise once again to call the other precincts to do likewise, Ravenwood at last arrived at his Upper West Side home for the night.

He spared little more than two or three words with the valet, doorman, and elevator operator, agreeing with each in turn that it was, indeed, a late night, but ending any attempt at small talk with a terse nod. He took note of the silence upon entering his spacious penthouse apartment, but paid it no further heed as he dropped his cane into an umbrella stand and walked casually across the front room in the dark.

A draft brushed past his ankles. He reached instinctively for the Luger holstered under his suit coat, whirling at the curtain rustling over the open balcony. Suspicion faded quickly to idle curiosity, though, as he recognized the silhouette outside.

Ravenwood set the binder of Ricci's investigations on a coffee table and turned to join the short, unassuming figure on his balcony.

"I expected you'd be in bed by now," Ravenwood said, stepping out into the night air. Though he never truly thought of the Nameless One as 'old,' in truth his age was as big a mystery as everything else about him. He was mortal by all evidence, so it still struck him as odd to see him up and about so late.

The venerable master looked out over Central Park, taking in the closest approximation the serenity the city had to offer. "Since you took your first steps on this road tonight," he began at length, "I have been trying to follow it. To see where it leads. But my visions are..." The wire thin strands of hair about his mouth and chin sagged as he frowned around the word, "Clouded."

"You've often said that the future is uncertain," the younger man countered.

"True, my son," he agreed solemnly. "But it is as if my Sight is blocked. Actively or not, I cannot say. I know only that I see nothing but darkness ahead."

"Then we shall face it," Ravenwood stated. "Together." There was no attempt at pandering in his tone. The words came as naturally as if observing that grass is green.

"*Always the Nameless One will guard you and your flesh,*" the mystic sage quoted. "That was my promise to your father, as it is to you. To that end I have taught you much so that you can defend yourself. For in your journey you will come to paths you must walk alone."

He looked up before turning to go. The conflict on his student's face was obvious. "It was not my intent to distract or worry you. Merely to caution: Tread carefully. You have much to prepare yet, so I will leave you to it. As always, remain focused on the present; on that which you can control, and let fate worry about the rest."

"As always," Ravenwood agreed. "Goodnight."

The occult investigator took a few more moments out on the balcony to clear his mind. Once accomplished, he immersed himself in research. First, he appropriated the study, wherein he organized

Father Ricci's files into a timeline, which he pinned to a large cork board that now dominated the room's décor. He then delved into his library, pulling a myriad of books on demonic legend and an almanac of the Abyss.

At one point, almost as an afterthought, he opened his gun cabinet and searched for a dusty case of custom made, iron coated bullets. Though shooting them meant a shorter effective range and less accuracy, lead alone was harmless to demons, no matter how large the caliber.

He was in the midst of procuring an array of compounds needed to detect and analyze traces of a Hellborne's presence when an unexpected presence of a more Earthly nature caught him by surprise.

"Sir?" a voice asked from the doorway.

"Good Lord, Sterling," Ravenwood exclaimed. "Go to bed."

The distinguished, gray haired butler returned his employer's gaze with equal measure confusion and concern. "With respect," Alexander Sterling began humbly, "I did. And then I woke up. I was just about to set out the marker flag for the early morning ice delivery."

It was only then that Ravenwood noticed the first rays of dawn peaking through gaps in the eastern skyline.

"When you didn't come home last night, I thought perhaps your date with Miss Hart went, uhm. Well."

Ravenwood shook his head regretfully. "Quite the opposite. In fact, get her two dozen roses from me when you get a chance. Best make it three."

"Ahh," Sterling acknowledged. "Work?"

He nodded, placing a vial of rosemary powder in a medical bag. "I suppose I should get some sleep. Please see that I am not disturbed."

"Of course, sir."

Ravenwood awoke a few short hours later, fully rejuvenated thanks to a yoga meditation technique which allowed his body to gain the benefits of a full night's rest; yet another invaluable skill gained under the tutelage of the Nameless One.

The remainder of the morning was spent in traffic. The investigator started his tour across Central Park at the 19th Precinct. He made his way south from there. The sun had long crested past noon when he checked the final address off his list upon leaving the 7th Precinct building.

At each stop, he and the detective assigned to the case repeated an aggravatingly similar ritual to the one he went through with Inspector Stagg. To an extent, he understood their reluctance to share official police documents with a stranger, licensed or no. And he recognized that his reputation would precede him at every station, unfounded or no. But the dance grew tedious after the second song.

Why anyone would actually do this for a living was beyond his reckoning.

Fortunately, every negotiation ended the same as well, once the officer in question realized he was offering to help solve an unsolvable mystery.

Every crime scene told the same tale; no forced entry, no fingerprints or trace of any kind. As they all happened months apart and scattered across so many different neighborhoods, police found no pattern to connect them. Though if not for the inclusion of the supernatural element, there would be no reason to look for one.

Even with that factored in, though, Ravenwood had trouble seeing the pattern himself. He knew it was there. It just remained elusive when viewed as a jumbled pile of typed reports.

These thoughts and more preoccupied the investigator's mind as the light turned green. Blaring horns prompted a Pavlovian ritual of shifting gears and easing forward across the intersection. A copse of trees rose to Ravenwood's left; a small park that filled a gap in the cityscape where the road ahead forked off. The convertible casually gained speed as the north and southbound lanes gently curved to merge into one street.

Until a voice thundered in his mind, *"STOP!"*

Ravenwood obeyed without hesitation. A symphony of horns blared in the wake of the Nameless One's warning and the roadster squealed to a halt; inches shy of a speeding Buick that careened out of his blind spot at well over forty miles per hour.

"Is it Sunday already?" Ravenwood wondered aloud.

He thought he heard the voice say more, but it became muted as his mind replayed a slow-motion reel of the near-collision. Somewhere during his next heartbeat, survival instincts demanded his attention elsewhere. On blind instinct, Ravenwood, shifted back into gear, and stomped the gas pedal.

The car lurched with a violent crunch. Ravenwood felt the custom Mercedes shudder from the impact of the sedan behind him, but its reinforced frame held, and its racing engine pulled him far enough ahead to deflect the brunt of it. He shifted up again, and flattened in his seat as the car surged with a mighty roar.

"My son," the Nameless One repeated. "There is a Hellborne entity inside that vehicle."

"I gathered as much," Ravenwood concurred. "One moment."

The runaway Buick had turned off the main thoroughfare only two blocks away. More accurately, its trajectory had lead toward it. Ravenwood had to make the same high speed turn at a sharper angle. He did so with deft precision.

"There wasn't much fear on display for a man going the wrong way down a one-way street," he continued conversationally. "The driver was focused far more on me than trying to keep his vehicle under control. Even this escape route appears premeditated. Not that he expected to need it."

His eyes narrowed as the distance closed between vehicles. Parked cars on either side limited maneuverability to zero, like racing down the barrel of cannon. There was nowhere to turn. Nowhere to hide. Ravenwood allowed a thin lipped smile to form. He shifted into top gear and peeled down the narrow road in pursuit of his prey at breakneck speed.

The sleek, souped up roadster easily overtook the bulky coupe. Ravenwood timed the chase perfectly, reaching the widening intersection in time to veer around and take the lead. The driver spun the wheel on reflex, barely avoiding the speeding missile that the sports car had become, but altering its course across an open patch of sidewalk.

And crashed off the foundation of Calgary Church.

The Buick bounced off the corner of the giant structure with a horrendous wrench of metal against stone, coming to land on the front steps as the wheel bent off its axle.

As it was, in fact, not Sunday, the landmark area was mostly devoid of pedestrians. The few people who had been enjoying an afternoon stroll ran well ahead of the crash, motivated either by the oncoming horns or the mysterious voice in their heads warning them to run.

The driver, a skinny middle aged man with a thin wisp of brown hair, managed to shove the dented door open. He started to pull himself out of the vehicle, but stopped in momentary panic. He looked down at the cement stairs; at the holy ground inches below his foot.

The demon snapped a glare at the plaque on the church's wall, then at Ravenwood, who had exited his own car and was running toward him. His sneer softened into a smirk. He snickered, then suddenly collapsed.

A collective gasp rolled through the onlookers as Ravenwood ran up to the wreckage. "Stay back! It's on fire!" someone yelled, pointing at the trails of reddish smoke wafting out of the windows. The occult investigator knelt over the body to check for a pulse. He released his held breath in relief upon finding one.

The driver came to with a start. "What happened. Where am...? Holy Jesus. He's gone!"

"Who's gone?" Ravenwood asked in earnest. "Did he give you his name?"

"It could only have been..." His words caught in his throat as he propped himself up straight. He blinked several times as if waking from a dream. "I tried to run you off the road. I could've killed you. Oh God forgive me. I'm so sorry."

Ravenwood's brow furrowed with concern. "You weren't yourself."

"But I..."

"You were watching the entire affair as if detached from your body," Ravenwood said reassuringly. "You tried to stop yourself, but you weren't in control."

"How do you…?"

Ravenwood shook his head abruptly. "I need you to tell me everything you can about what happened to you. No matter how insane you think it makes you sound." He took a breath and added in a gentler tone. "I know it's hazy. But try."

The man nodded fretfully, his forlorn gaze distant.

"Sir!" Sterling exclaimed. "Good to see you in one piece."

Ravenwood cast a wary glance as he plopped his medical bag down in the foyer. "It's good to *be* in one piece. Should I not be?"

"I heard of your auto accident on the radio," the butler replied, taking his coat and picking up the bag to store it more properly. "You gave us quite a scare."

"Us?" Ravenwood asked skeptically.

"Well, me at any rate."

"Exactly. Master told you I was okay, I presume."

"Or course, sir, but…" Sterling stopped and sighed as he watched his employer casually drop his cane in the umbrella stand and waltz toward the kitchen. "I was merely concerned when you didn't call. I didn't know if I needed to call a tow truck. Or when to make dinner. Or…"

"Sorry. I was at the police station most of the day. Which reminds me, the Mercedes has been impounded. It'll need to be taken to the garage anyway. Handle that, will you?"

Sterling took note of the instruction, but remained fixated on what was left unsaid. "The news reports were conflicting. One said you were nearly killed it a hit and run. Another claimed you ran a man off the road."

"Both true."

Sterling blinked. "Well," he settled on saying. "I trust your adventure was worth whatever the fine and repair bill will cost."

"More than," Ravenwood replied confidently, but added in frustration, "Well yes, and no. I now know the why, but not the how."

"You mean why this man tried to kill you?"

Ravenwood shook his head dismissively. "No, that much was obvious. I must be on the right track. He, or they, don't want me to get any closer to the truth. The important question is 'How'. He knew I would be merging onto Park Avenue South at that exact moment. How long had he been following me? How did he know I was investigating the thefts in the first place? But primarily, how did the demon get its hold on him?"

"I'm afraid that doesn't make any sense at all, sir."

"It didn't to me at first, either," Ravenwood went on as if they were having the same conversation. "I didn't think he fit the pattern. He wasn't on my list, because it was his place of business that was robbed, not his home. It turns out he's the proprietor of a pawn shop. But it had all the same hallmarks; no forced entry, no fingerprints."

Ravenwood's green eyes brightened as he paused for emphasis. "And then he told me that one of the items stolen was a framed dollar bill he had hanging behind the cash register. 'The first buck I ever made,' he described it, fondly."

Sterling returned his ebullient gaze with a befuddled stare.

"Don't you see? What do people sell at pawn shops?"

"Uh," the butler stuttered. "Watches. Old jewelery?"

"Heirlooms!" Ravenwood exclaimed so suddenly he startled the older man. "Sentimental jewelery and the like. Such items would create an ideal psychic conduit, especially for the downtrodden who only parted with their valuables out of desperation." He looked like wanted to say more, but the words caught in his held breath.

"Sir?" Sterling prompted with a hint of concern.

"His shop is on Delancy, right off the bridge." Ravenwood's eyes muted to a more earthen tone. "The danger may not be isolated to Manhattan after all."

"Still," Sterling offered into the silence. "You've made progress in solving your case."

"Knowing his motives is all well and good," Ravenwood mused aloud. "But, to what end is he targeting so many victims? Is he raising an army? Planting agents? Or is there an agenda at all beyond sowing chaos?" He shook his head ruefully. "Regardless, it brings me no closer to catching the actual perpetrator."

After a moment of awkward silence, Sterling went to the cupboard. "I always think more clearly on a full stomach. You must be famished."

"Thank you, no," Ravenwood replied absently. "I had supper with Vincent. After wasting all that time with the police, we spent the remainder of the day revisiting old cases. I inspected the homes of people he had exorcised, visiting under the pretense of checking in to see how they were faring, and to insure their dwellings remained safe from otherworldly threats."

"Were they?"

"Maddeningly, yes. Good news for the families living there, I suppose, but not at all productive for me. The only thing I took away from the experience was confirmation of what I already suspected. The only evidence of a Hellborne I found was in the room where the ritual was performed. Any trace magic in the rest of the house was latent, little more than an echo. Though there were variations, however faint, in isolated areas."

Ravenwood crooked his head and muttered curiously, "Mostly in the kitchens."

The occult investigator shot out of his chair and looked about. He stopped suddenly on his second rotation, and his eyes lit up as if he'd found something he'd misplaced.

"Sir?" Sterling asked hesitantly.

His employer flashed a grin, then strode out.

Ravenwood walked through the palatial living room of his penthouse with a marked spring in his step, and into the library. There, he made four phone calls. Each conversation seemed to brighten his demeanor a little more, until he stopped to consider making one more.

He took a bracing breath as the operator connected him.

"Stagg," said the voice on the other end in greeting.

"Iceboxes," Ravenwood stated.

A pregnant silence clung to the phone line.

"Iceboxes," Inspector Stagg finally replied.

"That's the connection," Ravenwood confirmed. "Being a delivery man grants our culprit open access to case his targets in relative anonymity. It's a detail of a home that is all too easy to overlook." He paused for emphasis before adding, "All of the victims used the same service."

Ravenwood frowned at the stubborn detective's noncommittal grunt. After another beat of silence, Stagg asked, "You got a theory how an ice truck driver got in and out without a trace when the tenants weren't home, smart guy?"

Ravenwood pinched the bridge in frustration. He knew that however the thief was breaking in would defy the Inspector's narrow definition of logic. "How much attention do people really pay to routine delivery men? Once inside, it's not impossible to make an impression of the key if one is clever and subtle enough."

The investigator could hear Stagg's mouth working as he mulled that over, searching for an objection. "An average civilian might not pay close attention to their movements, but they always know the guy who shows up to their door every week. I mean, you probably don't, but ask Sterling what your ice delivery guy's name is. Or the milkman's."

Ravenwood smiled, sensing he was making progress. "He wouldn't leave so obvious a trail. The buildings are too far flung to be on the same delivery route. We need to look for substituted schedules, people calling in sick and the like, say, within a month of the break-in."

Again, silence reigned.

"It'll take a subpoena to get business records," Stagg said. "I won't wake up a DA over a hunch. And I gotta confirm it myself or he won't sign it anyway. Tomorrow."

"Understood, Inspector," Ravenwood agreed. "Thank you."

He hung up the phone with an unexpected weariness. It seemed a Pyrrhic victory. Though he was glad to have convinced Stagg to help, he greatly disliked having to wait on the creaky wheels of justice. But more than that, the yet missing pieces of the puzzle gnawed at him.

On that note, he wandered out toward his balcony in contemplative silence. This far above the street, the cacophony of the city melted with the soft flutter of windswept trees into a distant hum. Here, he could think.

A faint scuff on the living room floor broke him from his pensive trance.

"Will you be needing anything else, sir?" Sterling asked.

"Put on a pot of Master's herbal tea. The green tin."

"Already brewing."

Ravenwood smiled at his loyal servant without looking at him. "Thank you, Sterling. That will be all."

"You seem troubled," the stodgy Englishman said. "I'd think you'd be in better spirits, now that you are closing in on this criminal."

"That's just it," Ravenwood explained. "The NYPD is only concerned about catching a thief. But that aspect barely scratches the surface of the case."

"If I may," Sterling offered. "Often when I look at a new list of tasks that need doing, and it seems overwhelming taken as a whole, I focus on the simplest of them first."

Ravenwood turned slightly to face his butler askew. "Not seeing the trees for the forest," he paraphrased. "Have you been spending time with the Master?"

"Not when I can help it, sir."

Ravenwood chuckled. "Goodnight, Sterling."

The Stepson of Mystery turned back around toward the city, losing himself in the deep shadows cast over Central Park by the setting sun.

Two kinds of people remained in the park this long after dusk. You had a range of miscreants who felt at home under cover of darkness; muggers, rapists, purveyors of illicit opiates. And you had their victims; some unsuspecting, some tragically willing, most destined to make tomorrow's headlines.

Predators and prey.

One who walked among the sparse nighttime denizens of Central

"Thank you, Sterling, that will be all."

Park had a hard time deciding which group he fell into. Though he more often associated with the former, recent events made him feel more and more like one of the latter.

He ducked off the paved walkway, through a gap in the foliage, and onto a natural trail, well out of sight of passersby even in the daytime. He took a circuitous route, doubling back to insure he was not followed, and soon found his way to a clearing surrounding a stone outcrop. There, he went about clearing brush off the base of the stone, exposing a wide, flat step. A carefully painted pentagram enclosed in an ornate circle appeared on its flat surface as he removed the last of the camouflage.

The fair haired, middle-aged man paused before the summoning glyph with a deep breath, then produced a pocket knife. He pricked the middle of his scarred palm and held out his clenched fist. A trickle of blood spilled onto the outer ring carved in the stone.

He bandaged his hand. And waited.

A pungent, black cloud billowed within the pentagram. It quickly spread, but rose skyward at the edge of the circle, as if filling an invisible cylinder. The smoke topped off eight feet above the stone, and curled in on itself until it formed a vaguely human shape.

"You..." the man said, taking an unconscious step back. "You called me here. How?"

The entity swirled as if tilting its head curiously.

Taking the silence as confusion, he added in a more dominant tone, "I summon *you*. You don't summon me. That's how this works."

"Is it now," a deep, gravelly voice resonated from the circle. "Then why are we here, Duncan Alistair McConnell?"

Without knowing why, Duncan blanched at the sound of the demon speaking his full name. "That doesn't answer the question."

"You seek more knowledge, then," the voice replied. "Are we reopening negotiations?"

"No," Duncan blurted so sharply he startled himself.

A haunting sound resembling a chuckle rolled from the smoke filled circle. "You fueled this portal to my domain with your blood," it said, as if the explanation should be self evident.

McConnell's urge to end the unscheduled meeting overrode

his concern over the implications of that revelation. "What do you want?" he asked flatly.

"To tell you that your window of opportunity is closing swiftly," it explained. "I cannot risk further delays. You must do as you agreed. Tonight."

"Tonight….why?" the thief stammered. "I haven't walked the route. The map alone only tells me so much."

"Do as I say or your soul is forfeit!"

McConnell fought the urge to cower, instead finding resolve in what he thought, prayed, was an empty threat. "No matter how I opened this portal, I can close it just as easily." He snapped his fingers for emphases. "With you still in it."

"You could certainly try." The entity looked around idly. One of its smokey appendages tapped on the invisible barrier around it. "But this arrangement serves my needs."

"All the more reason why I can't rush…"

"You're not listening. I give you this warning freely. A very dangerous man has put the authorities on your trail. If you are caught, you will fail to fulfill your debt to me. If you fail…"

McConnell mulled that over, but even the unspoken consequences of his deal with the devil didn't change the truth behind his hesitancy. "Crossing planes..." he began, the words heavy with exhaustion. "Each time takes more out of me. I feel..." Duncan bit back words like 'empty', 'lost', 'dead', and settled on saying, "I need rest. I can't. I just can't."

Something resembling a sigh emanated from the circle. "Do this final thing and I release you from your contract."

"I don't have my gear," McConnell countered. "The boxes won't unlock themselves. I can't get what I need, load the truck, drive there, and finish the job before dawn. It will have to be tomorrow. On delivery, you guarantee my escape from the city." He thought a second and added quickly, "Alive. I'll have a big enough score to set up somewhere new. I just need to get away clean to enjoy it. Then, I accept your offer. We're done."

"So be it," the demon growled, and vanished in a swirling flash of brimstone.

Inspector Stagg watched Ravenwood's Jaguar SS-100 race into view and screech into an empty parking spot with wry amusement. The door of the sporty roadster flew open before the engine had ceased churning.

Ravenwood's pace slowed as he approached on the sidewalk, concern darkening his curiosity the closer he got. "What? You called me, no?"

Stagg eyed the smartly dressed playboy, shifted his gaze briefly toward the new car, then back again. He wondered what it must feel like to have a different car for every day of the week, but kept that thought to himself not wanting to invoke the aloof man's patented innocent stare. "Yeah," he chortled instead. "You're gonna want to see this."

"So you found him," Ravenwood said, falling into step behind Stagg. "His name was on the delivery route ahead of each burglary, just like I told you. He lives here?" The occult investigator looked about as they crossed a tiny lawn and entered a two-flat house. He felt a twitch at the fringe of his senses as they ascended a flight of stairs.

"Your lead was solid," Stagg said, with no small amount of surprise. "But just finding his name written on a schedule wasn't enough to arrest him."

"But enough to get a search warrant, I see."

"Nope."

"Then what was?" Ravenwood asked, noting the uniformed police presence and forcibly opened door.

"When we showed up to question him, he high tailed it at first sight of us. We chased him a couple blocks, but..." Stagg grimaced. "He got away."

Ravenwood suppressed a grin spurred by the image of the stocky cop running two whole city blocks. "Which leads us here," he commented instead, intently scanning the thief's living room.

"Duncan McConnell," he read off an envelope. "I take it he wasn't home when you arrived."

Stagg shook his head, then lead them further inside.

The astute detective drank in details with each furtive shift of his bright hazel eyes. That odd sensation still tickled at the periphery of his sixth sense, but he couldn't place the source, and forgot about it entirely once he saw the contents of the next room.

Sheets of paper covered every last inch of all four walls; incredibly details sketches, hand drawn maps. A desk bore stacks of ledgers outlining behavior patterns.

1705: Mr C home from work +/- 7 mins!
1715: Mrs C walks dog - 15 min tops
8/30 (sunset 1925): Dinner at Basillico's — Drive x 2 + meal = 55 min
Waiter on schedule 8/30 = Mario – PRICE to slow service?

"He was in the Navy," Ravenwood mutttered idly.

"Yeah. An engineer. How'd you know?"

"The twenty-four hour time markers in his no..." Ravenwood swallowed the last word and asked, "Is that what I think it is?"

Stagg followed Ravenwood's gaze to the largest of the maps laid out on the drawing table. "If you think that's Midtown National, then yeah. Looks like he was getting too big for his britches, planning a bank heist. So much for that, huh? But, hey. That's not what I called you all this way out here to see. C'mon. In here. It looks like your kind of abracadabra hooey."

Ravenwood froze in the doorway. His eyes flickered with an amber hue as they fell upon the floor, where five razor straight lines formed a perfectly symmetrical star, enclosed in a circle that consumed a full third of the room. Black candles adorned the five points of the pentagram. Sunlight filtering through the dirty window glinted off bits of silver in the chalk.

"So, what?" Stagg prompted after he'd had enough of the silence. "This guy a devil worshiper or something?"

"After a fashion." Ravenwood focused his thoughts on that tinge of magic that had been nagging him since he entered the dwelling, trying to translate it into something his other five senses could commit to memory.

"Of course," Stagg sighed. "Well at least he won't be robbing any more houses. Or a bank for that matter. If he's got half the brains all that planning out there tells me he's got, he'll be on the other side of Jersey by now. His notes should give us something to go on. It looks like he bribed a waiter for help on the Cochran job. Maybe this Mario fella can... Hey!"

Ravenwood ignored Stagg's protest and marched past him. He stopped just as suddenly in front of McConnell's notes on his victims' daily routines.

"Sunset," he muttered.

"Yeah, he was pretty obsessed with details," Stagg said as if in agreement. "Kinda hard to rob a place blind during the day."

Ravenwood turned to come face to face with the Inspector. "You said you pursued the suspect, but he got away," he said hurriedly. "How?"

"Shadows!" Ravenwood exclaimed triumphantly.

The Nameless One knelt in meditation on a small rug. He opened his eyes to acknowledge his student in the open doorway to his room, but his gaze remained distant, unfocused. Beside him, candles flickered briefly from a breeze with no apparent source.

"It's how he escaped the police by fleeing into an abandoned tenement," Ravenwood continued without being prompted. "It's how he gets inside his victims' homes. I deduced that he could walk through walls, but not how. A portal would be too bright, too flashy. It would leave a much larger mystical footprint behind. Taking on an intangible spirit form would make carrying out his ill gotten gains a needless challenge. That's not how he thinks."

The ancient master's brow pinched a fraction. "You don't know who your enemy is, only his name, yet you know how he thinks?"

"Based on the pattern of his crimes, and having seen his lair first hand, I've come to understand the kind of man we're dealing with. Yes. I suspect that every time McConnell robbed a home, the Hellborne pulling his strings was paid with one of the victim's personal affects. Maybe he knew the true reason behind it, or maybe he was duped into thinking he was simply giving his accomplice a cut of the action."

"He could be possessed himself," the Master said.

"True," the student conceded. "But his behavior is too methodical, too carefully planned. His strategy suggests experience in his craft. He chooses his targets, studies them, then acts only at an ideal time. A demon rarely demonstrates that level of patience or meticulous thinking."

"Rarely," the Nameless One echoed, letting the single word serve as its own statement.

"Meaning they can," Ravenwood concluded. "I just have yet to encounter one. My instincts tell me otherwise, Master."

The old man bowed his head, his expression still neutral. Whether it was a gesture of agreement or concession, he couldn't tell.

Ravenwood paused in search of his original train of thought. "The thief always struck after sunset," he went on. "And the telltale magical energy I detected was always where rooms would be darkest when the lights were out. You see? Shadows are extraplanar soft spots. They can serve as gateways with proper effort, and require only minor magical talent to employ."

"Or none," the Nameless One commented darkly. "If the power is bestowed."

"The ability to walk through darkness undetected is something a burglar might well sell his soul for. Fortunately I don't have to. I think I've discovered how to duplicate the effect."

"Think upon your next words carefully, my son." The venerable master raised his deep-set, hooded eyes. "You seek to breach the Veil through the realm of shadow."

"Without using Infernal magic," Ravenwood amended. "You taught me better than that."

"Have I?"

"If I am to catch this villain, I must learn how he operates. He's going to strike again tonight. I know it. I will need this knowledge to prevent another escape."

"You laud his intelligence, yet think him a fool."

"He is meticulous, yes. Were he acting alone, he may well have fled the city. But you saw that rune same as I. You felt the latent dark magic surrounding it. So yes, he is a fool if he willingly communes with demons. If he bargained with one, then he's not the one in charge, whether he likes to think so or not."

"You found his plans laid bare. Foiled them."

"Demons only deal in one currency," Ravenwood countered. "It will not let him simply walk away. Not with hundreds of safe deposit boxes full of people's valued treasures at stake. All those unguarded channels into unsuspecting human souls. No. He will find a way."

The Nameless One closed his eyes again, absorbing the argument, and the passion in its delivery. "The space between shadows feeds on fear," he said. "Being immersed in it; simply staying focused in its fluid terrain would tax even your considerable defenses."

"McConnell must be highly disciplined to navigate it," Ravenwood agreed. "And uniquely bold, insane, or desperate to keep going back. Though I imagine it gets easier with practice, it must take its toll. He'd need protection. A ward of some type."

"Or writ of safe passage from his benefactor." The Nameless One locked Ravenwood's soft blue eyes. "You will have neither."

"I'll take every precaution."

"You abandoned caution the moment you consulted the forbidden texts."

The words struck Ravenwood as surely as if his master had slapped him in the face. He was unaccustomed to hearing rebuke in the Nameless One's tone.

"You foresaw this course of events the moment I took the case," Ravenwood said at length. "If this path is truly so dangerous, then show me another way."

The Nameless One took a deep breath, closed his eyes, and exhaled slowly. "The path ahead is yours to choose. I stand always at your side. Neither leading nor following."

"Does that mean you'll help me?"

"No."

This time the word held no admonishment. It was a simple statement, neither warning or judging, left open for the investigator to infer *can't* or *won't* for himself.

Nor was he trying to stop him.

"For in your journey you will come to paths you must walk alone."

Ravenwood bowed, and left the master to his solitude.

Night settled over Midtown National Bank. The final vestiges of the sun's purifying rays had long receded, leaving the artificial yellowish hue of of the city in its stead.

Duncan McConnell watched from afar as the security guard locked the door behind the last of the janitors to leave. He nodded to an NYPD patrolman stationed out front. He yawned in reply.

The police presence around closing time had worried him at first. The maps in his apartment made them nervous enough to send two squad cars and an Inspector to make a show of looking into the bank. But as the hours stretched and twilight faded, they redefined their idea of beefing up security to include one lone, bored flatfoot checking the front and side doors every now and then.

Had Duncan needed either of those entrances that might have been a problem.

Just after eight o'clock, the thief climbed into his truck and drove in a wide loop around the block, coming to a stop in an alley down the street, running parallel with the alley behind the bank. He peered down a connecting gangway, checking his wristwatch. Right on cue, the cop walked by as per the pattern he'd followed all evening. Next, Duncan knew, he'll loiter out front, where at least there were passing cars to watch. Just like clockwork.

McConnell shifted an oversize blue duffel on one shoulder, carefully holding a toolbox level in the other hand so as not to shift its noisy contents, and duckwalked down the gangway. Upon reaching rear wall of the bank, he measured several steps east, then stopped and looked around in the dark.

He squeezed his eyes shut, then reopened them to a world lit in shades of green, as if filtered through a colored lens. Any dim light reflecting off a surface seemed to glow with a soft, pale radiance.

He both saw and felt shimmers in the air. He allowed his sense of sight to blur out of focus, imagining himself riding on those waves. All at once, his awareness expanded; to the sliver of light emanating through cracks of a drawn shade from an apartment window, to a pair of headlights plowing through the dim streets, to the security guard inside lighting a cigarette.

The first time he did this, he'd nearly lost himself. The sheer expanse of what he could "see" was breathtaking. Na'qhasu told him it was but a tiny taste of what magic could do. He thought he wanted to know so much more. Now he just wanted his life back.

Duncan reined in his mind on the immediate area. He studied the fluctuations in the air more closely, quickly noting a pattern. Their frequency increased the farther they flowed from a light source. His eerie green eyes narrowed as they detected distinct shapes in the curvature of the ripples, tracing them to a convex aperture hovering in the air.

He pictured the floor plans, conjuring details of its interior with precise detail in his mind. He mentally traced a path through the brick, through the steel beyond that, through the safe deposit boxes lining the wall. And walked into the shadows as if wading into a pool of ink.

An instant later, McConnell stood inside the vault. The thief's glowing eyes literally brightened at the sight of countless rows of steel boxes. He allowed himself a grin, and set about unloading a case of locksmith tools.

Within minutes he had the first box open. He haphazardly scooped out thousands in jewelry and savings bonds and tossed them in his bag. On to the next. Rinse, repeat. By the fourth lock he'd already found his rhythm.

When suddenly a searing light flooded the vault. The thief howled and clutched his eyes. He tried to will his darkvision away, through the pain in his temple made it impossible to concentrate. The bank's guard couldn't have heard him all the way at his post in the lobby.

He hadn't heard the vault door open. *How was it possible?*

His vision finally cleared, no longer cast in pale green but warm blue shining off the gray walls. He looked up from where he knelt. Right into the barrel of a Model 1929 Luger.

"It's over Mr. McConnell," said Ravenwood.

Duncan squinted up at the dapper gentleman holding the gun at his face. His gaze bounced from it to the fancy glowing stick in his other hand. "So you're the guy he was trying to warn me about."

Ravenwood's brow arched. "Apparently," he said.

"You're not getting nothin' outta me." Duncan carefully rose to his feet and moved to the back of the vault, keeping his hands in sight. "I'm already dead."

"What if I said I could protect you?"

Duncan laughed. "Only way you can do that is let me leave with what I came for."

"You truly believe he'll let it end there?" The wording gave McConnell pause, so Ravenwood pressed. "You're only now beginning to realize just how out of your depth you are. You are not a stupid man, Mr. McConnell. You suspect you're being used. And you're right. It's not too late to undo this."

The thief struggled with the glimmer of hope Ravenwood was offering, but shook his head. "What could you possibly do against something like him?"

"Well not me, precisely," Ravenwood admitted. "But I..."

"No," Duncan rasped. His eyes widened to saucers. "He's here. I wasn't going to tell him anything. I swear!"

As the cowering man's anxiety mounted, so did the gnawing of Ravenwood's sixth sense. He realized that McConnell was not staring at him, but over his shoulder. Where his body cast a narrow shadow in the light cast by his cane.

Ravenwood whirled around, Luger at the ready, but his gun arm slammed into a force that nearly ripped it from its socket. The pistol clattered against the far wall. Gritting through the pain, he spun back around, this time leading with the enchanted weapon in his off hand. It struck something solid, eliciting an inhuman howl of pain.

Ravenwood caught a brief glimpse of a vaguely human shadow

floating in midair before it caught fire and vanished in a puff of blue smoke. The occult investigator frowned as he scrunched his nose and smelled nothing. No smoke. No sulfur. More telling was the lack of any trace of a supernatural presence to his mystically attuned senses.

"Idiot," Ravenwood muttered to himself. He turned to face McConnell, who now held his own gun on him. "An illusion," he said; his tone a unique blend of snide and impressed.

McConnell smirked. "Sure felt real though, huh. Still think I'm outta my depth? Talking down to me like I'm some kinda rube. I've been robbing people like you blind all my life."

"Even when you were serving your country?"

Duncan shrugged. "Not everyone knows what they want to be when they grow up. It turned to a stepping stone toward my true calling. Europe was a gold mine."

"That's where you met your new ally."

"And a whole lot more. Secrets you wouldn't believe. Well, maybe you would, but the average Joe sure wouldn't. *That's* what this new joker in Germany's really after if you ask me. There's so much buried all over that continent."

"Even more in Asia," Ravenwood said.

"No doubt," McConnell agreed. "But that ain't got much to do with our current predicament. Does it?"

"I suppose not. So what now?" asked Ravenwood. "I cannot allow these people's possessions to leave this plane. And you can't shoot me. You know the sound of a gunshot in here would alert the guard stationed in the front lobby. These walls are thick. They're not *that* thick."

"Then I guess we'll just have to do this elsewhere."

With that, darkness engulfed the vault. Ravenwood's walking stick continued to glow, but the light it shed reached two or three feet behind his reach. McConnell bolted to his left and vanished. Suddenly the room was again bathed in soft blue light, but the thief was gone.

Ravenwood's eyes flashed crimson.

He clasped a talisman that hung about his neck, a souvenir from one of his many trips to Indochina imbued with properties ideal for channeling the flow of mind and spirit. He pictured his Luger pistol, imagining every detail with crystal clarity. Given how long the weapon had been in his possession, the imprint of his aura shone like a beacon through the ether.

Ravenwood extinguished the light radiating off his cane. The world drowned in black for an instant, then lit in hues of pale red as seen through his eyes. The Stepson of Mystery tightened his focus on the strand of energy that linked his mind to the weapon still in McConnell's hand.

"There you are," he whispered. He marched forward, oblivious to the wall in his path and intoned, *"Hēi'àn de zhámén dǎkāi,"*

The darkness itself enveloped him.

The occult investigator braced himself for the ambush he knew awaited him the moment he crossed back to the material plane. But he didn't feel the usual sensation of freefall that accompanied being mystically transported, as before. Instead he found himself, as McConnell had put it...

Elsewhere.

His surroundings appeared in ever-blending smudges of gray. He could see impressions of the physical building around him in negative contrast, like on a roll of film, almost transparent within plumes of black smoke. He knew, though, based on his studies of this realm, that it was not merely a reflection of the physical world, but an entirely separate reality, complete with its own natural terrain. The floor beneath him was gone, replaced by moist earth, peppered with gravel. Clouds of smoke rose in distinct patterns, not as walls so much as dense foliage on a rolling landscape.

Cold permeated Ravenwood's body. Not a chill like one feels on a bitter winter night, but an immeasurable absence of heat. An absence of life. An all consuming, unnatural cold that made it clear he was trespassing where mortals did not belong.

Duncan McConnell stepped out into the open, pulling the trigger on Ravenwood's Luger. A blue shield flared to life on instinct. The bullet ricocheted into the endless night.

"You are mad!" Ravenwood shouted.

"Says the madman who followed me here."

"Using this place as a bridge is dangerous enough. To linger in the space between reality is suicide."

"It's not your soul on the line, pal."

"No. Only the souls of the innocents you would sell."

Another gunshot thundered in the darkness. Again Ravenwood spotted his assailant at the last instant and deflected the shot. Barely. The investigator weighed the odds of the same outcome against the number of bullets left in the magazine.

"I didn't know that's what was happening," Duncan wailed in protest.

"Of course you didn't," Ravenwood said in mock pity. "What possible harm could come of colluding with a spawn of the outer realms?"

Ravenwood caught movement in his peripheral vision and darted to the side. He skirted the edge of one of the clouds that had them penned in. And recoiled as he felt his arm freeze to the marrow.

Inky black tendrils lashed out, numbing his hand where they touched flesh. Ravenwood yanked free, staring dumbstruck at the hypnotic strands of dark force as they unraveled and melted into back into ethereal smoke. The cadence of his heartbeat tripled. Sensation returned steadily with each pulse of blood, but he felt little desire to wait for feeling to return fully.

The tendrils lashed out again. Blind reflex urged Ravenwood to curl half-frozen fingers around the hilt of his cane and unsheathe the nimble sabre concealed within. The glyphs etched into the wooden scabbard began to light the area in soft blue. The blade sliced cleanly through the serpentine appendages in a single stroke. The same unearthly cry he heard from the shadow creature in the vault rang out as the things recoiled and vanished.

Ravenwood bit out a curse and immediately snapped the blade back in place to quell the light, but feared the damage of his foolish reaction had already been wrought.

McConnel's bemused chuckling emanated from the darkness. "You're used to having more control over your environment I imagine. You're not in charge here."

Inky black tendrils lashed out...

"If you think *you* are," Ravenwood said, "Then you're an even bigger fool than I wagered."

He almost didn't hear them over the pounding of his own heart. Disparate shuffling sounds echoed in the distance, punctuated by heavier footfalls. He noted two distinct sets. Then four. Then more. And more still, until he lost count.

Ravenwood frowned, acknowledging the irrational tide of fear welling within him, but refusing to lend it strength. Instead he channeled it into his search for McConnell. And for a way out of this unholy place. He kept the reflection of a familiar street corner in sight, and marched briskly toward the nearest patch of open ground.

"You expect me to believe that you control the denizens here," Ravenwood shouted. "An amateur who learned a few parlor tricks after begging for power from a demon?"

The irony of his own words caught in his throat. Though the Nameless One was no demon by any stretch of his imagination, their relationship was not dissimilar. Ravenwood possessed knowledge, senses, a modest arsenal of enchanted weaponry, and a modicum of innate talent. But he knew full well that his repertoire of skills amounted to little more than parlor tricks themselves, compared to the power of the threats he faced.

But that never stopped him before, and it would not stop him now. Nameless One's presence in the fight or no, he could not sit idly by when evil threatened his world.

The eerie shuffling, now a rumble, remained unseen behind the pall of gloom, but clearly grew in strength and speed. The cadence of his heartbeat grew with it. Ravenwood looked around frantically. Again, he'd almost lost sight of his escape route. The terrain was indeed fluid, disorienting, taxing his defenses, just as his Master had described.

And no matter how much McConnell boasted to the contrary, his mortal mind was just as susceptible to it. With that flash of insight, Ravenwood pivoted at a bend in the smoky maze. He focused his thoughts on his enemy. He felt his presence more than saw him, and ran. The thief responded to the sight and sound of the approach, shooting wildly at his position.

Ravenwood veered out of the field of fire, but kept coming. On his next step, he attuned his chi to the natural vibrations of the shadow portal through which he first entered the mystical realm, keeping his other senses honed on McConnell. Then he willed himself to close the distance.

The Stepson of Mystery appeared directly beside the thief, wasting no time in throttling the back of his head with his cane and sweeping his legs out of from under him. By the time McConnell realized he'd been hit, he lay flat on his back. Ravenwood's knee pinned his gun arm to the ground. A slender sword tip pressed against his jugular.

"The game is over," Ravenwood snapped. "Die here. Or cease your games and return to our world where we belong."

Duncan sneered in response. "Or stay here debating about it until we're both devoured alive. I told you. I'm already de…"

Ravenwood ended the debate with a knockout blow to the face. He quickly sheathed his sword, reclaimed his pistol, and hefted the man over his shoulder in a fireman's carry. Out of the corner of his eye, the gloom seemed to writhe to life as the charging creatures grew close enough to be discernible. He focused his will for another jump back to the material plane, but the cold, the chaos, and the fear permeating all six of his senses mounted.

Suddenly a distant flare bathed the area in warm golden light. The rampaging footsteps on Ravenwood's trail faltered in a fit of screeching. Even the black smoke retreated and the oily surface of the ground sizzled and evaporated.

Ravenwood steeled himself and ran toward the light. Over the course of his next several breaths, he found the strength to refocus his aura, and sprinted into a dingy alley in Midtown Manhattan. His eyes widened in shock as a cement wall appeared as if out of nowhere. Unable to halt his momentum, he threw himself into a rolling fall and tumbled hard into a row of trash cans.

For a moment he just sat there on the filthy pavement, propped on his good arm, slowing his thoughts and breathing in order to confirm that he was, indeed, alive.

The Nameless One regarded him coolly.

Ravenwood blinked at him. "I thought you weren't going to help me."

"And I didn't," the Master replied simply, and vanished.

Ravenwood blinked again, musing on the riddle. He smiled. Indeed, his Master had not helped him perform the specific task for which he'd sought his aid.

It occurred to him that perhaps a being such as the Nameless One, so in tune with the forces of nature, with living energy, was quite literally incapable of entering the place he had just been. The tiny bit of light shed by his magic infused weapons attracted shadow creatures like moths to a flame. What would the presence, even the astral presence, of a true Master of chi sorcery have done, he wondered, if he'd been able to bridge through shadows in the first place.

His placid blue eyes fell upon the stirring form of Duncan McConnell. That much of the threat to the city was over. A smile stretched across Ravenwood's face as screeching brakes and wailing sirens filled the air.

Father Ricci hiked down the trail through Central Park with marked trepidation. The flashlight in his hands shook a little more with each step.

"You're certain it's this way?" he asked.

"The map in McConnell's notes was fairly precise. Though your reaction confirms we are on the right path." Ravenwood pushed aside a bit of brush that served as a gate of sorts into the clearing ahead. "The earth has been defiled by repeated summonings. It is reacting to your presence."

"Not mine," Ricci corrected. "His."

"Semantics," Ravenwood said, clearing the camouflage off the ritual circle. "Are you sure you're up to this, Vincent?"

The priest whispered a short prayer and nodded.

With that, Ravenwood placed five candles in the stone at each point of the etched pentagram, softly incanting a variation on

McConnell's ritual in Old Tibetan. The carefully constructed modification eliminated any implied servitude or motivation for calling on the demon's name, and more importantly, did not require a blood rite.

"*Na'qhasu wǒzhàohuàn nǐ.*" The occult investigator circled a second time, this time lighting the candles. "*Na'qhasu wǒ zhàohuàn nǐ,*" he repeated. Then a third, infusing his will into the flames before coming to a stop next to Ricci. "*Na'qhasu wǒ zhàohuàn nǐ!*"

A column of swirling black mist filled the circle.

"Ravenwood," it said, drawing out the syllables. "Not that I am dishonored by your request for an audience, but do you know what it means to call my name thrice without paying fealty?"

"I seek no accord with you, demon" Ravenwood said, his cordial tone darkened by a faint growl in his voice.

"And yet you are about to ask me for something."

"Not ask. State. You will leave this world and never return."

A single, jovial laugh erupted. "Or what?"

"Father," Ravenwood said. "Proceed."

"Ah." The semblance of a head tilted curiously. "Padre. Didn't see you there."

Father Ricci began to recite a prayer of sanctifying in reply.

"Don't you want to hear my master plan first?" the Hellborne asked sarcastically.

"Not particularly," Ravenwood answered dryly. "Whatever designs you had on this city are about to be rendered moot."

"Oh I'm afraid not," he said. "My minions are everywhere. And they've told me all about you. I've been looking forward to meeting you for some time, in fact. Tis an honor."

Ravenwood did not dignify him with a response.

The demon chuckled. The smoke coalesced into a more humanoid shape, squaring its shoulders with Ravenwood in a show of continuing to ignore Father Ricci. "I don't know what you hope to accomplish here. You never should have offered Duncan Alistair McConnell protection. His soul belongs to me. I can take it whenever I wish, whether this portal remains open or not."

"That was his choice," Ravenwood said dryly. "But you won't harm any more innocents."

"Innocent? You don't spend much time outside your ivory tower, do you?"

Ravenwood's brow furrowed curiously. "Baiting me to keep me distracted from your approaching 'minions' as you called them? And here you claimed to have so much respect for me."

"Alas, thus far you are failing to live up to expectations."

Ravenwood shrugged, scanning the tree line with feigned disinterest. "Neither are you."

"I am Na'qhasu!" the entity roared. "Lord of the Firth House of Kaziel. My name is spoken in trembled whispers." With every word, the smoke solidified, taking on an auburn hue. Soon the two men gazed upon a monstrous creature.

The demon stood fully eight feet tall, with impossibly wide shoulders, on bestial legs with cloven hooves. A pair of wings folded across his back like a leather cloak. Its thickly muscled arms ended in taloned hands larger than a man's head. Reddish white horns curved out of its temples, and tusks jutted from its craggy jaw. It craned its neck back, as if stretching after along nap, then settled its head back to look back down upon the mortals. Four red eyes narrowed angrily.

Father Ricci broke from his incantation, though his voice never wavered. "You are powerless in the light of the true Lord of Heaven and Earth."

Na'qhasu regarded the priest like a gnat. "We shall see."

The foliage at the edge of the clearing rustled in patterns to unnatural to be merely the wind. Ravenwood adjusted the grip on his walking stick, causing the carvings along it to glow faintly. He assumed a ready stance next to Ricci, and whispered. "Tell me you don't have to start over."

The strength of Ricci's tenor rose in response as he picked up the rite where he left off.

Two men burst out of the night. Ravenwood sprang to intercept them. The first went down with a single stroke of his cane. The second doubled over from a swift kick to the midsection, crumpling the rest of the way from an elbow to the base of his neck. Two more rushed at him as if from nowhere, meeting the same fate in a flurry of cane strikes. A fifth charged Father Ricci from the far side of the clearing. He fell in a heap as Ravenwood speared him with running tackle.

Three more emerged through the brush.

"You can't keep this up all night," Na'qhasu said. "My thralls are legion."

Ravenwood ignored him, flipping a possessed minion head over heels into the path of another with a spinning arm hook. His momentum carried him into a graceful spin, and the trailing attacker jerked backwards with a crack of wood against this skull.

Two more appeared. One with a gun in his hand.

He heard at least one more behind him.

Ravenwood unholstered his Luger and snapped off two shots. Both men in front of him flopped backward in death spasms. He whipped around and flung his cane in the same breath. The spinning club pounded one man in the chest, bouncing into the head of another with nearly the same force as the bullets.

"*Huílái*," Ravenwood barked, and the enchanted weapon returned to his outstretched hand.

"Good show." Na'qhasu broke into bemused applause. "How long, you think, before the constable arrives to investigate the sound of gunfire?"

"Longer than you have left," Ravenwood said, keeping his pistol trained on the perimeter.

As if on cue, Father Ricci boomed, "*In inférnum detrúde. Ámen!*" The air crackled. For an instant, the dim moonlight reflecting on the grass brightened, then washed away on a warm breeze flowing outward from the stoic priest.

Crickets in the park hesitantly resumed their chirping.

Within the confines of the summoning circle, Na'qhasu looked about idly. At length he raised his hands, quaking in mock surrender.

"I don't understand," Ricci muttered. "Why is the portal not closed?"

The demon pointed. "Because he invited me here." Ravenwood's deep amber eyes darted between the Hellborne and his friend. Na'qhasu laughed. "For such a learned scholar you know so little.

You see, Father, when he invoked this gate, it created an imbalance. One he willfully neglected to fill. In doing so, he granted me open access to your world. And more importantly, the power to do this."

The demon's fists clenched as he crossed his arms. Eldritch energy flowed off its body, filling the cylinder it stood within. It whipped its hands apart, sending splinters through the invisible barrier. A second strike shattered it like a fragile wine glass.

"It also," Ravenwood added. "Gave you a physical body of flesh and bone, allowing me to do this." He raised his Luger, and emptied it into the monster's chest.

Na'qhasu reeled backwards, flinching with the impact of each iron coated slug. The weapon clacked open after six pulls of the trigger. The demon steadied itself, spread its wings and roared in unbridled rage. It marched forward, undeterred by the streams of black ichor lining its chest.

Ravenwood took full advantage of the arrogant Lord's posturing by calmly replacing the spent magazine, relocking the breech, and firing eight more iron rounds into the beast's torso. The barrage halted the demon's charge at the edge of the stone table, though it stood its ground with defiance literally burning in its eyes.

"You insignificant flea!" Na'qhasu screamed. It took a single step forward, stomping its hoof with the force of a stone pile driver, sending a shockwave across the breadth of the clearing that knocked both men off their feet.

The sanctified ground under the Hellborne's foot began to smolder. It laughed despite its ragged breathing and incanted a terse phrase in an inhuman tongue. The air crackled as before, this time blasting a frigid wind outward that wilted the grass in its wake.

"Now!" shouted Ravenwood.

Na'qhasu whirled to face the occult investigator. And froze. Its twin rows of eyes widened in an expression that seemed entirely alien on a creature of such evil. Fear. Father Ricci looked up, confusion warring with panic. He followed the gaze of the demon, which was not focused on Ravenwood, but past him. Looking at nothing.

"You," the demon rasped. "It's impossible. You're dead."

The Nameless One allowed himself a small smile at the Hellborne's shock. Without further ceremony, a deluge of energy flooded from every corner of Central Park. It formed a swirling vortex around the ancient master's astral projection. Then with a single, swift gesture, he channeled the wellspring of pure lifeforce into a geyser that slammed into Na'qhasu with a thunderous explosion.

Father Ricci shielded his eyes from the sudden flash of light that engulfed the demon. By the time he dared to look again, only wisps of red smoke remained. All around them, the fallen disciples of the minion stirred. The same red smoke wafted off all but the two who'd been killed.

Ravenwood rose, pulling an errant branch from his lapel pocket. "Well done, Vincent."

"Well done…?" Ricci stammered. "What just happened?"

"We defeated the villain," Ravenwood said. "Well, banished him at any rate. I suspect not for the first time." He glanced idly at the Nameless One's astral projection, then added, "Though hopefully the last within my lifetime."

"This was your plan all along," Ricci said, gesturing at nothing in frustration. "Whatever _this_ was. What was I then? Bait? A diversion?"

"Nonsense," Ravenwood objected flatly. "The effort he expended to defile the ground you hallowed made him vulnerable. I would never needlessly put your in danger, my friend."

Vincent struggled to put his cluttered thoughts to words, but ultimately gave up and chuckled. "You're not going to tell me who the demon was talking to, either. Are you."

Ravenwood nodded. "It's probably best that way."

The two men looked up at the sound of sirens closing in on them. Ricci glanced around at the disoriented men trying to sit up around them, then finally on the two dead. He frowned and regarded Ravenwood darkly.

"I had no choice, Vincent," he said.

"I know that," Ricci assured him. "I was just thinking that your plan also accounted for the presence of a priest when you tried to explain all of this to the police."

Ravenwood pursed his lips. He could only return the reverend's stern, accusing look with one of apology.

Father Ricci nodded at length as the shouts of the clamor of the authorities grew closer. "Let me do the talking," he said.

Ravenwood smiled. "Agreed."

The End

WHO IS RAVENWOOD?

So Ron invites me to write a story for Airship 27, and I'm taking a look at his library of characters. One name jumps out immediately. Ravenwood. Supernatural craziness in the 1930s. That's a unique era for the genre nowadays, where everything is either set in an older historical period or the 21st century. I'm all over that.

Thing is, my only frame of reference for an occult investigator is John Constantine, or the Winchester brothers. But this guy is an aloof playboy. He knows the world is not what people think it is. He knows that magic and creatures of folklore are real. He knows what lurks in the shadows. And he takes that in stride with a ready quip and an easy smile. I found that dichotomy fascinating, especially for a classic pulp character. Challenge accepted.

At fist my take on him was actually a little too light hearted. Ravenwood came across a bit too dorky in the first draft. The interaction between him and Stagg played out like a comedy routine. As you (hopefully) picked up on, I like healthy doses of humor in my stories, but only delivered in ways that fit the tone of the characters. Ron set me straight on that early on, and I readjusted the image in my head of who this guy was. He started to resemble something closer to Roger Moore's rendition of James Bond. Things started to fall into place easier with that in mind.

The plot came first, as is the way of pulps. I've always loved the creepy idea of shadow dimensions, another literal world that lies just on the other side of the darkness. Down every alley, around every corner. And I saw a perfect opportunity to run a connecting thread through my other anthology stories. Look for Na'qahsu to show up again in different adventures.

But how would this hero handle the threat? Sure the story is plot driven, but the focus is still on Ravenwood. Without an interesting hero to follow, it all falls apart. A lot of the character centric scenes really kind of wrote themselves. The more I thought about how this guy would react to the events around him, the more he intrigued me.

First there's the fact that he's so filthy rich. In the middle of the Great Depression, that alone is significant thing that sets him apart from the world he lives in. Everyone sees the way he dresses and the sports car and immediately writes him off as some elitist playboy... which he is. I can't imagine anyone outside of his circle of equally rich socialites liking him very much. But he's also the guy keeping your kids safe from the boogeyman. Often literally.

That's why I knew his relationship with Inspector Stagg would be gold. A blue collar New York copper and an Uptown rich kid would be like oil and water.

But even though the original pulps played Stagg off like a kind of Keystone Cop, I couldn't bring myself to do that. I have too much respect for the badge and I've loved cop shows my whole life. Stagg is my kind of character. It's true, he can't possibly wrap his mind around the things Ravenwood deals with. And either through plot convenience or willful ignorance, he gets to live in denial of those things he can't explain. But he's not an idiot. I definitely wanted to spend time with those two.

By hook or crook, I was going to have a car chase. I did quite a bit of research on New York of the era for landmarks to use. And I just couldn't pass up the scene where Ravenwood drives up in front of Stagg in a brand new hideously expensive car the next day after trashing his old one.

And of course, there's The Nameless One. He's a toughie. The hero of the tale is Ravenwood, a mortal man with at most a modicum of magical knowledge. So you don't want The Nameless One to be the cop out solution that makes your main character look inept. But you can't ignore him and expect a guy with so little raw power to fare well against creatures above his weight class either.

I saw the two as teacher and student, not weird old guy who annoys Sterling and lucky kid who inherited a life debt. They are a team, like Remo and Chuin, but with obviously different chemistry. The idea of putting them at odds over a case struck me as interesting, and something I don't think anyone else has done, at least at the time I started writing it.

So that's a peek inside the process. If you can call it that. Hope you had as much fun reading the story as I had writing it.

L.R. STAHLBERG - After surviving college and a decade of trying to fit in the world of traditional wisdom, Lance wandered the fringes of the comic book industry. First as an indie self-publisher, than as a distributor for a few years.

He has since joined the New Pulp movement with novellas in the crime, spy thriller, superhero, and supernatural genres. Nominated for 2014 New Pulp Awards: Best New Writer.

You can find him at LRStahlberg.com.

THE RABBI'S SCOURGE
by DeWayne Dowers

"Inspector, inspector, over here," called a shadowy figured tucked under the entrance to the mausoleum in an effort to stay dry in what was turning out to be a hell of a storm.

"Shut your mouth you fool. I see you," whispered Inspector Horatio Stagg "And get that flashlight out of my eyes."

Inspector Stagg was awakened with a start at 2:45 a.m. with an unsettling report of a grave being vandalized in Queens. It was the kind of thing that was disturbing in the best of times, but these weren't the best of times and there wasn't anything normal about this call. For the last week, it had been as if someone had torn the sky in half and offended the heavens causing all of God's wrath to be poured out in wind and rain and hail and in freakish occurrences.

Inspector Stagg shined his flashlight into the mausoleum. Its dark oak doors were splintered and ripped from their hinges revealing muddy footprints that led into its dark recesses. There were two sets of footprints that seemed to move in and out of the monument and then a third set that was almost indiscernible. "What happened here?" asked Stagg. The patrolman started to answer but the Inspector cut him off, "That was a rhetorical question."

The inspector raised his flashlight overhead and read the name that was hewn into the stone of the mausoleum. It read 'Masseria'. "For the love of everything that is holy," spat out Stagg "I'm guessing that's Joe Masseria, the dead mob boss."

"Yes sir, I believe so," responded the patrolman.

"Shut up, I wasn't asking you," blurted out Stagg. "Of all the dead ginnys in this god forsaken place they pick Joe Masseria's tomb to mess with."

"It's a little more than that sir," said the patrolman.

Rain poured into the mausoleum causing the already unsavory smell of death to wrap about you like a pungent shroud choking the air from your lungs. The patrolman gagged and felt his supper lurch forward. Inspector Stagg dismissed him with a wave of his hand. He reached into his overcoat pocket and pulled out a half-eaten bag of peanuts. They were stale and most likely had been hidden away in his coat for several weeks. But the salty crunch provided a needed distraction from the grisly scene. Stagg looked down into the open coffin of former mob boss Joe Masseria.

"They cut off his head," Stagg mumbled out loud but there was no one around to hear him. Stagg raised the bag of peanuts to his lips again taking in a mouthful. "His hands are missing," he whispered pushing at the torso of Masseria with his flashlight. "They disemboweled him as well," said Stagg. "This city is a diseased lot, full of deranged pukes." Stagg turned to walk out of the Mausoleum and his gaze fell upon a tall, specter standing across from the tomb. His eyes were burned brilliantly despite the torrential rains.

"Hey, stop," Stagg yelled out as he pushed his way out of the mausoleum but the shade was gone.

"I've got to get going," she said as she eyed the alarm clock sitting on the dresser. It read 4 a.m.

"If you leave, you will break my heart," said Ravenwood. His eyes flashed green reflecting an insatiable appetite for the curvy redhead that was pulling away from his grasp. "Stay and I will have Sterling fix you an unbelievable omelet. You really can't beat the fresh tomatoes and peppers. He grows them himself."

"I don't think Sterling cares for me," she said as pulled on her blouse and began searching for her shoes. "And he certainly wouldn't care for me if you had him fix me breakfast at such an odd hour." She was not the kind of girl that spent night with strange men nor was she the kind of girl that slinked out of their homes in the middle of the night but there was something different about Ravenwood. He was like cool water to parched lips. His wavy brown hair and entreating eyes had left her mesmerized causing her will to be subjugated to his desire.

"Sterling doesn't care for anyone, really," Ravenwood said as he leaned back against a pillow and struck a match. It caused an orange glow about his face revealing his smile and dimpled cheek but then she noticed that his eyes had turned gray possibly with the disappointment of her leaving. Ravenwood sucked down on his cigarette and let out a puff of smoke that wafted across the room. "He likes me possibly, but I doubt anyone else."

She picked up her purse and tucked it carefully under her arm. "Goodnight, Ravenwood." She smiled. It had been a good night. She knew that she would probably never see him again but she didn't regret what she had done. Some things simply had to be experienced. She thought to herself as she started for the door, how could one describe a star if they had never seen one or how could someone describe the smell of fresh cut grass, if they had never taken a deep breath on a summer morning? No some things simply had to be experiences. Hunger, thirst were all God given longings she thought but she knew the hungers that she had satisfied this night were more devilish in nature.

"Goodnight," Ravenwood said as he watched her close the bedroom door behind her. Ravenwood extinguished his cigarette and rolled over to his side. His eyes were heavy with sleep and soon he was dreaming but they weren't dreams of red hair and pale skin. These dreams were more visceral and vile.

Ravenwood was drawn into the world that exist between life and death that place that we hover only for the briefest span of time. He was pulled into that place where reality is ill shaped by our own desires and where futures cry out through our pangs. He saw a holy man drenched in another's blood walking through vacant streets. A dark, ominous shadow followed him limping with an unusual gait. Ravenwood's ears were filled with the flapping of birds' wings. He was startled awake by his dream.

The Nameless One stood in the corner of his bedroom silently.

His sackcloth vestment was stained with dirt and dappled with caked on blood that appeared almost black. The sleeveless garment barely covered him with its crudely stitched hem falling just above mid-thigh. A singled strand of coarse rope cinched the makeshift robe at the waist. His feet were bare and stained with blood and mud as well. Candles did little to illuminate the dank, tenebrous chamber but in the faint light his muscular arms shimmered as he strained to hold the frantic ram in place. He turned his face to the left revealing a pink scar that ran from just below his eye and down his cheek bone as he tore open the throat of the ram allowing its life to pour out onto a mound of earth and stone. He uttered words that weren't from this world but from a world that had long ago faded into the archaic. Soon, the animal no longer struggled but lay still, its dead eyes were fixed on the holy man.

"I will not. You can eat what I have prepared," said Sterling.

"The god who made the mouth will provide the food," said the Nameless One as he dismissed Sterling's argument by waving both hands at him in exasperation.

"Well, he can cook it as well because I am not searching all over the market for Foo Gwa," Sterling said a little too loudly. "I have prepared a crown roast with a peach-ginger sweet potato, and cinnamon apple sauce and you are welcome to join Ravenwood for dinner," said Sterling but the Nameless One had vanished. "I did pick up the corbaci peppers that you requested."

"I think he has left, Sterling," said Ravenwood startling his butler.

Sterling jumped and exclaimed, "He is quite impossible," and with that he excused himself to the kitchen muttering as he went.

Ravenwood seated himself at the mahogany dining table and picked up a glass of wine that Sterling had poured in anticipation of his arrival for supper. He considered briefly calling on Iris but those thoughts were interrupted by a voice that he could only hear.

"Calvary cemetery. Queens," whispered the Nameless One to his thoughts.

"Can I have dinner in peace first?" Ravenwood said out loud. "It's bad enough that you invade my dreams and now you interrupt my dinner?"

"I sensed your distress and came to you as I have sworn," whispered the Nameless One "but I did not send the visions."

Sterling returned to the dining room carrying a silver charger with a bronzed, perfectly charred crown roast. The smell of the seared flesh and roasted herbs filled the penthouse fueling the hunger pangs of an already ravenous Ravenwood.

"Eat quickly. Stagg was at the mausoleum early this morning. He may return," said the Nameless One.

Purring up the drive, the convertible coupe rumbled to a stop just outside of the second addition of Calvary cemetery. Countless thousands had been interned in Calvary cemetery since the first shovel of dirt was overturned. Some more memorable than others but by far one of the most infamous stiffs was Joe Masseria. None other than Lucky Luciano allegedly murdered him. This was a hornet's nest and Ravenwood knew it. He would rather trek across a few hundred acres than his car be seen parked next to the defiled grave of a former mob boss.

The torrential rains had stopped and the dark clouds had given way to a bright low hanging moon. Ravenwood slid out of the convertible with his cane in hand and his hat pulled down low. It was unlikely that he would be noticed but if he was noticed it was more unlikely that he wouldn't be recognized. No reason to take chances he thought.

"No indeed," responded the familiar voice of the Nameless One.

"I may never get accustom to that," said Ravenwood.

"Ahh, to find god while searching for a stone," whispered the Nameless One.

"Or that," sighed Ravenwood, "Why exactly am I here? Since when is it my business to get involved in the interworking of the families?"

"Darkness is merely the absence of light. Evil however can corrupt the holy," said the Nameless One.

Ravenwood shook his head and strode into the darkness. He discovered Masseria's tomb within the hour but it wasn't because he read the name emblazoned in marble. It was because several thugs stood outside the entrance guarding the mausoleum. One of the gangster's squatted smoking a cigarette staring off into the distance while two others leaned against the stonewalls of the tomb. Ravenwood picked up a couple of stones and flung one behind the unwitting gangsters. The rock bounced off of a marker and landed solidly in a puddle.

"Go check it out," snarled the gangster that had been squatting. He stood and took a long drag off of his fag and flicked it away. He pulled a revolver from his waistband and followed after the other two mobsters.

"That is less than adequate. They will return," said the Nameless One.

"I know," mumbled Ravenwood as he closed the distance quickly so that he was leaned against the entrance to the mausoleum when the mobsters turned from checking out the noise. He lit a cigarette allowing the glow of the match to reveal his position.

"What the hell?" said one of the thugs.

"We have us a wiseacre here, boys," said another.

"Sal Grillo is the name of the one that just spoke. He was muscle for Masseria. Luciano has plans of sending him to Chicago but has him here for the time being as a sign of goodwill between him and those that still have some allegiance to Masseria," said the Nameless One.

"Sal, is that anyway to treat a friend," said Ravenwood.

"You're no friend of mine," said Sal Grillo.

"Maybe not a friend of yours but a friend Mr. Luciano," said Ravenwood "He asked that I take a look in on things."

"The boss never mentioned anything about anyone looking in," said Grillo.

"I don't mean to put you in a hard place," Ravenwood turned to leave "I'll just let Mr. Luciano know that I wasn't allowed inside the crypt. No worries, Sally."

Sal Grillo cursed. Ravenwood turned again and walked into the mausoleum of Joe Masseria unopposed by Luciano's men.

Ravenwood stepped just inside of the crypt and stood quietly, solemnly. His lips were pressed together tightly as he allowed the lingering shades to tug at his consciousness. It was a horrid bouquet of scents that pulled him in at first that of blood and earth then he was overcome by cold shiver that reminded him of stone or granite. Shortly after, an intense feeling of apprehension flooded his mind that almost forced him from the mausoleum but it was soon replaced by nausea and a deep-seated fear.

"They have been disquieted and refuse to rest," said the Nameless One.

"What could have possibly disturbed them in such a manner?" asked Ravenwood.

"Ya say something in there, bud?" asked Sal.

The Nameless One refused to answer Ravenwood's query, as was his custom. "Nah, just thinking out loud," mumbled Ravenwood.

"I'll take the drop," said Fat Tony "I'm meeting up with the banker later." Fat Tony snatched up two large satchels filled with cash. Louis Vacca ran a small casino over on 87 East Fourth Street in the Village for Lucky Luciano and it had been a lucrative two days.

"Take Little Tony with ya. I don't want any surprises," said Vacca. He struggled to open the middle draw of his beat up cherry wood desk. He was a lithe little fellow in a tawdry suit. His easy demeanor suited him well for the job but hadn't made him a favorite amongst his peers. Regardless, Luciano saw something in him and had entrusted with the casino. "I don't want any trouble," said Vacca.

"Ya, ya, no trouble," said Fat Tony.

"I'm serious," said Vacca "No screw ups."

"I heard ya already," said Fat Tony as he pushed open the door at the rear of the building and stepped out into the alley.

"Tony," called out Fat Tony, "Tony, Vacca wants you to ride along." No one responded.

"Tony," again Fat Tony called out. The air stood still and the humid New York summer night seemed to close in about Fat Tony. "Alright, quit screwing around," he called out receiving the same response as previously. Tony dropped one of the satchels and pulled a .38 revolver from the waistband of his pants. "Tony," he called out again. He turned opening the screen door and pushed the satchel he had dropped inside then sat the other one beside it. Fat Tony froze in place when he heard footfalls behind him. He waited a long moment before slowly turning around.

"It's you," said Fat Tony. He stared into a set of eyes that resembled flames on a hearth. The man staring at him had silver hair that was cropped close to his head and a long flowing beard. A pink scar trailed down his cheek from just below his left eye. A sackcloth robe was cinched tight about him with a single cord of rope. "You scared the hell out of me," said Fat Tony, "What the hell are you wearing? Why are you out here? Tony?"

Fat Tony slid his gun back into the waistband pants feeling relieved that it was only a crazy old fool in the back alley. As he turned to recover the satchels, he noticed the mangled body of Little Tony balled into a heap by stoop. He fumbled to retrieve his gun but when he looked up the old man was gone.

"Vacca, Vacca, get out here," screamed Fat Tony as he backed up against the screen door trying retreat into the building. That's when it emerged from the shadows moving slowly toward him. He raised his revolver and squeezed off the first shot and then followed immediately with a second. Both bullets tore into its chest but it continued to lumber forward. Fat Tony fired a third round and then a fourth both having similar affect. The monstrosity reached for Tony and he screamed as it lifted him from the ground by his head holding him suspended between heaven and earth. Tony writhed about trying to free himself from its grip. One of his brown and white wingtip shoes came lose and fell to the step. It closed its fist about Tony's head crushing the gangster's skull as if it was wadding up a piece of paper. Blood trickled down the monsters arm leaving red blotches on the discarded shoe.

"Inspector Stagg is waiting at your car. He has been there for some time," said the Nameless One.

"How did he know where?" asked Ravenwood.

"He's not entirely clueless. It seems that he followed you from the penthouse," said the Nameless One.

"Anything else I should know?" asked Ravenwood but there was no response. "No fitting proverb?" But the Nameless One was gone.

"Inspector, I had no idea that you were a fan of sports cars?" asked Ravenwood.

Inspector Stagg leaned against the door of the convertible and stared at Ravenwood for a long moment. His shoes were caked with clay-like mud, and he seemed more disheveled than usual. Stagg's overcoat was slung open and his revolver was visible to all that might look.

The Inspector finally spoke, "I had no idea that you enjoyed hanging out in graveyards at night." Stagg didn't offer to move but remained perched against Ravenwood's car door.

"We can learn much from the past and little exercise never hurt anyone," said Ravenwood as he made a point to stare at the waistline of the inspector.

"What were you trying to learn from a dead mob boss' grave?" asked Stagg.

"Inspector, you don't want to get mixed up in this. This is an evil hoodoo," warned Ravenwood.

"It's my job to get mixed up in this stuff," Stagg rebutted as he stood to his feet. "And that's a load of crap and you know it. Hoodoo? It's more of the same. Someone is trying to get things stirred up between the families and I plan on finding out who that someone is and I'm going to arrest them."

Ravenwood stepped past the grizzled detective and climbed into his car. "I would seriously take a pass on this one Inspector Stagg. It would be for your own good."

"You threatening me, Ravenwood?" snarled Stagg.

"No. I'm just trying to help."

"I don't need your help and if I find out you are involved in this, you'll end up in jail," barked the Inspector.

Ravenwood nodded and started up his car. He left Stagg standing in the glow of his taillights. Something had disturbed the lingering shades of Calvary cemetery and not only disturbed the spirits but caused a prevailing sense of fear, almost panic amongst them. Ravenwood wondered what cause the dead to panic. He turned onto the highway and headed back toward the penthouse. He thought that Inspector Stagg was going to be a nuisance in the very least and at most might get himself killed.

"What in the world is a matter with people?" asked Stagg shuddering in disbelief.

"Eight dead from what we can determine," reported Sergeant Tom Coker.

"What," said Stagg "from what you can determine?"

Fat Tony, otherwise known as Anthony Lanza, was decapitated and laying on the stoop halfway into the building and halfway out. Little Tony's, born Tony Tannenbaum, back was broken and he was folded into a bloody mess next to the dumpster.

"Parts of some of the victims are missing," said Coker.

"Missing?"

"Yes, sir missing or scattered. We are still trying to figure out what happened."

Stagg bent down and removed a red ribbon from the bottom of his brogue oxford. It was covered in dark blood. Stagg swallowed hard as it dawned on him that it was a child's hair ribbon. "Canvas the area. I want to know if anyone saw anything. I want to know if anyone else is missing and get every available patrolman here now," commanded Stagg. He shoved the bloody ribbon into his pocket. His anger quelled his sorrow as he stepped into the gambling hall. He next discovered Vacca, the boss of the operation, pummeled to death by what could have only been enormous fists. "Nothing human could have done this," he whispered to himself. Vacca's body was twisted and resembled a man only in the vaguest sense of the word. He stepped through the small, clammy office that reeked of death and followed a long hall into the main gambling hall. Tables were turned over, chairs were splintered, and death was everywhere.

"What could have done this?" Stagg mused. A rookie was working over in a corner trying to cover a lady who should have been at home last night instead of this less reputable establishment. The young man held a handkerchief over his face and was visibly shaken.

"Hey rook, what's your name?" asked Stagg.

"Malone sir. Jacob Malone."

"Malone, they need help outback. I need to you to rope the area and keep the press out of here," ordered Stagg. It was simply no way for a young officer to spend his first day on the job.

"Yes sir," said Malone and he hurried out of the building.

Ravenwood stepped out of the shower and reached for his robe. Inspector Stagg handed it to him.

"I could not prevent him, sir," insisted Sterling from the other side of the door.

"He has two officers in the penthouse and he has back up stationed on the street. He thinks you were involved in a multiple homicide across town," said the Nameless One in a voice that only Ravenwood could hear.

"Its fine, Sterling. Offer the officers some coffee. We will be right out," said Ravenwood as he pulled the robe about himself.

"How did you know there were there?" queried Stagg.

"Because you would have never made it past Sterling if you had been alone," answered Ravenwood. "Now if you don't mind, please wait for me in my study."

"I do mind. I'm not leaving you alone until we have had the opportunity to talk."

Ravenwood stepped past the Inspector and led him out into the bedroom. "What exactly are you wanting to discuss?"

"Where were you last night for starters?"

"You know exactly where I was."

"After that, where did you go after you left Calvary?"

"I came back to the penthouse. I ate a late supper of mutton with an unusual curry sauce. Not exactly to my taste."

"Can anyone confirm your story?"

"Of course, Sterling served me," Ravenwood slipped on a pair of slacks. "What is all of this about?"

"Was anyone else here?" Stagg looked around the expansive bedroom.

"I don't see how that is any of your business."

Stagg pulled the red ribbon from his pocket that was still caked with dry blood. It was immediately obvious to Ravenwood that it belonged to a child. Ravenwood's muscles tensed and his lips straightened into a narrow expression of anger.

"I need your help," Stagg admitted at last.

"You have a hell of a way of asking for it."

Stagg turned his back and walked toward the bedroom doors. "Eight dead. Torn into pieces. A little girl is missing. She is most likely dead as well," Stagg elaborated. "Excuse my lack of decorum."

Ravenwood stepped into his study wearing a pair of dark slacks and a crisp white shirt. His white gold and ruby studded cufflinks matched his red silk tie. He wore a pair of red and white spectator shoes that were shined and peeked out from under the cuff break of his pants. His Luger was strapped under his left arm in a shoulder holster. "What sort of help are you looking for?" He seated himself behind an enormous rosewood desk with gilded lion feet that was littered with archaic text and weathered journals.

Inspector Stagg sat on the edge of a button back burgundy chair facing Ravenwood. "What happened in the East Village is indescribable! It wasn't human."

"What wasn't human?"

"Whatever it was that did all this."

"I'll need access to the building," Ravenwood explained.

"That's not possible," offered one of the officers accompanying Stagg.

"I will arrange it," Stagg relented.

"But Inspector, he's probably involved. He's knows more than he is telling us," protested the same cop.

"I can assure you I don't…but I will soon," Ravenwood promised. "And you are going to need my assistance."

"Like, I said, I will make the arrangements," Stagg repeated.

"Also, I don't need anyone getting in my way. No one tailing me. I don't want anyone getting hurt. Not me and not them," said Ravenwood.

"Just stop whatever is doing this!" pleaded a desperate Stagg.

A wide drag of blood, dirt, and gravel led down the steps into the dark recesses of the damp, musty chamber. The trail led to a stark altar with candles scattered about it burning low. A giant, lifeless figure was slumped prostate across the table. It was more than nine feet tall, misshapen, and grotesque. Malevolence clung to the beast like a shroud.

"Your sins be my sins," breathed a man with short-cropped silver hair and a long flowing beard. He placed his hands upon the monster wiping

"What kind of help are you looking for?"

the splattered blood from its awful figure and smeared that blood upon his face then his chest. "Your transgressions be my transgressions," he said in a louder voice as he rubbed the gore into his beard. "Forgive the unnecessary results of the necessary violence," he moaned standing naked before the creature with his sackcloth robe cast off in the corner. He placed his finger into a bullet wound whirling it about in a circular motion then he knelt with his hands up raised and began chanting in an obscure dialect.

Ravenwood pulled up in front Abram's Butcher Shop in his deep red Delahaye convertible coupe. He linger a moment allowing the rumbling of its V12 engine to gather the attention of everyone inside. He paused a moment longer to give everyone the wrong idea. His eyes flashed bright blue as stared at the bustling storefront. He knew there were six customers inside; all of them were there to pick up their weekly orders. Henry, the owner's son, worked behind the counter and was unarmed. There was a long barrel shotgun laid under the far counter but well beyond Henry's reach. Ravenwood also knew that there was a clutch of mobsters gathered in the stockroom but no one over a lieutenant was present. He grabbed his cane and walked briskly into the butcher shop ignoring everyone around him.

"They are in the back Mr. Ravenwood," said Henry.

"Thanks Henry," said Ravenwood "I'll be just a moment." Henry wondered why he had said that and was even more confused about how he knew Ravenwood's name. He shook his head and disbelief but didn't feel it necessary to stop him from entering the stockroom.

"Boys, don't get up," Ravenwood directed. "I have just a few questions for you." Ravenwood held his cane loosely in his left hand and his suitcoat was unbuttoned. A solider type for the Genovese crime family was leaned back in his chair against the wall. He rocked slowly forward setting all four legs of the chair on the ground. The solider was powerfully built and well over six foot tall. His thick brown hair was slicked straight back and a butt of a cigar dangled from the left side of his mouth. "There's no reason for trouble, fellas," Ravenwood added.

The solider leaped to his feet reaching for a revolver that was holstered at his side while two other mobsters did the same. Ravenwood swung his cane low catching the solider at the knees and upending him. Then faster than what should have been possible Ravenwood reached the table that the mobsters sat around and flipped it upwards and drove it into them pinning them against the wall.

"I tried being polite but I'm guessing courtesy is wasted on a lot like you."

The solider that initially drew on Ravenwood had regained his feet and was bringing his weapon to bear on him. With incomparable speed, Mr. Ravenwood pulled his Luger from its holster and aimed it between the eyes of the Genovese thug. "Toss your gun over here," said Ravenwood. The thug complied without argument. "Now sit down."

Henry stepped into the stock room. "I've closed up shop like you asked, Mr. Ravenwood."

"Very nice Henry, thank you," nodded Ravenwood. Henry stood there with his shotgun resting against his hip. It was pointed at the gangsters pinned against the wall by the table.

"You want me to keep an eye on these guys, Mr. Ravenwood?" asked Henry.

"Yes, Henry. If any of them move or even flinch without my approval, blow off their knee caps." The young man concurred but felt very strange about what he was doing.

"Gentlemen, I know that you are in one way or another associated with Lucky Luciano," said Ravenwood. "And I know that some terrible things happened at one of his business ventures last evening. What I don't know is why? And what I don't know is who?" Ravenwood realized that this lot would not be privy to this kind of information. They might have their own personal theories but they would be void of any real information. This was all exhibition because Ravenwood to get the five families attention.

"Now let us sit down like men and discuss these matters," he continued. His eyes flashed green and gray. The gangsters gave a simple nod.

Ravenwood walked into his study with only more questions. It was difficult to ascertain if anything that he had discovered tonight was true or even possible. Lucky's men had regaled him with tales of a beast that stood over nine feet tall. A mindless monster that crept out of the shadows attacking indiscriminately all that were unlucky enough to cross its path. They said it had the strength of fifty men but wasn't a man at all. Ravenwood removed his fedora and tossed it onto his desk next. He laid his cane next to it and removed his gloves. As he walked around his desk and took a seat, he saw the Nameless One standing in front of the fireplace.

Ravenwood bowed his head slightly and the Nameless One responded in kind. "I have no idea what I'm up against," Ravenwood confessed.

"No one does," said the Nameless One.

"You don't know what I'm up against?" asked the occult detective, surprised by this admission on his teacher's part. Sterling entered the study carrying a silver platter that held a bottle of scotch and a single glass. "Thank you Sterling. I'll take it by the hearth."

"Of course, sir." Sterling set the platter between a pair of leather French club chairs that faced the fireplace. Sterling did not acknowledge the Nameless One but promptly exited the study.

"You said no one knows what I'm up against?" repeated Ravenwood.

"If you want to know what a tiger is like, look at a cat," suggested the Nameless One.

Ravenwood poured himself a glass of scotch and took a long contemplative sip. He looked down at his shoes recalling the clay like substance he found inside of the mausoleum. He also recalled the fear that the shades felt. Only an abominable act could have stirred the dead in such a way. "You are maddening most days." Ravenwood stood and walked back toward his desk.

"So you have said."

"But you may actually be onto something." Ravenwood set his glass on his desk and searched for a particular text. He looked up and his mentor had vanished.

Ravenwood spent the remainder of the night searching through ancient medical journals and archaic text that examined the darkest of practices of both medicine and magic. His eyes changed colors almost as often as he turned pages flashing from green to gray to blue and mixtures thereof. He mouthed the words of incantations silently and memorized spells with ease. The Nameless One looked in on him sporadically as Ravenwood searched for the cat that resembled his Tiger.

Sterling carried in a breakfast tray at exactly 7:15 AM with poached eggs, dry toast, and fresh squeezed orange juice. His New York Times was neatly tucked between the breakfast charger and the pitcher of juice.

"Sterling, Inspector Stagg is at the door. Show him in please," said Ravenwood.

"Sir, how do you…" Sterling was cut off by a stern look from his employer. "Yes sir, of course."

Ravenwood jotted a few notes down into a tablet pausing often to devour his breakfast.

Sterling stepped into the study several minutes later announcing Inspector Stagg. He looked like he gone without sleep as well. His overcoat hid the greater transgressions but his shirt and pants were crumpled stained with dried food indicating that he had spent the night in his car.

"Inspector," greeted Ravenwood. The Inspector grunted instead of offering a salutation. "Coffee, orange juice, maybe something for breakfast?"

"No thanks. Why am I here, Ravenwood?"

"Inspector, you called upon me. Remember?"

"True but I had a distinct impression that you wanted to see me. The impression was so strong that I left my stakeout and drove over," responded Inspector Stagg. Ravenwood smiled at him and pushed his hair back with both hands. "Exactly," said Stagg "Now, why am I here?"

"I've spent the night doing some research," Ravenwood informed the copper.

"I also heard that you roughed a few of Lucky's boys at the meat market," said Stagg.

"Like I said, I've been doing some research and we need to pay Joe Masseria a visit."

"His mausoleum or is the body that you want to examine?" .

"The body."

"The body is at the city morgue. What are you looking for?"

"I'm looking for a cat."

"Mr. Buchalter, do you have a moment that I could speak with you?" asked Rabbi Rash.

"Rabbi, I'm in a bit of a rush here," said Louis Buchalter.

"It will just take a moment of your time," pressed the Rabbi.

Buchalter motioned for his driver to bring the car around while ignoring the Rabbi's insistence. They stood outside of Zito's Bakery over on Bleecker Street. A young man was bringing fresh bread from the street level entrance of the cellar. Bread was stacked high in the storefront window below a sign that read five-cent loaves. Rabbi Rash had short white hair that was cropped close to his head and long flowing white beard. His black overcoat was buttoned up and he held his black derby in his hand along with a tall staff that might have been a walking stick. His shoes were stained with mud and clay. "Lepke, all I'm asking for is a moment of your time," repeated the Rabbi.

"I'm sorry old man," reiterated Louis 'Lepke' Buchalter of Murder Inc. "I'll send someone with nice contribution to the synagogue. Here's a bit to tide you over." He tucked a twenty-dollar bill into the Rabbi's coat pocket and started to walk away.

"Your money be damned with you," curesed Rabbi Rash.

Louis Buchalter spun around squaring off with the Rabbi. "What the hell did you say to me?"

"I said your money be damned with you!"

Buchalter laughed at the audacity of the cleric. "You shouldn't have said that old man." Buchalter reached to grab hold of the rabbi's lapels but Rabbi Rash slid out of his way and was suddenly standing behind Buchalter.

"You'll no longer practice your trade in Brooklyn or blood will fill the streets as it did in the East Village," declared the Rabbi. "You'll no longer hire the young boys as couriers, you will not enslave your own people within those textile factories, and you'll not spill blood again to gain filthy lucre."

Buchalter was outraged and pulled an ice pick from his coat. His intentions were clear but his target became a shapeless blur. Lepke struck at nothing.

"Man that is born of woman is of few days and full of trouble," intoned Rabbi Rash.

"I went to synagogue as a child. It didn't suit me," Lepke retorted as he turned himself about to face the Rabbi. Lepke started for the Rabbi once more but noticed that his driver was in a crumpled heap leaning against the car and stopped short.

"Let's see if you are faster than my gat." He pulled a 1911 .45 from its holster. The time he spent pulling his gun from its holster was more than enough time for the Rabbi to close the distance between them. Lepke was upended by a sweeping blow from the Rabbi's staff and now he was looking at him from his back on the concrete. Louis 'Lepke' Buchalter, head of Murder Inc., stared into the face of Rabbi Rash and for the first time noticed his fiery eyes and the pink scar that ran down his cheek from just below his eye.

"Ransack!" said Lepke in horror. The Rabbi smiled at Lepke and then vanished.

Inspector Stagg and Ravenwood were deep within the winding halls of the city morgue. Medical exam tables were littered with the remains of the victims from East Fourth Street. It was a gruesome jigsaw puzzle with bloody parts and missing pieces. Inspector Stagg pulled his handkerchief from his pocket and placed it over his mouth. Ravenwood's chameleon eyes scanned the scene pausing momentarily to exam each body.

"This may very well be more beneficial than we had expected," said Ravenwood to the Inspector.

Dr. Raymond Purvis stepped into the exam room a bit puzzled. "Mr. Ravenwood, I have prepared everything as you expected I hope." He stood nearly six foot tall and was a handsome sort. He had cool blue eyes, a stern chin, and a straight back. Dr. Purvis was the Chief Medical Examiner for the city of New York.

"Thank you Dr. Purvis. We would also like to discuss with you the remains of Joe Masseria." Ravenwood smoothed his lapels.

"Of course," Dr. Purvis heard himself agree but was disturbed as to why he would agree. "Right this way, gentlemen." Ravenwood and Inspector Stagg followed the Chief Medical Examiner over to an exam table against the far wall. "Mr. Ravenwood, this is irregular to say the least. I have no idea why I feel obliged to help you."

Inspector Stagg spoke up, "Because of this badge, that's why!" Stagg flashed his badge that was pinned to his chest.

"But Inspector I do not feel it necessary to help you. I feel driven to comply with Mr. Ravenwood's request," Dr. Purvis clarified.

"To the matter," Ravenwood pointed to the remains of Joe Masseria.

"Of course, Mr. Ravenwood. Joe Masseria, died April 15, 1931, cause of death multiple gunshot wounds. The killers used .32 and .38 caliber weapons."

"We are familiar with those details. What did you discover after he was exhumed?"

"His head was removed with a jagged instrument. Possibly a saw. His heart, liver, intestines were all removed along with his hands and feet."

Inspector Stagg took a step back from the examining table. "I'll meet you out front," he told Ravenwood.

"If you can wait, I'll be just a moment longer," Ravenwood replied. Inspector Stagg huffed and returned to the examination table.

"All incisions were crudely done," continued Dr. Purvis. "The individual you are looking for had no medical training."

"Thank you for your time Dr. Purvis." Ravenwood and started to shake the man's hand.

"Before you go, I prepared something for you." The Chief Medical Examiner handed a file and a small bag to Ravenwood. The Stepson of Mystery examined the contents of the bag and smiled. "Thank you, this will be most helpful.

The noon day sun threatened to interrupt the meditations of the Nameless One as he sat alone in the park adjacent to Sussex Towers. It was a rare occasion that he ventured out from the penthouse but today was such an occasion, with Sterling being in a terse mood and Ravenwood searching for clues, he needed a few moments to reconnect with sources of power beyond most men's comprehension. He sat under an elder poplar tree with his legs crossed in the lotus position. Within a few short moments, noisy midday Manhattan vanished and the nameless one was walking along a barren path. He could feel the warm sun against his back as he strolled through the mountainous crags of Burma. Suddenly there was a warning shout and then the crackle of gunfire. It was the very first time that he had laid eyes on the young master. He had vowed to protect Ravenwood from that day forward.

"The sun shines even on a cesspool," said an elder gentleman.

The Nameless One contemplated for a moment whether the voice that spoke to him was corporeal. He was reluctant to return so soon to this plane that was filled with despair and woe.

"The sun, too, shines into cesspools and is not polluted," the Nameless One opened his eyes and found himself staring directly at Rabbi Rash.

"Ahhh, but we know that's not true. This cesspool affects all that come in contact with it," corrected the Rabbi.

"Light will never be affected by darkness," argued the Nameless One as he stood to his feet. "It is my pleasure to make your acquaintance, Mr. Rash."

"And you are?"

"A man with no name and a person of little consequence."

"We know that is not true as well." Rabbi Rash lunged toward the Nameless One. The Nameless One spun out of the way as if he had foreknowledge of the attack.

"Darkness is persistent but every night, no matter how determined or how dark, gives way to the rising sun," the old monk smiled.

"I am the sun and I will burn away the chaff of this world. I will scorch the wicked and utterly consume the corrupt," growled the black clad rabbi. He whirled his staff overhead and brought it down upon the Nameless One. The staff struck the ground hard but the Nameless One had vanished. "Arrggh," yelled the Rabbi. "I was drawn here for a reason. You have the answers that I need, Yogi."

The white ceramic tile floor was broken up by round tables that were littered with fresh flowers and baskets of day old bread. A cruse of olive oil set in the middle of each table along with cracked pepper and tiny sauce dishes for sopping the thick-crusted loaves. A neon sign that simply read Gertrude's hung outside over the front entrance of an otherwise unremarkable storefront. Wood planks had replaced the large glass pane windows during the Castellammarese War of 1930.

"Are you certain it was Ransack?" asked Lucky Luciano.

"I'm telling you it was that same crazy Jew that ransacked all of your stash houses three years ago," said Lepke.

"I thought that was taken care of," snarled Lucky Luciano.

"It was but it wasn't," Lepke nodded. "He has a nasty scar running down his cheek where Philly almost took his head off. After that he laid low, so we thought it was over."

Lucky sat a table in the northeast corner with his back to the wall. A hefty portion of pasta and gravy rested between Luciano and Lepke along with a healthy serving of sausage and peppers. Business never interfered with Lepke' appetite making his responses sporadic and sluggish.

"I want it over," Luciano declared. "I want that deranged Jew's head on a spit." Lepke didn't respond but continued eating. Luciano threw up his hands in frustration and then motioned for Sal Grillo, who was standing in the back against the wall with other family members, to come over.

"Sal, when Mr. Buchalter finishes his dinner, I want you and him to make Ransack dead."

"Sure thing boss," said Grillo.

"He's not that easy to kill," reminded Lepke.

"Dead, do you understand me? Dead," shoured Lucky.

"Boss, there might be another issue," Grillo pointed.

"What?"

"The other night some sort of cop or detective showed up at Masseria's grave.,"

"So,?"

"Boss, he wasn't your typical private dick but he wasn't a cop either. So we looked into him."

"Well?" Luciano's patience was wearing thing.

"His name is Ravenwood and he works with Inspector Stagg. He's some kind of spook detective who lives in the Sussex Towers."

"Lepke might actually finish eating before you reach your point," anger covered Luciano's face..

"Word on the street is that he's trouble, Boss. Big trouble."

"Bullshit. If this guy gets in the way, kill him. If tries to link us to the Masseria thing, kill him. Is that clear enough for you, Grillo?"

"Sure, Boss. I got it. No sweat."

Ravenwood stepped into the opaque serenity of the Nameless One's retreat. Immediately Manhattan vanished as he was swept from the moorings of reality by swelling tides of pure energy. He rarely ventured into this portion of the penthouse affording his teacher and guardian a private, sacred place of meditation and prayer.

"Sit with me like we have in times past," welcomed the Nameless One in a voice only Ravenwood could hear. The student folded himself into the lotus position as his teacher commanded. They sat together for a great while without speaking a word. For men of lesser understanding, it might have appeared queer and wasteful but to the Ancient Yogi it was necessary and timely.

Ravenwood and the Nameless One set high atop the apex of Loi Leng in the distant lands of Burma. Sterling, the penthouse, Sussex Towers, Manhattan, New York City had all been peeled away like the cornhusk is pulled back from the ear. Wisp of gray clouds wrapped themselves like long tendrils around the mountains' base as the evening sun crashed into the horizon.

"You have learned many things today but you still know nothing," said the Nameless One.

"I know more than what I did."

"Do you?"

Ravenwood didn't respond but watched a redheaded vulture circling below him in a never-ending search for food. He thought of his father and his mother who both were torn from his life by the plague at a young age. He missed them greatly. He looked at the Nameless Once recalling the day that his teacher and protector had come for him.

"I know nothing," the student relented.

"Life's cry is soon replaced by death's sobbing," quoted the Nameless One.

"We are all born and then we all die."

"And if what was dead lives again?".

"Then the natural order is disturbed." Ravenwood was confused. "But who could bring the dead back to life?"

"And if what never lived then has life?"

"So you are saying that someone wasn't raised from the dead but a monster was created? Given life?"

"I haven't said anything, my son."

"There were bits of clay and rock on the body of Masseria," recalled Ravenwood.

"Certainly not uncommon for a victim of ghoulish grave robbers."

"All of the victims from East Fourth Street had the same residue."

"Death deserved and undeserved. Timely and unseemly. Sepulchers' gapping mouths fed with the innocent and the once godly consumed by hate," concluded the Nameless One. Then it was as if a curtain fell across a stage. Suddenly, Ravenwood was pulled back into the dark room at the penthouse in Sussex Towers and he was sitting across from his master.

Bony fingers broke through the darkness inside of D'Angelo's Shoe Store and flipped the open sign to read "closed." The shoe store was perched on the corner of Kenmare and Mulberry Street adjacent to Alfonse Grocer.

Ravenwood was pulled back into the dark room...

There was a barbershop caddy-corner to the grocer where the old men gathered to tell tales, a produce stand next to it where ladies gossiped and bartered what they could, and several other shops lined the street in the heart of Little Italy.

Rabbi Rash squatted down against the wall outside of D'Angelo Shoes with his black derby pulled down over his eyes. His overcoat was draped about him and he mumbled indiscernible words of power as his long white beard nearly touched the sidewalk while he drew various symbols on the ground with his staff.

A paunchy gentleman and his frail wife locked the door to D'Angelo's behind them as they stepped out onto the sidewalk. His newspaper was tucked under his arm and he carried a small sack containing the day's receipts. His wife was weary and completely unconcerned about anything but getting home. The fat, little fellow however immediately noticed the odd figure squatted down outside of his store.

"Can I help you?" inquired Mr. D'Angelo.

"I have already discussed my concerns with Mr. Buchalter," answered Rabbi Rash.

"Mr. Buchalter?" asked D'Angelo. Rabbi Rash didn't respond. He didn't look up but continued chanting and striking the ground with his staff. D'Angelo motioned for his wife to go on without him.

"The name Buchalter doesn't carry any weight in this part of town," said Mr. D'Angelo "Do you understand me?"

Rabbi Rash looked up at D'Angelo. "I understand more than you know."

D'Angelo stared into the face of the rabbi taking notice of his eyes that seemed to burn with fire, the pink scar that ran down his cheek, and the long white beard. "Ransack!" muttered D'Angelo. Rabbi Rash stood to his feet whirling his staff overhead in wide arc and then violently struck the sidewalk with its butt. It seemed almost simultaneously that the sun dropped below the skyline and a thick darkness settled into Little Italy. D'Angelo fumbled with his keys trying in desperation to unlock the door.

"You should have escorted your wife home," laughed Ransack. The air became thick with the smell of death and rotting flesh as the monstrous golem stepped out of the shadows. He stood well over nine feet tall and his arms dangled low to the ground. Two ram's horns twisted backward from its skull giving him the appearance of the scoundrel himself. Where there should have been a nose and ears were only open sores. His mouth gaped wide revealing broken shards for teeth as he slowly stumbled forward toward D'Angelo. The storeowner swung open the door but it was too late.

The golem grabbed him by the back of his neck crushing his spine with a single hand. "Your sins be my sins, and your transgressions fall upon me," shouted Ransack. The golem raised his fists overhead and brought them down violently against the entrance to the store. Glass shattered and wooden beams splintered at the will of the golem.

Ransack followed his golem into the shoe store knowing that it was a hub for all of Lucky's bookmaking operations and that it would be heavily guarded. He wasn't disappointed as men poured from the basement but instead of guns they were wielding axes, meat cleavers, and machetes. "You fools," laughed Ransack. "All you will do is anger it." The mobsters rushed forward with their weapons high overhead and the golem killed them all. Ransack's monstrosity was soaked in blood and as he tore his way through the back of the shoe store, he still held onto the arm of one of his victims.

"You can rest now," Ransack told the golem as he followed it into the alley but the golem neither slowed his pace nor heard what the rabbi had said. "Return to the shadow," yelled Ransack but the golem lumbered forward down the alley and into the street directly in front of Alfonse Grocer. Ransack rushed forward with mystical speed and struck the golem with a heavy blow from his staff at the back of the leg. The golem wasn't slowed in the least but simply swatted at his maker like one would swat at a fly. "I command you to return to the shadows!" yelled Ransack. But instead the golem drove his fist through the front entrance of the grocer and yanked the hefty doors from their frame. He lifted both hands once more overhead and brought them down ripping a hole in the front of the building. Alfonse scurried down stairs with his wife and two small children following behind him.

"Damnable creature why have you come!" yelled the grocer in fear.

"Get your family and get out of here now," responded Ransack.

"Alfonse," yelled his wife. But the grocer stood there paralyzed by fear as the golem reached and grabbed him by the ankle lifting him from the ground. Alfonse's wife screamed in terror as the golem shook the life from her husband and then tossed him aside. She scooped her children up in her arms and she began to speak, "The Lord is my shepherd, I shall not want." The golem was upon them before anything could have been done to save them.

Ravenwood stood beside Inspector Stagg outside of Alfonse Grocer. Neither spoke a word as Stagg dug at the sole of his shoe with the blade of his pocketknife. Any animosity or doubts that he had concerning Ravenwood had vanished for a moment because he simply wanted to remove today's sorrow from under foot.

"It's a golem," Ravenwood announced.

"A what?" mumbled Stagg.

"It's a mystical construct made from inanimate material that is capable of unthinkable destruction." Inspector Stagg didn't respond. He closed his knife and shoved it into his pocket.

"All magic has a signature and magic of this magnitude will have a very distinct signature," Ravenwood added. "No mere novice could pull off anything remotely kin to this."

"How do we stop it, Ravenwood?"

"A golem is like a marionette."

"So, we have to cut the strings."

"In the simplest of terms, yes, we just have to cut the strings."

Inspector Stagg turned his face back toward the ghastly spectacle. Crumbled brick and splintered timbers littered the street and water poured onto the sidewalk from a busted main. A man from the coroner's office was knelt down over the body of one of the children and he was scribbling something on his clipboard. Alfonse's bare feet protruded from under the sheet that covered his remains.

"What can we do to help?" asked Inspector Stagg.

"Find a name for me," Ravenwood replied. "He's a Jewish Rabbi and an associate of mine had a run in with him. He has short white hair, a long beard, and a pink scar that runs down his cheekbone from under his eye."

"A Jewish rabbi?" the Inspector scratched his chin.

"Yes and be careful. Just get me the name."

Ransack lifted the cross member from the bare floor and dropped it into place securing the round top door. Letters and symbols were scrawled upon the walls in what was most likely dried goat's blood. Two sconces burned brightly illuminating the narrow entrance to the room that contained his monster. He bowed his head and placed his hand upon the center of the door while reciting an incantation. The sconces flared signifying that the magical wards that he had spelled for protection had snapped in place.

The Rabbi wearily climbed the long spiraling staircase to his study in the east tower of the synagogue. His golem rested securely in a basement below the tower that was unfamiliar to everyone except himself. Scrolls and parchments written in Hebrew and Aramaic littered a large oaken table that also contained several tomes stained by years of use. Candles burned in every corner illuminating the stately room in an eerie amber glow that lent to the mystical tenor of the tower. The old Jew had tapped into creative powers that hadn't been practiced in centuries but had failed to establish control over his beast once it was unleashed. He removed his overcoat and hung it on a chair. He pulled his white starched shirt over his head revealing the raised flesh of multiple scars across his back and chest. Rabbi Rash had lived many years and fought many battles all of which were represented by the heavy scarring and wounds that dotted his formidable physique.

"I made you with my own hands and yet you will not obey me," muttered Ransack. "I spoke words of great power over your lifeless form for many hours and yet you will not heed my instructions," he yelled. "I am a fool. I am old fool whose heart is filled with hate."

Ransack leaned over the table peering at the parchments with his hands outstretched nearly to the corners holding himself up. His fiery eyes leaped from the crude drawings that he had sketched of his golem to the pages of spells that had brought the golem to life to the writings of a Hindu priestess about reincarnation that he had found on one of his pilgrimages.

"I'm thirsty," said a faint voice from a dark corner of his study.

"Hush child," the rabbi growled. "I gave you water." Ransack never looked up from the table.

"I knocked over the pitcher while you were gone," said the little voice.

"I should feed you to my golem for dinner you troublesome wart," snapped Ransack. The child didn't respond but stayed very still because the golem scared her immensely. The old Jew sighed and then walked over to her. He pulled her into the light so that he could see her. Her cheeks were wet with tears and clothes were soiled because he had forgotten her in the tower for at least a day maybe longer. "You are a mess child," he grunted. She didn't respond because she was so very afraid of him. Ransack picked up the pitcher and walked away. He soon returned with the pitcher of water and a little food. He also brought with him a washbasin and a rag. He poured a small portion of the water into the basin. "Clean yourself up," he commanded.

"Thank you," said the child.

"Save your thanks for those deserving of it." He strode back over to the large oaken table and picked up the writings on reincarnation. He then remembered the powerful being he had encountered outside of Sussex Towers at the park. He had been drawn to that park but had never pondered why he was drawn to it. Ransack didn't fully understand the attraction until now.

"Sally boy," smiled Lucky Luciano "I'm glad to see that you are still with us."

"I thought he was dead," Lepke said.

"Me too," Benjamin "Bugsy" Siegel joined in.

"But he's not," Lucky stated the obvious. "He's right here."

"So I'm guessing if he's standing here," Lepke guessed, "then Ransack must be dead."

"Of course he's dead," Bugsy chuckled. "Why else would Sal Grillo be standing in front of us? He's come to tell us that Ransack is dead."

Sal Grillo swallowed hard and did not speak for a long moment. Sweat gathered along the curl of his lip and his palms were moist with fear. He didn't have anything good to tell Lucky and his lifelong friends that made up Murder, Inc. He knew that they might actually kill the messenger. Finally Grillo spoke, "D'Angelo is dead as well as Alfonse and his family," Gertrude's was vacant other than Lucky Luciano, Bugsy Siegel, and Louis "Lepke" Buchalter and of course, Sal Grillo. "We figured that D'Angelo's would be next on Ransack's list so we were ready for him," Sal explained nervously.

"You were ready for him," echoed Luciano.

"We moved all of your money and everything else, Boss. We completely moved the entire bookmaking operation to a different location."

"For sure, he was ready for him," Lepke grinned.

"I brought up guys from Harlem and from Jersey," Grillo said as he took a step backwards. "All the guys had instructions not bring any iron."

"No guns?" Bugsy was puzzled.

"No guns. They don't work against the monster." Grillo unbuttoned his double breasted coat revealing his piece strapped to his side. Grillo didn't trust Lepke or Bugsy and he wasn't going to get rubbed out unceremoniously without a fight.

"Sally Boy, no reason for the hostility." Lucky got to his feet and stepped around the table. He extended his arms and said, "Come here." Grillo was hesitant but to refuse would be an open act of aggression. He stepped forward and kissed Lucky on his cheek. Bugsy pulled his heater from its holster and laid it on the table with Lepke following suit. "See everything is ok."

"Alright, Boss. I just didn't want," but before he could finish, Luciano interrupted him.

"Shhh, no worries Sal. Do we know where Ransack is now?"

"A friend of mine followed him to Sussex Towers in Manhattan. He's still there now."

Luciano raised a hand. "Bugsy, Lepke, go!" They grabbed their guns and started toward the door. Grillo nodded at them as they walked past. "Oh, there's one more thing that the boys wanted to discuss with you, Sal."

Sal Grillo reached for his for gun but before it could clear the holster Lepke hit Sal with a slapjack between the shoulders and dropped him to his knees. Bugsy grabbed a handful of Grillo's hair twisting his head back and said, "Alfonse, was a friend of ours." Bugsy brought the butt of his gun crashing down into Sal's face knocking him to the ground. It was unfortunate for Grillo that the blow did not render him unconscious. Lepke and Bugsy kicked and stomped Grillo as he crawled toward Lucky Luciano. Finally, Lucky held up a hand and Murder, Inc. ceased from tuning up Grillo.

"Sally Boy, the next time maybe you will follow orders."

Rabbi Rash sat on a park bench across from Sussex Towers watching the sun decline behind the Manhattan skyline talking to himself. "You will not walk amongst the living tonight my child." A dark colored sedan was parked a block down from Ravenwood's residence but in view of both the Towers and the adjacent park. Another similar sedan driven by Bugsy Siegel pulled up behind it. The Rabbi smiled to himself. "I wish that you were here by my side my child. There are so many that need to taste god's judgement but not tonight I guess." He watched a young man dressed in a business suit walk into the Towers escorted by his wife and young child.

Ransack crossed the busy street and entered Sussex Towers. Four gentlemen in suits followed closely behind the rabbi.

"We have company," declared Ravenwood. "Please show them in and then make yourself scarce."

"Yes sir," said Sterling.

Ravenwood pulled on his coat, popped his cuffs, and picked up his cane. "This evening should prove very interesting."

"Do not underestimate the mystic," warned the Nameless One as he appeared in Ravenwood's study. "He's accessed dark, archaic powers."

"It's not my custom to underestimate my enemy."

"Yes, but you have not faced someone as old or as powerful as this Jewish mystic," cautioned the Nameless One.

"Noted." Ravenwood walked out of his study into his expansive living room. A baby grand piano rested in the far corner with a large floral tapestry hanging over it. A crystal vase filled with orchids sat upon the lid of the piano. A multi-tiered crystal chandelier hung from the ceiling in the middle of the living room hovering above a lavender Queen Ann sofa. The entire living room was wrapped with layers and layers of crown molding that trickled down the wall from the ceiling several feet. High back chairs encircled a brick fireplace that had a perfect flame burning in its midst almost magically. Rabbi Rash stood in front of the fireplace admiring an oil painting of a civil war solider.

"Mr. Ravenwood, Rabbi Rash," said Sterling.

"No need for formal introductions," interrupted Ravenwood "I believe we will have more callers shortly."

"At least four gentlemen and I believe they are armed," said Rabbi Rash.

"Friends of yours I suppose."

"Admirers."

"I doubt that very seriously. Why have you come, Mr. Rash?"

"I need to talk with your teacher. I met him in the park." He held his staff loosely and began mumbling indiscernible words in Hebrew.

"He's not much of a conversationalist. I'm afraid that will be quite impossible."

"That's a shame...for you." Rash whirled his staff overhead and spoke the word 'RUACH'. He brought down his staff with both hands slamming it into the floor causing all of the air in the room to be pulled toward the middle and then rapidly expelled knocking Ravenwood from his feet and slamming him into the opposing wall. "I do not want to hurt you but I must have the old one's assistance."

Ravenwood pulled the blade from his cane and lunged forward at Rash in a whirlwind attack. His speed and accuracy was uncanny but Rash was faster. Rash's simplistic movements evaded every strike of Ravenwood's sword. Rash countered with a low sweeping blow that took his feet from under him. Rash lifted his staff overhead and commanded the winds once more by speaking the word 'RUACH.' A torrent blew through penthouse causing Ravenwood to skid across the marble floor and into the wall.

"Summon your companion," cried Rash "or I will be forced to destroy you."

"He's currently unavailable," groaned Ravenwood as he gathered his bearings "Why not come back tomorrow?"

"I have pressing business," retorted the maniacal rabbi "and you are wearing on my patience."

Rabbi Rash pointed his staff in the direction of Ravenwood and yelled the Hebrew word, 'ESH.' Fire leaped across the room from the staff in a spiraling arc scorching everything in its path. The Nameless One emerged from a haze and deflected the fiery coil with magic of his own.

"I was hoping that you might show up," Rabbi Rash bowed.

The Nameless One did not respond but pulled Ravenwood through an interdimensional passage landing them in the park in front of Sussex towers. "Another thing that I will never get used to," the occult detective muttered.

"I warned you about the mystic," reminded the Nameless One. "When two tigers fight, one dies today and the other tomorrow."

"Unless one tiger is smarter," Ravenwood ad-libbed. "Take me back, but this time through my study."

The Nameless One let out a sigh and took Ravenwood by the arm. The two vanished from the park and reappeared in penthouse study. By this time, Ransack was fully engaged with the gangsters that had followed him there. Ravenwood pulled his Luger from its holster and rushed into the fray firing his weapon. He hit Ransack in his left calf dropping him to the ground. Ravenwood was an expert marksman and after the recoil of the weapon there was a thud and then the snapping of bone. Ransack would be at a distinct disadvantage in any future altercations. Ravenwood squeezed off two more shots. One hit Bugsy Siegel in the shoulder and the other tore through the Lepke's hip. The gangsters couldn't afford to wage a war on two fronts especially since Ransack could have easily killed them all if it hadn't been for Ravenwood wounding him. Ravenwood flipped over a large credenza and ripped off two more shots at Luciano's men. The gangsters retreated.

"I'm afraid I have bled all over your rug," apologized a groaning Ransack as he secured a piece of cloth that he had torn from his shirt around his bloody shin.

"I'll have my man send you a bill to have it replaced," said Ravenwood.

"Very good." Ransack pulled an odd little bottle from his coat pocket and dabbed a portion of its contents on the wound. It soaked through the cloth and he winced as it penetrated the bullet hole. "I did not realize that you were acquainted with Mr. Buchalter and Mr. Siegel." He placed his hand on the bullet wound and muttered the word 'RAPHA.'

"I thought they were friends of yours." Ravenwood closed his eyes allowing his senses to reach past his physical location to where Ransack was ducked down.

"Oh, I have known them for a long time. Since they were children in fact," claimed Ransack as he rose to his feet.

"You heal quickly," noted Ravenwood still hunkered down behind the credenza not willing to allow Ransack another open shot with his elemental blast.

Rabbi Rash called upon his mystical powers once more with great anger and frustration. He bellowed words in an unknown language and pointed his staff toward Ravenwood. The credenza was caught by an updraft of wind and flipped end over end into the study. Ravenwood had sensed Ransack's intentions and had rolled out of the way a split second before the blast. Ravenwood was now kneeling with his Luger pointed at Ransack's chest while he stood there helpless trying to recover from wielding such enormous power. Ravenwood squeezed off a shot hitting Ransack in the chest. He pulled the trigger a second time and the bullet tore into the mantle over the fireplace.

Then Ransack was gone.

The Nameless One appeared in the great living room next to Ravenwood. He lifted Ravenwood to his feet. "You wounded him, my son. You must follow him and finish this before he is able to unleash the golem."

"He heals too quickly," Ravenwood pointed out. "I shot him in the chest. He should be dead."

"We all die a little each day, but we are reborn each morning."

"Morning," muttered Ravenwood, "there is a reason that foul creatures, like his golem, prefers the night." Ravenwood retreated to his study and began searching through the scattered text that now littered his floor. After much searching, he picked up a particularly aged tome and began rifling through its pages. "Dusk is like a floodgate for magic. The sun sets and all

"You wounded him, my son."

manner of evil has the ability to roam freely on the earth. But dawn, the morning, has the opposite effect.

"I need…"

"Hyssop and Myrrh," interrupted the Nameless One.

"Yes."

"It will not kill it."

"I don't need to kill it."

Ransack was slumped over the golem's incredulous form gasping for breath. The bullet from Ravenwood's gun had missed his heart but had nicked one of his lungs. Blood trickled down his chest onto the golem as his life poured out of him. "I underestimated that one," gasped Ransack. He reached for his odd little bottle of ointment but it was shattered and the contents wasted in his pocket. Ransack dabbed up the remainder with his finger and then pushed his finger into the hole in his chest. The rabbi screamed in agony as he tried to coat the wound with the salve. Ransack whispered, "RAPHA" before slipping into unconsciousness.

Black mold crawled its way from the floor to the walls and up to the ceiling at the abandoned house in Harlem that served as a fallback safe house for the Luciano crime family.

"He used us as a distraction," accused Bugsy Siegel "He knew we were there the entire time."

"I don't understand how something like this can happen," Luciano said confused. "He is nothing more than a rabbi from the old neighborhood."

Bugsy Siegel slouched in a chair holding a bandage over the gunshot wound that had been inflicted by Ravenwood. Lepke was stretched out on a card table with a man under Lucky's employ attempting to remove the bullet from his hip. "He was able to do things, Lucky."

"What kinds of things? Is it something that a bullet couldn't stop?"

"Boss, he was hurling fire at us," Bugsy related. "And that Ravenwood character appeared out of nowhere rattling off rounds without missing,"

"He couldn't have been that good. You are both still alive."

"That's the thing Boss," responded Bugsy. "I don't think he was aiming to kill us. He just wanted to wound us."

"Did you guys hit Ransack at all? Both of you are a bloody mess. Did we even get close to killing him?"

Bugsy looked into the stern face of Lucky Luciano and then at his childhood acquaintance Lepke, who was yawping in pain, and shook his head. "We didn't have the opportunity but Ravenwood slammed a bit of lead into his chest."

"So he's dead then. Why didn't you say that in the first place?"

"Not dead," corrected Bugsy. "I saw the rabbi get shot but then he vanished. Gone."

Lucky slammed his fist onto the table where he was sitting. His frustration with the situation and his hatred for the rabbi and now Ravenwood was only amplified by the ridiculous accounts that his most trusted man rehearsed for him. He stood suddenly and flipped the table over in an outburst of rage.

"Every solider, every friend of ours," breathed out Lucky in huffs "everybody, do you understand me? All of them will converge on that synagogue tonight and we are going to kill that rabbi and destroy his monster!"

Bugsy nodded as he continued to press the blood soaked bandage against his wound his eyes trailed from the outraged Luciano to Lepke, who lay bleeding also on the card table. He thought that was a bad idea.

Ravenwood poured a steaming concoction from a beaker into several vials. The odorous amalgamation was unsettling to the sensitive nose of Sterling and it was only after having sent Sterling on an errand was he able to finish his medieval apothecary. He secured corks in the open mouths of the vials and placed several vails inside of his suitcoat pocket. Others he placed in a leather satchel along with a few extra rounds of ammunition, a large blade made of the darkest steel that was twisted in a most peculiar fashion, and an amulet inscribed with Hindu runes.

"A ram's horns can face but one direction," reminded the Nameless One.

"My fight is with Rabbi Rash," said Ravenwood. "The Luciano crime family is of no concern to me at the moment."

"That's why you are bringing more bullets," pointed out his guardian. "Bullets will not stop the golem or Rash. They must be intended for the gangsters."

Ravenwood ignored the old man's comments. He had no idea what he might be walking into. He had sensed earlier that Luciano was mobilizing an army against Rash and he knew they stood little chance against the man much less his 'Frankenstein' monstrosity. If this was to be resolved, it would have to be up to him. As he walked out of his study, the Nameless One was perched in the middle of his desk in the lotus position. He knew that the ancient Yogi would not allow him to be harmed to any degree if possible.

"Strike first and often," instructed the Nameless One in a voice that only Ravenwood could hear. Ravenwood closed his eyes and nodded then tossed the leather satchel into the back of his convertible. He settled in behind the wheel of the Delahaye and gripped the steering wheel. In a moment, all twelve cylinders were firing as he rumbled toward the mystical tower located in Lower East Side of Manhattan.

As Ravenwood arrived, he noticed that Inspector Stagg was leaned against his car as if he was waiting on someone. "Ah, Ravenwood. How did I know that I would find you here?"

"Inspector, I really think you and your men might want to sit this one out."

"Not a chance." Stagg pulled a red ribbon from his pocket. "We got an anonymous tip about the child that went missing."

"Very smart."

"What?" asked Stagg.

"We need to move, Inspector. We have company coming."

"We need to wait on backup. I mean, I need to wait on backup."

"Then I cannot afford to wait with you. I'm going to see a man about a horse." Ravenwood vanished into the night. He moved effortlessly across the manicured lawn and through a maze of hedges that led to the rear entrance of the synagogue. "A very big horse." Layers of stone wrapped around the double oak doors that made up the rear entrance and was the only access point to the eastern tower where Rabbi Rash was held up. It was a choke point. Rash and his monstrosity could defend off entire battalions from this location.

"Rash, give up the little girl and release control of the golem," Ravenwood called out loudly. There was no response but he was certain that the rabbi heard every word. Ravenwood spoke a couple of indistinct words in Latin and passed his hand over the door pull. The heavy doors swung open wide in dramatic fashion slamming against the doorstops. Death and earth wrenched together by the reprehensible magic of the Jewish mystic caused an awful odor of blood, rot, and clay to saturate the pristine synagogue. Ravenwood choked on the acrid odor sucking down the distasteful stench.

"Rash, what would cause a man such as yourself to dabble in such dark arts?" Again, he knew that Rash was listening but chose not to respond. Ravenwood stooped low and pulled the dark steel dagger from his satchel. He poured one of the vials carefully down its blade and whispered the words, "ET LUCEM VITAE". A shimmer of light danced down the edge of the blade and then vanished a second later. Ravenwood held the awful dagger in one hand and his cane in the other. He knew his cane sword would prove little use against the golem but hoped that this dreadful blade coated with the purifying magic might provide the advantage he would need.

"I had hoped to enlist the help of your master," Rabbi Rash finally responded.

"Why do you think he would help you?"

"To prevent the loss of innocent lives."

Ravenwood's chameleon eyes changed colors rapidly as he scanned the long corridor leading to Ransack's tower. He could clearly see the golem lurking in the shadows waiting on his master's command. He took note of Rash standing further back armed only with his staff. He could sense that Inspector Stagg was moving toward the front entrance and that there was an army of gangsters lurking around the grounds waiting for the unwitting police to enter the synagogue.

"No one associated with me would ever assist you rabbi."

"That's a shame, young man. It was my earnest hope that we could work together to rid this city of its worst sort."

"You've killed innocent people," rebutted Ravenwood. "You have unleashed a mindless monster upon the city."

"Not upon the city, but upon those that deserve god's judgement."

"You aren't the one to make that call. An innocent family was murdered. You were most likely standing there."

"I can see that we will never come to terms."

"This has all been a ruse. He was merely waiting on the Inspector to enter the building and for the gangsters to gather," voiced the Nameless One in Ravenwood's mind. "He's been gathering his strength. He's is about to unleash the golem."

"Not if I can stop him." Ravenwood dropped his cane and pulled his Luger from its holster. The first shot that Ravenwood squeezed off hit Rabbi Rash in the thigh. Rash had anticipated the attack and was moving before Ravenwood could pull the trigger. It was only Ravenwood's chameleon eyes and quick reflexes that allowed him to hit his target at all. Rash was gone before he could pull the trigger a second time.

"You have much larger problems to deal with now," whispered the Nameless One.

A loud thump echoed through the corridor and then another thud. The golem had been unleashed and was striding slowly toward Ravenwood. The dark, empty pits that were the golem's eyes stared at Ravenwood as its nine foot frame lumbered forward with its mouth opened wide like a vulgar chasm filled with broken teeth. It was stained with death and left a muddy trail in its wake. The golem was repulsive in every way having no nose or ears but only festering sores in their place. Two long ram's horns twisted back from its skull marking it as the deceiver himself.

Ravenwood pulled several vials from his satchel and tossed them into the golem's path. He then pulled his Luger from its holster once more but this time Ravenwood emptied the clip into the golem. The bullets sank deep into the golem's skull, pierced his eyes, and shattered its teeth but did little to slow the monster. Ravenwood slammed another clip into his Luger and raised his weapon at the golem once more but just then one of Stagg's men stepped into the corridor from the tabernacle. He had his weapon drawn and lined Ravenwood up in its sights. He fired without warning and the bullet sank deep into Ravenwood's shoulder.

"I could not get to you," the Nameless One's thoughts reached him. "The entire building is warded with some sort of protection spell."

The impact of the bullet whirled Ravenwood around knocking the dark dagger from his grasp. He staggered and then slumped to the ground holding his shoulder. His chameleon eyes scanned the area for the dagger but he was quickly distracted from the search by the terrible death of the patrolman. Rash's golem grabbed the copper by the neck lifting him from the ground and snapping his head nearly from his shoulders. The golem shook the patrolman and then tossed his lifeless form aside. Two more of Stagg's men appeared from the tabernacle through the side door but before Ravenwood could shout a warning the golem snatched them up and shook them angrily beating them against floor. The golem let out a startling growl that would have caused lesser men to faint from fear.

"More innocent men die at your hand Rash," cried Ravenwood. "I will not only destroy you but I will destroy this illegitimate son of yours."

"Those men died because you refused my request."

The golem lunged forward and stepped on one of the vials that Ravenwood had tossed into its path. A white, cleansing flame burst from the vial scorching the golem. It was staggered for a brief moment. Ravenwood scrambled to reach his satchel and almost intuitively the mindless beast realized that it was in danger. The golem leaped forward placing himself between Ravenwood and the satchel. Ravenwood flung the remaining vials that he had stashed in his pocket at the golem. Each of the vials burst against the monster in a brilliant explosion of white flame. Each time the golem seemed to be staggered by the cleansing concoction.

"It's not enough," thought Ravenwood. "I can only slow it." The Nameless One did not respond.

Men poured into the corridor from different directions. Luciano's gangsters entered the synagogue through the maze of hedges that Ravenwood had followed while Stagg and his remaining patrolmen poured out of the tabernacle and into the corridor from the opposite direction. Gunfire erupted in successive waves from every angle. Inspector Stagg shouted out orders to his men and they responded by taking cover where they could find it. The patrolmen fired upon the golem exclusively unless one of the gangsters engaged them. Luciano's men were disorganized and became scattered. They were fodder for the awful beast. The remaining vials were destroyed by foot traffic having little or no effect on the golem.

"This won't last long," sent the Nameless One. "If you want to know what a tiger is like, look at a cat."

"I'm staring at the tiger."

"You are looking at the cat, my son. Rash is the true danger."

"I'll never defeat Rash." Ravenwood's left arm dangled limply by his side. He had holstered his Luger and held his cane in his right hand. Blood soaked his left sleeve and trickled down his fingers on to the floor. Silhouettes danced against the walls as the orange blast of gunfire illuminated the many figures that filled the hallway. There were so many ways to die crammed into such a confined space. Ravenwood scoured the corridor as his eyes changed colors from gray, to blue, to green, to a brilliant fiery hue and finally he spotted the dagger tucked into the waistband of one of Luciano's thugs.

"Of course," he said. He focused his attention on the gangster for a moment and his eyes flashed a gold and brown.

"Ravenwood," yelled the gangster. "Catch!" The gangster pulled the dagger from his waistband and tossed it at Ravenwood's feet. The young hood wondered how he'd known Ravenwood's name or why he'd given him the dagger.

"Thanks." Ravenwood picked up the dagger and shoved it into his coat pocket. The golem turned to face the Stepson of Mystery somehow sensing that he was a threat once more but the golem was quickly distracted by a blast from one of the gangsters' shotguns. Ravenwood shouted to Inspector Stagg, "Stay out of reach but keep this thing occupied while I deal with the rabbi."

"Sure thing," agreed the Inspector as he fired off a couple of rounds from his rifle into the midsection of the golem.

Ravenwood mustered his remaining strength and sprinted past the golem through barrage of bullets. "I don't get paid enough for this," Ravenwood mumbled as he made it to the bottom of the spiral staircase. He glanced over his shoulder before heading after Rash and noticed immediately that more men lay dead on the floor than those that still wielded weapons. Broken glass glittered like diamonds in the reddish-brown pools of blood as the living warred against the dead or more fittingly the soulless. Ravenwood pulled his blade free from the cane and sprinted up the stairs.

"My child," Rash addressed his captive. "Can you climb?" The little girl didn't offer any response besides a nod of her head. "Good." He led her to an open window that looked out over the city from his study. Rash picked her up and pushed her matted hair out of her face. "I was trying to protect you," told her just as Ravenwood entered the study. "I wanted you to be safe from the corruption that tainted your parents." Rash lowered her onto a trellis. "Climb little dove and once you get down. Run, run far from here." The little girl disappeared into the night.

Rash whirled around pointing his staff in the direction of Ravenwood and unleashed hell's fury upon earth. Fire belched from his staff in a colossal wave that ran along the floor devouring everything in its path. Stone flooring melted, furnishings burst into white ash, and the wood wrapped ceiling exploded into flames. The tower shook from the impact of Ransack's magic. Ravenwood escaped being incinerated by chance only to be scorched by the heat of the spell. "You are out of your depth young apprentice. You should have allowed the adults to discuss matters with civility."

Ravenwood leaned against the sofa that he had leaped over to escape the path of Rash's spell. "Every spell has it cost. How much has it cost you to conjure that golem?"

"I didn't conjure anything. I formed him with my own two hands. I am not practicing necromancy. My magic is my birthright. Something you heathen would never understand."

"So he is a true golem."

Rash did not respond but pointed his staff in the direction of Ravenwood and called upon the winds casting a hideous gale in the direction of the stepson of mystery. The Victorian sofa slammed into the adjacent wall landing in a broken heap from the force of Ransack's spell.

"You need to work on your aim," chided Ravenwood.

"Indeed."

"Of course I understand your need for such spells. You were unable to face Lucky Luciano and Lepke so you created a golem to do your dirty work." Rash didn't respond but stared at Ravenwood with his flaming eyes. "I mean, they did give you that nasty scar, didn't they?" Ravenwood moved closer to Rash whipping his sword from side to side. "And now you are unable to face me, I get it."

"I am centuries old and will not be talked to with such insolence." Rash whirled his staff around to purpose.

"Excellent." Ravenwood attacked Rash with a large arcing slice across his body. Rash parried the attack with his staff and drove the butt end into Ravenwood's left side shattering a rib. Ravenwood stumbled backwards with his left arm still dangling limp by his side and useless.

"This really isn't a fair contest," said Rash. "You are hurt. There's little glory in dispensing of a wounded foe."

"Dispense of me first, then worry about glory."

"As you say." Ransack spun the staff overhead in a circular motion and then bounded toward Ravenwood bringing the staff down in an overhead strike. Ransack's staff crashed against the floor but Ravenwood was unable to counter the attack. He was weakened from the loss of blood and the shattered rib robbed him of his breath. Ransack swept Ravenwood's feet out from under him landing Ravenwood on his back. A smile spread across the face of Ransack as he pressed the end of his staff into the throat of Ravenwood. "You are fading quickly, Ravenwood."

"Why create the golem?" asked Ravenwood in mock curiosity.

"I watched Buchalter, Siegel and Luciano grow up. I watched as they were corrupted by infernal influences," recalled Ransack. "I watched them abandon the old neighborhood then exploit it."

"So you created that monster." Ravenwood slowly worked the dagger out of his coat pocket. Its gnarled steel was of the darkest sort and it had been forged with cruel intentions but now it was imbued with cleansing fire.

"No I created the monster when they started recruiting young boys from our neighborhood, when they robbed local merchants, and turned innocent girls into whores," Ransack spat out. "I decided to create the golem when a young mother's life was snuffed out not two blocks from here by these putrid leeches."

"And how many lives have you…" Ravenwood was interrupted by a queer silence.

"What has happened." Ransack turned himself about puzzled by the quiet. The angry monster wasn't bellowing, there were no gunshots, and no more shouting men. It was a disturbing calm. It seemed as if it was almost by design when Ravenwood curled his body upward toward Rash with amazing agility and drove the dagger deep into the back of Rash's thigh. A cleansing fire poured from the blade and rippled through the old Jew knocking him to his knees.

"It's said that this particular dagger was used upon Julius Caesar," gasped Ravenwood as he struggled to gain his footing. "It is particularly suited for ridding the world of evil tyrants and golems."

Ransack struggled to pull the dagger from his leg but the task was impossible in his severely weakened state. Ravenwood shoved Rash forward with his foot causing the rabbi to smash into the floor face first. The Stepson of Mystery pulled the dagger from the back of his thigh and blood ran out of the wound.

"But I don't personally believe in such wives' tales, so I imbued the dagger with hyssop and myrrh."

"I'm constantly underestimating you," groaned Rash as he rolled to his back. His black overcoat flailed open revealing a sweat stained white shirt and odd talisman hanging from his neck in the shape of the Star of David. A crude vial was bound to the necklace and it seemed to be filled with a dark, thick liquid.

Ravenwood stood over Rash. He was covered in his own blood and felt as if he might slip into unconsciousness at any moment. He reached into his suitcoat and pulled his Luger from its holster. He aimed it downward at Rash and his face spread into what one might judge to be a smile if it didn't resemble a grimace. As he started to squeeze the trigger, the silence was interrupted by a tremor that shook the synagogue causing the floors to crack and the walls to tremble. It felt as if the building was being torn in half.

"The golem is trying to break free from the building," warned the Nameless One. "But the same spell that keeps me out has the golem trapped. Rash did not want the golem roaming free tonight."

"The spell might contain him but it does nothing to protect the structure," said Ravenwood out loud.

Rash whirled his legs about in a circular motion that swept Ravenwood's feet out from under him and landed him on his back once more. The rabbi stood over Ravenwood with his staff pointed downward and began to mumble words in Hebrew but before he could finish his spell Ravenwood pulled the trigger on his Luger. His weapon spit fire as the bullet left its chamber and found its mark.

Darkness draped the grisly scene in shadow hiding a great deal of the carnage. It was a favor that would soon be repealed by the dawning of a new day. Sunlight would shine through the shattered glass, broken doors, and the walls that were riddled with bullets revealing the blood and other stains that were associated with so much death. Broken bodies were strewn up and down the corridor that barely remained standing separating the tabernacle from the outside world. Gangster and policeman alike had died fighting against a soulless monster that killed without prejudice.

The golem was now crumbled into a pile of rock and clay minus its ominous form. Its terrifying horns were now just goat's horns and its broken teeth were now merely rocks scattered across a bloody floor. Frankenstein's monster had fallen at the hands of the angry villagers or more appropriately at the hands of Ravenwood.

"Inspector, I'm glad you survived," Ravenwood grinned.

"I don't know how I did," confessed Inspector Stagg. "This thing had killed all of Luciano's men and most of mine when it decided to start pounding on the exterior wall. It tore timbers free. Brick and mortar just crumbled under its massive fists."

"But it didn't escape."

"No. One of Lucky's men was killed near me so I grabbed his tommy gun and filled it full of lead. I knew I couldn't kill it but maybe I could distract it." Stagg had worked to free himself from a massive mound of rubble. "It turned to face me and was coming right at me when all of sudden it just collapsed and fell on top of me."

"You were very lucky." chuckled Ravenwood.

"Where is Rash?" asked Inspector Stagg.

"Gone."

Ravenwood stepped out of the corridor and into the tabernacle. The ark sat at the front of the building with two seraphim perched on either end with their wings extending over the mercy seat and covering their faces. Their heads were bowed low. Candelabras stood at each corner of the platform like golden sentries illuminated with hundreds of candles. Golden inlays covered the beautifully carved archways as well as the pillars that reached to the ceiling.

"Beautiful," sighed Ravenwood.

"You left the policeman there?" asked the Nameless One, referring to Stagg.

"He wasn't injured."

"Everyone will believe that he stopped the golem."

"Another reason I left him there," laughed Ravenwood as he drove back to Sussex Towers. "Any luck locating Rash?"

"No, but he hasn't left the city."

Ravenwood sped down the highway lost in thought. When the Luger's round crashed into the talisman, it broke the spell that had animated the golem. Rash realizing that the golem was no more had vanished into the night. Ravenwood was in no shape to pursue him. That would have to wait for another day.

The End

THE RABBI'S SCOURGE ESSAY

There is nothing that I enjoy more than having the opportunity to breathe life into a character and then walk with him down uncertain paths in search of an even less certain destiny. Such an opportunity was afforded us by Ron Fortier and Airship27 Productions in this particular tale about Ravenwood, the Stepson of Mystery.

Our first task was becoming acquainted with Ravenwood. He was admittedly unfamiliar to me when we began this process but I quickly fell in love with the backdrop that others had carefully painted of the occult detective and his posse. It was easy to imagine a character such as Ravenwood facing any number of foes. He is smart, well equipped, gifted with peculiar abilities, and has a knack for seeing what others miss. The first few days we spent reading material that was provided to us by our publisher. It gave us a solid foothold in the world of Ravenwood then we branched out searching for covers and images of any sort of the occult detective. Finally, we read some past works while taking notes on what we liked and didn't like.

After becoming more familiar with the hero of our tale, we went to work on our antagonist. Our initial concept we had to scrap after discovering that something very similar was already on the market. We were definitely sorrowful to toss the Nazi Necromancer and his legion of soldiers into the wastepaper basket. So from there with the help of our editor, we decided to pit Ravenwood against something so hideous, so completely monstrous that he couldn't possibly defeat it and his only hope would be to contain it. It was easy enough to combine all of our childhood fears into the grotesque golem that terrorized New York City. But with every puppet that has to be a puppeteer.

The creation of Rabbi Rash was my favorite part of telling this tale. Rash was inspired by an early episode of the Sopranos where Tony Soprano is accused of being a golem. Rash is an ancient cleric that is torn by his desire to correct the injustice that surrounds him and the absolute devastation that his golem causes. Hopefully you will see Rash crop up again from time to time.

All in all, it was an awesome privilege to be involved in this project and I had fun with it.

DEWAYNE DOWERS - lives on a small farm nestled in the midst of the Ouachita Mountains with his wife, Ann Marie, of 23 years and two beautiful children. He graduated from the University of Arkansas with a degree in Psychology before there were laptops, cell phones, or the internet. DeWayne proudly served his country during Desert Storm. He enjoys authentic Louisiana cuisine, Brazilian Jiu-jitsu, and playing with his wolf-dog Leah. It is rumored that he maintains a secret identity as a project manager for an industrial maintenance group. Follow DeWayne Dowers on Instagram @thedecided

VOICES IN THE DARKNESS

By Michael A. Black

Ravenwood felt the sudden feeling of impending danger as he looked into the crowded audience in the auditorium. There were well over two-hundred people who had come to hear him speak on the "Occult of the Orient," and he had almost completed his lecture. Suddenly, the troublesome premonition surfaced like dark storm clouds intruding upon a sunny day. Despite the abruptness of the feeling, trying to narrow down the impression was problematic at best. He hadn't noticed anyone new entering the auditorium during the speech, but perhaps they'd come in through another entrance. Or maybe they were standing in the hallway. He poured some water from the carafe that had been graciously provided for him on the lectern and brought the glass to his lips.

Are you sensing the peril, my son? the Nameless One's voice asked him sub-vocally.

Indeed, I am, Ravenwood replied telepathically. *But I'm having a bit of trouble pinpointing it.*

In time, the Nameless One's voice said, *all shall become clear.*

A man slipped out through the doors at the rear of the auditorium.

Ravenwood set the glass down as he continued to survey the audience. The threat had lessened, but it had not totally dissipated. He smiled and spoke into the microphone.

"This concludes my lecture for tonight. If any of you are interested, signed copies of my latest books are available in the lobby."

A round of applause emanated from the crowd. As Ravenwood started to move away from the lectern, a woman's voice emerged from amongst the fading clapping.

"Sir, wait. I wanted to ask you about the bridge to the spirit world."

Ravenwood paused and looked. The voice belonged to a young woman, who was in the aisle near the front. She was a pretty young thing, and Ravenwood immediately was intrigued. A young man stood by her side with an expression halfway between anxiety and embarrassment. Apparently, from their close proximity and his consternation, she was spoken for. Still, there was the premonition of danger that still pervaded

102

the room. Ravenwood stepped back to the microphone and addressed the young woman.

"That certainly is an interesting topic, Miss," he said. "But one better left to another time. Goodnight."

He turned and left, cognizant that she'd called out to him again, but he was content to let her question get lost in the fray of the departing crowd. The premonition was growing stronger again, but was indistinct, save for one thing: Death was in the air.

Ravenwood went through a stage door on the left that led to a hallway. The proprietor was standing there with a broad smile on his face. He held out his open palm and congratulated Ravenwood on "an exceptional speech."

"I found it very informative," the proprietor said. "And very moving, as well."

Ravenwood shook the man's hand. "I'm flattered you found it so."

The proprietor jerked his thumb toward the lobby. "You're going to go out there and sign copies of your books, aren't you?"

"The books have already been signed. And I fear I must be going."

"Going?" The man looked disappointed. "But —" He ended the sentence with an inflection that indicated their unfinished business.

"As I said," Ravenwood said. "I must leave as soon as possible. Another matter of the utmost importance is pending."

A hint of disappointment invaded the proprietor's smile and he ushered Ravenwood into an office on the other side of the hall. Seating himself behind a large mahogany desk, the proprietor opened the desk drawer, withdrew an envelope, and handed it over the desk to Ravenwood.

"Your fee," the man said, "as agreed upon. I'll have my secretary send you a report as to the book sales."

"That would be fine," Ravenwood said.

The Nameless One's telepathic voice echoed inside Ravenwood's head: *My son, the alley... There is much danger present.*

I know, wise one. I sense it, too.

Ravenwood looked at the manager. "Is there a rear exit that I might use?"

"Certainly," the fellow said, getting up from his chair. "Want to avoid the crowd of adoring fan's fair, eh?

Ravenwood accepted the check and thanked him, declining to give any justification regarding his choice of egress. He then went to the rack by the door and retrieved his coat, top hat, gloves and walking stick. As he finished slipping on his overcoat, the premonition continued, stronger with each passing second. Great violence was imminent. Ravenwood paused, taking in the full extent of the vision, letting the feeling wash over him.

"The rear exit," he said. "I must get there without delay."

"Of course. I'll take you there."

"And afterward, would you be so kind as to call the police?" Ravenwood pulled open the door and held it, showing his urgency.

"The police? What for?"

"There's a crime about to occur," Ravenwood answered, holding his hand toward the doorway.

The proprietor looked perplexed. "A crime?"

"There's no time to explain. The exit, if you please."

His host nodded as they walked down the hallway to the rear door, the man's hand dipping into his pocket and emerging with a large ring of keys. "A crime... Of course."

Ravenwood ignored the fellow's skepticism as they strode toward the exit. The premonition almost had reached its apex. There was little time to waste.

The proprietor's hand shook as he tried to fit the key into the slot on the door, just below the knob. The clicking of metal scraping on metal jarred Ravenwood's concentration.

It's happening now, he thought. *In the alley.*

The man's fingers fumbled with the jangling keys. He inserted the key and twisted, but the lock held. "Must be another key," he said, flashing a weak smile. "Don't use this door very often."

There was precious little time to waste. Ravenwood reached out and placed his left hand on the proprietor's chest. With gentle pressure, he moved the man back, and then raised his right leg upward toward his chest. In a motion almost too fast to see, Ravenwood's foot shot out and crashed against the door. Wood splintered and the door flew opened, bouncing against the concrete wall and almost returning to its former position as Ravenwood pushed through it.

"My door!" the manager yelled.

"Take whatever you need to repair it from the profits from my book sales," Ravenwood said. He stepped out into the darkness of the rather warm spring night and found himself on an elevated porch with a set of wooden stairs descending to the floor of the alley below.

About forty yards ahead a set of automobile headlights illuminated six people. Ravenwood canted his head to better distinguish the figures. The young woman who had asked the question about the spirits was being held by a rough looking hoodlum, her arms pinioned behind her back. Three more hoods were working over the young man who had been with her. His arms were pinned as well, as the two men in front of him delivered repeated blows to his body. The young man's grunts of pain mixed in with the ambient cacophony of sounds of the city by night.

Ravenwood leapt down the steps, landing with the grace of a cat, and ran toward the struggling figures. He reached them in a few seconds and lashed out with his walking stick, striking one of the assailants in the left knee. The burly hoodlum buckled and Ravenwood delivered a quick right cross to the jaw. As that man crumpled to the alley floor, Ravenwood jabbed the second assailant in the face with the walking stick. The man's nose burst open with a torrent of blood. Turning, Ravenwood brought the long cane down on the third hoodlum's head, striking the thug behind his ear. This man howled in pain as he, too, fell to the ground, releasing his hold on the young man. He sank to his knees, blood dripping from his mouth and nose.

"What the hell?" the fourth hood said as he held the struggling girl.

"Let her go," Ravenwood commanded. "Now."

The hood's mouth twisted into a snarl and he muttered an obscene reply.

As Ravenwood took a step toward him one of the hoodlums on the ground sprung upward. Ravenwood whirled to meet the new threat.

A flash of silver glinted in the hoodlum's right hand, accompanied by a clicking sound.

A switchblade, Ravenwood thought.

Ravenwood immediately moved back, placing a bit of space between him and the knife-wielding hoodlum.

"Stick him, Tony," the hoodlum holding the girl urged.

Tony grinned and lumbered forward. He was a big man, perhaps outweighing Ravenwood by a good fifty pounds. The stepson of mystery shifted his grip on his cane and swung it hard into the advancing man's knee joint. The big hood did a stutter-step and Ravenwood followed up by bringing the cane down hard on the hand holding the knife. As the hood yelped in pain, and the knife clattered to the ground, Ravenwood delivered two more telling blows to the hoodlum's body and temple.

The big thug collapsed.

Ravenwood turned back to the hoodlum holding the girl. Her face held a look of sheer terror in the glow of the headlights.

"I believe I told you to let her go," Ravenwood repeated.

The hood's eyes flashed, his hand reaching inside his coat.

Ravenwood knew that the time it would take to draw his Luger would leave him on the short end of the equation. Instead, he stepped forward and hurled the walking stick like a javelin. The point of the cane hit the hoodlum in the throat and he fell back gasping, his pistol clattering to the alley floor. The hood grasped his neck and, at the same time, shoved the girl away. She screamed as she fell into Ravenwood's arms. The wail of an approaching siren sliced through the night, and the hoodlum glanced around warily. With one hand still holding his throat, the thug bent down and reached for his gun.

Ravenwood was too far away to intercede, plus he was now holding the young girl. He backed up, literally carrying her away from the fray while he reached for his own pistol.

The thug grasped his gun, a large .45 semi-auto, and pointed it at Ravenwood. Suddenly, both Ravenwood and the terrified girl were whisked to the side, out of harm's way just as a foot-long burst of fire exploded from the barrel. The hoodlum's shot had gone wide… Or had it?

Ravenwood heard the Nameless One's voice ask, *Are you all right, my son?*

I am, he answered back. *Thanks to you.*

Ravenwood's fingers curled around the handle of his Luger and he withdrew it from his shoulder-holster in one smooth motion. Just as the hoodlum's arm was bringing the .45 toward them for a second shot, Ravenwood pulled the trigger. His bullet hit the gangster in the upper body, and the man's gun hand lowered, firing another round into the pavement. The other two were regaining their feet. One pulled out another weapon, this one a long-barreled, blue steel revolver. Just as the hoodlum was about to take aim, Ravenwood adjusted his aim and shot the man between the eyes. The gangster fell like a marionette whose strings had been cut. An official sounding voice, accompanied by a flashlight beam, came from the side of the vehicle.

"Police. What's going on here?"

The last hoodlum, who had a gun as well, whirled and fired at the voice. The flashlight fell to the ground, the policeman tumbling downward after it.

Ravenwood fired another round at the shooter. The hood grunted, whirled, and fired off four shots in Ravenwood's direction. The bullets zinged off the brick building in back of Ravenwood. He pushed the girl to the ground and shielded her with his own body. Her young man companion was lying on his side, his breathing shallow and rapid.

The sound of more approaching sirens became audible. The last remaining hood scrambled into the car, exchanging a few more shots with Ravenwood. Their vehicle lurched forward and Ravenwood dropped his gun and grabbed the prone young man by the ankles, managing to pull him to safety as the hoodlum's car surged past them. Ravenwood watched the red taillights disappearing down the alley in the opposite direction of the approaching police cars. He centered himself in the alley and took careful aim, adjusting his sight picture to the rear windshield just above the left taillight. Ravenwood squeezed the trigger and watched as the fleeing car suddenly slowed and then drifted the left, smashing into a set of garbage cans and sending an arch of sparks as it sideswiped the adjacent building.

The vehicle came to rest, the horn blaring. Ravenwood replaced the pistol in its shoulder-holster and went to check the girl and the young man. Seeing that they were all right, he ran to the fallen police officer. The copper had an entry wound just under his right eye. A good portion of the back of his head was broken open like a ruptured melon.

Ravenwood gently closed the police officer's eyes and stood up, lifting his arms over his head as a swarm of police approached shouting commands.

"Stay where you are," he said, turning to address the young couple. "Don't move. You're safe now." He turned back to the police, adding, "I'm afraid one of your own has been shot."

The next morning the three of them sat in Ravenwood's living room as Sterling, the butler, brought in the silver coffee pot to refill their cups. The young woman, whose name was Laura McArthur, was very pretty. She appeared to be around twenty, and had the unusual combination of dark hair and blue eyes. The young man, Thomas Parker, looked a few years older. He continued to gaze adoringly at her, despite his swollen left eye and heavily bruised face. After Sterling had refilled each cup, he left and returned with a tray containing an ornate silver container of sugar and a small silver pitcher of cream. Both Laura and Thomas used the tiny tongs to drop a cube of sugar into their cups.

Sterling straightened and asked, "Will there be anything else, sir?"

Ravenwood shook his head.

The butler turned and walked out of the room.

Ravenwood noticed Laura was staring at him and she blushed.

"I'm sorry," she said. "I was… trying to figure out the color of your eyes."

Ravenwood smiled. "It's a condition known as heterochromia. I'm afraid their color fluctuates from time to time."

"Well," Thomas said. "Whatever color they are, I'm glad you were keeping them on us last night." He grinned and then winced in pain from the movement.

"Tom's right," Laura agreed. "How can we ever begin to thank you?"

"That's not necessary," Ravenwood said.

"We have no idea why those men targeted us," Thomas went on. "But one thing's certain. They were up to no good."

"If you hadn't been there, there's no telling what would have happened," Laura added.

"And you said you hadn't noticed the men following you prior to the incident?" Ravenwood asked.

Laura shook her head, as did Thomas.

"Of course," Ravenwood said with a smile, "you probably were looking at each other and not to anyone who might have been following you."

Thomas blushed this time.

Ravenwood watched them both carefully.

The young man guessed, "It must have been a random act of violence."

"Do you think they intended to rob us?" Laura asked.

Again, Ravenwood hesitated before he answered. There were too many unknown variables for him to formulate any hypothesis as to why the attack had occurred, but he doubted the motive of the three hoodlums was robbery. They had been too heavily armed for mere stick-up men. Additionally, they were also in possession of guns and a vehicle, which indicated that the incident had been planned in advance. The premonition of danger that Ravenwood had experienced, along with that of the Nameless One, still lingered in his psyche. This further convinced him that this mystery and the danger were far from over.

"Regardless," Ravenwood said. "It's time for you two to get on with your lives. What are your plans?"

The young couple exchanged an extended glance, then Thomas turned and said, "We're going to get married."

Ravenwood nodded. "Ah, capital. I wish you much happiness."

"We're going to announce our engagement this weekend," Laura informed. "At my debutante's ball."

"We'd be so honored if you'd attend," Thomas invited. "As our special guest."

Ravenwood's eyes scanned both of their faces. They seemed so innocent, so naïve, yet he sensed some apprehension in the young man's visage. "Well, this is rather short notice. Is it here in the city?"

"No, I'm afraid it's at my family's country estate." Laura clenched her lower lip between perfect teeth. "It's a ways from here. Upstate. But we do have two buses leaving from the Empire State Building on Saturday morning. They're bringing my friends and some kitchen personnel and the band that's going to play at the ball."

"You'd be most welcome to ride along," Thomas said. "I'll be there to make sure you don't have to travel with the hired help." His face had a rather pinched, anxious expression.

Ravenwood laughed. "That wouldn't be the first time. And I'm sure whatever accommodations you've arranged will prove most satisfactory."

"Then you'll come?" Laura pleaded.

"I'd be delighted."

"Wonderful," she smiled. "There are so many things I wish to ask you. I can't wait for you to meet Prince Mubashir. He's an occult scientist and he's able to bridge the gap between the spirit world and this one."

Ravenwood raised an eyebrow. "You've witnessed him doing this?"

Laura had a look of ecstasy on her face. "My mother... She perished three months ago. I've been trying to establish contact with her. The Prince has been able to do that."

"I see," Ravenwood steepled his fingers. "And Prince Mubashir will be at this party?"

"Oh yes," the bride-to-be elaborated. "We're going to hold a séance there."

Thomas cleared his throat and spoke. "And the invitation is also extended for one of your lady friends, of course."

Laura seemed beside herself with joy. She thanked him again and said she'd send over the information shortly. Thomas excused himself for a moment and left the room. When he returned, Ravenwood and Laura got to their feet and Ravenwood walked the two of them to the door. He noticed the young man reaching into his pocket.

"I look forward to seeing you on Saturday, sir," Thomas said, turning and extending his hand. "And thanks again for saving our lives."

As they shook hands, Ravenwood was cognizant that Thomas was passing a note to him. Ravenwood's eyes narrowed, but he was able to read a beseeching expression in the young man's face. Palming the note, Ravenwood slipped it into his pocket as he lowered his hand. After a few more goodbyes, they left and he retrieved the note and read the hastily *written* scrawl.

Mr. Ravenwood, I need your help again. I believe the attack last night was planned and that Laura is in danger. I wish to speak with you privately Saturday on the bus. T.P.

He heard the doorbell ring and wondered if Thomas had returned. Sterling entered the living room once again and said, "Sir, Inspector Stagg has arrived and wishes to see you."

Ravenwood shoved the note into his pocket and nodded. He positioned himself by the window to contemplate the situation. Presently, Stagg entered the room. He was a rather short and stout man, wearing an overcoat and had a smoldering cigar in his mouth. He held a brown paper bag, which he thrust toward Ravenwood.

"I brought back your gun," Stagg said. "Now I want some answers."

"Answers?" Ravenwood accepted the bag and took out his Luger and the accompanying magazine. The slide was up, indicating that the weapons was unloaded. Ravenwood held up the pistol and smiled. "Much appreciated, by the way."

Stagg nodded and puffed copiously on the cigar. "'Twas the least I could do for you after you took care of those murdering skunks that shot that copper." Stagg removed the cigar and frowned. "He was a good man. Left a wife and three little ones."

Ravenwood kept his expression neutral. "Let me give you a check for the widow and orphans."

Stagg nodded again. "That'd be appreciated, of course, but I want something more." He replaced the cigar and the end glowed red as he drew in more smoke. "Like I said, I want answers. Who put them gunmen up to it? It didn't have the earmarks of any robbery to me."

"I agree," Ravenwood nodded. "But as far as answers, I'm afraid I don't have any for you as of yet."

Stagg's frown deepened.

"Have you any plans for this weekend?" Ravenwood inquired.

"Huh?" Stagg's jaw sagged and the cigar almost tumbled out of his mouth.

"If you wish to find out who was ultimately responsible for the murder of your fellow officer," Ravenwood continued, "I'd like to suggest that you accompany me this weekend to upstate New York."

"Upstate?" The space between Stagg's eyebrows showed double creases. "What for?"

"There is an aura of evil in the air, Inspector." Ravenwood let the man hang for several seconds before adding, "Accompany me so that we can run this mystery, and hopefully those behind it, to ground."

Thomas Parker was standing next to the first bus outside the Empire State Building at ten o'clock Saturday morning. He welcomed Ravenwood with a warm handshake and smile, which caused him to wince.

"Still feeling a bit sore, I see," Ravenwood pointed out.

"A little," Thomas admitted. He glanced around and leaned close to Ravenwood. "I do hope we'll have time to confer once we get to the mansion, sir."

"Undoubtedly, we shall." Ravenwood stepped back and held out his hand, palm upward. "May I present one of my manservants, Horatio. I have very special dietary needs and he often accompanies me to tend to those duties."

Stagg's face reddened and his lips compressed into a tight line.

"Would he be more comfortable in the second bus then?" Thomas asked. "With the kitchen staff and the band members?"

Stagg's face turned an even darker shade as Ravenwood turned toward him with a broad grin. "Perhaps that would be more appropriate."

"Come on, Horatio," Thomas said.

"If you'll give us a minute, sonny," Stagg replied. "I need to confer with my *boss* in private."

Thomas nodded and went back to supervise the loading of the luggage and band equipment.

"Hey," Stagg's mouth twisting into a near snarl. "What's the big idea telling him I was your servant?"

"You're supposed to be working incognito, remember," Ravenwood reminded the homicide detective. "And what better cover could you have than that of a servant? You'll have the full run of the place to watch over things."

Stagg pursed his lips and considered this, then grunted an agreement. "Just don't expect me to peel no potatoes."

"I wouldn't dream of it," Ravenwood chuckled.

"And why did you tell him my first name?"

"If I called you Inspector Stagg any listening villains might put two and two together. After all, you do have quite the reputation in certain ignominious circles."

Stagg snorted. "Igno—what?"

"Nevermind," Ravenwood said. "Just go along with the charade."

Stagg frowned and was about to say something else when a female voice calling out Ravenwood's name intruded. Both men turned in time to see a comely red head ambling toward them carrying a small suitcase. She was a pretty woman in her late twenties, with long, elegant legs and a superb figure. Ravenwood recognized her as Allison Hayes, aka *Allison H*, of the *New York Post* newspaper's society page.

"What's she doing here?" Stagg asked in a hushed whisper.

"I have no idea," Ravenwood said, but he flashed a welcoming smile. He'd called Allison the day prior asking her assistance on researching Laura McArthur and her family. When Allison had called him back with the information from the newspaper morgue, she'd been full of questions, most of which Ravenwood had declined to answer. Now, apparently after having smelled a story, she'd come to insinuate herself into the investigation.

"My, you do look exceptionally lovely, my dear," Ravenwood complimented, executing a slight bow.

"Yeah," Stagg said. "You do. Now scram. We got official business to take care of."

Allison's smile was unfazed. She walked up next to Ravenwood and planted a quick kiss on his cheek, saying a louder than normal voice, "I'm so sorry I'm late, darling. But when I got your invitation, I just had to make sure I had an appropriate dress to wear."

"I'm sure it will more than appropriate," Ravenwood stepped back and held his hand toward the open door of the first bus.

"You ain't thinking of letting her tag along," Stagg blurted. "Are you?"

"You remember my manservant, Horatio, my dear?" Ravenwood's smile was broad and wicked.

"Of course," Allison said. Her smile was equally sharp. "I just didn't recognize him without his... uniform."

Before Stagg could say anything more, Thomas Parker strolled up and

"What's she doing here?"

tapped him on the shoulder. "Are you ready to go to the other bus now, sir?"

"Please," Ravenwood said. "Call him Horatio." He winked at Stagg as he spoke, and then indicated Allison. "And may I present my companion for the ball, Miss Allison Hayes."

"My, it's certainly a pleasure to meet you, ma'am," Thomas said.

Stagg glared all the way as Thomas escorted him back toward the servants' bus. Ravenwood's smile seemed etched on his face. He leaned close to Allison and whispered, "You really ought to reconsider, my dear. This could be dangerous."

"Another of your premonitions?"

"You could put it that way."

"Well, not on your life, buster. I smelled a story yesterday when you called me, and I'm not passing up this chance on a big scoop."

"Very well," Ravenwood gave-in, placing a hand on her back and guiding her toward the bus door. He handed her suitcase to the driver, who was packing things in the luggage compartment. "But stay close to me. As I said, this could be dangerous."

"I'll stay close, all right," she grinned. "Just don't let it give you any ideas."

"Heaven forbid."

Once they were seated on the bus Ravenwood allowed Allison to take the window seat and then sat next to her, placing his arm around her shoulders and leaning close to her ear.

"I trust you brought the articles I requested?" he asked in *sotto voce*.

"Right here in my purse," she took out a large envelope.

Ravenwood quickly opened it and reviewed its contents. True to her word, Allison had brought the latest clippings on the McArthur clan. After making sure that no one was watching them, he quickly scanned the articles. Three of them were typical society page fodder detailing Laura's departure from the family estate to attend college, her completion of her schooling, and the announcement of her debutant's ball. Another article dated two years hence mentioned the remarriage of Elizabeth McArthur, Laura's mother, to one Sir Henry Wordsworth Yarborough III, an English gentleman who had swept the rich heiress to the McArthur fortune, off her feet. This clipping was followed by an obituary detailing the tragic drowning death of Elizabeth McArthur in a yachting accident off Hudson Bay three months ago. It mentioned that she was survived by her daughter, Laura, and her second husband, Sir Henry. Ravenwood shuffled to the last article in the stack.

"I thought you'd find that one most interesting," Allison smiled knowingly.

Ravenwood glanced at the headline, which was dated seventeen years prior:

Millionaire Magnate Goes Missing in South America. Presumed Dead.

Well known explorer and philanthropist, Dr. Clarence D. McArthur, was reported missing and presumed dead while on an expedition in Brazil. The renowned Dr. McArthur, president of the McArthur Foundation, had been on a trip to the South American country to investigate claims of a remarkable plant that as capable of healing all diseases. McArthur, who leaves behind a wife and a three-year-old daughter, had been with a group of local guides when he mysteriously vanished. A massive search was undertaken, during which time some of McArthur's clothing and belongings were found in the dense jungle. Due to the presence of blood stains on the recovered clothing, it was conjectured that McArthur had wandered away from the campsite and been attacked by one or more of the wild animals that are plentiful in the forest. A comprehensive search was conducted to no avail, and was called off after ten days without result. Officials said they intended to mount another search after the conclusion of the rainy season.

Ravenwood folded the articles and replaced them in the envelope, which he handed back to Allison.

"Well," she said. "What do you think?"

"I think," Ravenwood removed his arm from around her and reclined back in his seat, "that we're in for an interesting time at the ball."

After what seemed like an interminably long drive, the bus finally turned off the highway and onto a series of well-maintained side roads surrounded on either side by a thick forest of tall trees. As the long vehicle slowed to make a sharp right turn, the forestation thinned appreciably and a view of the vast McArthur Manor became visible. The estate was on what appeared to be an island, separated by a long channel of water at the bottom of a significant cliff of perhaps one hundred feet or more. A sturdy looking bridge, replete with an extended roof, spanned the clef between the mainland and the island.

"Wow," Allison exclaimed, shaking Ravenwood's arm as she looked out the window. "That place looks like something out of a Charlotte Bronte novel."

"Or one of Nathanial Hawthorne's." Ravenwood agreed. "But it does appear to have more than just seven gables."

The huge, three-storied brick mansion was centered among successively smaller additions. A colonial style quadruple set of massive white pillars lined the front entrance, and there were towering pine trees on either side of the road leading from the bridge to the mansion. The bus slowed even more as the driver executed the turn off the roadway and onto the bridge. Some of the girls on the bus squealed in unison. Allison looked out the window again and then back to Ravenwood.

"Looks like quite a drop. I hope this bridge is in good shape."

"So do I," Ravenwood added. "Otherwise we might have to swim home."

Allison glanced at him. "What?"

He chuckled. "I was merely pointing out, that from the looks of things; this bridge is the only point of egress."

After they had traversed the bridge the bus wound along a serpentine roadway toward the big house. Substantial rows of tall pine trees lined the winding path like enormous sentries.

"There it is, everybody," Laura called out from the rear of the bus. "My late father's family christened this place Green Lake Island, but I've always called it sleepy hollow." Her subsequent laugh sounded like musical charms.

"I like that," Allison remarked. "I'll have to use that in my story."

"I've been meaning to talk to you about that," Ravenwood whispered. "Remember you are here at my largess, and therefore I claim the right to set the rules for our weekend."

Allison cast him an alluring, sideways glance. "Oh? Exactly what does that mean?"

"It means, you're to keep the true nature of your presence here to yourself. And absolutely nothing gets printed without my prior approval."

She smiled and looked at him. "Is that all? I figured you were hoping for a bit of romance."

Ravenwood smiled too. "Well; after all, we are supposed to have a ball, aren't we?"

She canted her head and shot him a look that was rife with ambivalence.

The thought of spending time with Allison was a desirable diversion, but he was there to work. There was evil afoot.

Laura came strolling down the center aisle, talking as she walked, with Tom at her side.

"The manor was built in 1858 by my father's grandfather. He was, as you might infer, a great admirer of gothic architecture and medieval castles. When I was a little girl, some of my fondest memories are of coming here and playing in the many hallways and rooms. There are thirty-two separate bedrooms, by the way."

The bus slowed to a stop and Laura and Tom turned toward Ravenwood.

"The four of us can disembark here," Tom suggested and then raised his voice to address the others. "The driver will pull around back and the servants will unload all the luggage and show you to your rooms."

The other bus, containing the band members and servants and the imposturing Inspector Stagg, continued on the road toward the rear of the immense structure.

Ravenwood was watching the front of the house. A large man in a butler's uniform stepped out of the front door and held it open as a handsome, mustachioed man smoking a pipe stepped through and headed for the bus. He appeared to be around fifty, with well-clipped brownish hair, parted down the center showing a hint of gray on each temple. His tweed smoking jacket was unbuttoned, and did little to conceal a rather broad chest and substantial shoulders. He nodded to the butler as he exited and strode purposefully toward the bus.

"That has to be Sir Henry Wordsworth Yarbourgh III," Allison said. "I recognize him from his pictures."

"Undoubtedly," Ravenwood nodded.

The bus came to rest and the driver opened the doors. Laura trotted down the steps and gave Sir Henry a perfunctory hug. He then shook hands with Tom. Ravenwood and Allison made their way off the bus and Laura introduced her stepfather to Ravenwood as "the man who saved us."

Sir Henry transferred the pipe to his left hand and offered his right. "May I offer my sincere thanks to you, sir, for saving my step-daughter and her fiancé"

Ravenwood shook the man's hand, noticing his rather substantial grip, and introduced Allison as his "friend and companion."

Sir Henry executed a curt nod and welcomed her. He turned to the hulking butler and said, "Jarvis, do go round the back and supervise the unloading of the luggage."

Jarvis nodded and left without saying a word.

"He's a big one, isn't he?" Allison commented.

"Yes, he certainly is," Sir Henry concurred. "Our family butler was recently injured in an unfortunate accident, and Jarvis came highly recommend. We were fortunate to be able to procure his services on such short notice." He held his hand toward the main entrance. "Shall we?"

They walked up the limestone stairs onto a raised porch situated just behind the row of pillars. Sir Henry opened the door and they stepped through into a huge, circular foyer with elegant tables and vases on either side. At the end was a long, winding staircase with an ornately carved banister and fencing. A magnificent chandelier hung from a vaulted ceiling in the center of the foyer, and two, life-sized pictures hung on opposite walls. One was of a rugged looking man in a tan suit. The other was of a beautiful woman with black hair and azure eyes— the same coloring as Laura, who had apparently noticed Ravenwood staring at the paintings.

"That's my mother," she told him.

"She was very lovely," Ravenwood said.

"She was, wasn't she?" Laura's eyes welled up with tears "Oh, how I wish she were here for this."

Sir Henry took a half-step closer to her, but didn't touch her. "As do we all."

"Who's that in the other painting?" Ravenwood asked.

"My long, lost father," Laura explained with a trace of bitterness lacing her tone. "The manor was built by his grandfather, as I mentioned on the bus."

Tom moved between them and put his arm around Laura's shoulders. "Perhaps it would be a good time to go upstairs and—"

"Upstairs? Nonsense," a rather intrusive, but feminine voice interceded.

Ravenwood turned and a stunningly beautiful woman, also with jet black hair and blue eyes, moving down the winding staircase. She was wearing a black evening gown with a circular opening in the front that displayed a hint of cleavage. A cigarette smoldered between the fingers of her left hand as she strolled toward them with an elegant grace.

"Aunt Phyllis," Laura greeted, her tone ebullient once again. She ran toward the woman and they embraced. Tom Parker and Sir Henry exchanged quick glances that Ravenwood detected as anxiety laden. Laura held her aunt's hand as they approached the group and the introductions were completed. Phyllis Lundgrin, younger sister of Laura's late mother, Elizabeth, smiled as she was introduced. Ravenwood noted that it was a rather dazzling smile. He felt Allison pinch his arm slightly as he professed his pleasure at making Phyllis Lundgrin's acquaintance.

"Has the Prince arrived yet?" Laura asked.

"He has," Phyllis replied. "I was just upstairs helping them unpack."

Laura turned to Ravenwood. "I can't wait for you to meet him. I'm sure you'll have much to talk about."

Before Ravenwood could inquire further, he saw a man wearing a turban and clad in a garish looking bright purple robe enter the foyer from a rear door. A nice looking woman in a bourka and long gown followed several steps behind him. As the man drew closer, Ravenwood noticed his rather swarthy complexion.

A Levantine, he thought.

The woman also appeared to be of that nationality.

Laura ran forward and grabbed the turban clad man's hands.

"Oh, Prince Mubashir, there's someone I want you to meet."

She led the Prince over to the group. "May I present Prince Abdul Aleem Mubashir, prophet to the spirits."

The Prince bowed slightly.

"Abdul Alleem," Ravenwood said. "Servant of the everlasting. Mubashir, the spreader of good news."

The Prince raised an eyebrow. "Do you speak Arabic?" His voice was tinctured with a foreign accent.

"Only a little," Ravenwood confessed. "In order to further my studies."

The Prince's eyes narrowed. "I see you are a man of great vision, and also of great courage." He cocked his head slightly and his eyes closed to slits as he rocked back and forth. "And I also am sensing something more… You have demonstrated this courage quite recently…" His eyes closed completely, and he was still for perhaps twenty seconds, then he assumed his previous, normal expression. "You are the one who rescued Laura and her fiancé from a gang of outlaws."

Ravenwood merely nodded and said nothing. He noticed that the prince was wearing a bit of makeup.

"Isn't he amazing?" Laura asked. She turned to Ravenwood. "He's helping me to bridge that gap between the spiritual world and our own."

Sir Henry frowned, as did Tom. They exchanged another troubled glance.

"It was hardly a gang, Prince," Ravenwood said. "I'm afraid the reports of my exploits have been a tad exaggerated."

"Nonsense," the Prince scoffed pleasantly. "You do not do yourself justice."

"I thought you were still upstairs," Phyllis interrupted.

"We came down to inspect the ballroom," the Prince explained. "It will be necessary to make some adjustments to our presentation."

"We can talk about that later," Sir Henry said. "But right now, our guests have had a long ride and may very well wish to freshen up a bit."

As if on cue, Jarvis appeared in the hallway.

"We have the luggage unloaded, sir."

"Ah, capital," Sir Henry continued. "Why don't you take the ladies upstairs, while we men retire to the library for a cigarette and a bit of sherry?"

Ravenwood glanced at the Prince who shook his head.

"Regrettably, I must attend to my other duties, Sir Henry. It is almost time for my afternoon prayers."

"Ah, yes," Sir Henry rememebered. "My apologies. I totally forgot that your religion frowns on the practice of imbibing."

The Prince merely nodded.

Sir Henry's expression was neutral. "Very well, then. Mr. Ravenwood, Thomas, would you two care to join me?"

The three of them walked down the hallway toward a large wooden door with a rounded top. Sir Henry twisted an ornate doorknob and shoved it open. Once inside, he closed the door behind them and walked over to a table in front of a massive fireplace made of squared, limestone slabs. A glass decanter of amber liquid and several glasses rested on a silver serving tray. Sir Henry removed the stopper, poured three glasses, and handed the drinks to Ravenwood and Tom. He picked up his own glass, held it in front of him, and said, "Cheers."

All three of them downed the sherry. It had a sweet tartness to it that Ravenwood appreciated. When Sir Henry picked up the decanter and held it with a questioning look, Ravenwood nodded.

Sir Henry refilled each glass, replaced the decanter, and opened a finely carved wooden box that contained long, European style cigarettes. Both Tom and Ravenwood declined. Sir Henry took one, crimped the extended paper base into a filter, and lighted it with a gold lighter. He exhaled a plume of smoke and sighed.

"I may as well tell you, Mr. Ravenwood," he brought the cigarette to his lips once more. "Thomas and I don't trust that bloody Prince one bit. I think he's a charlatan and out to take advantage of my step-daughter's naiveté, and her grief at the loss of her mother."

"I take it that was the basis of the note you slipped to me?" Ravenwood asked, looking at Tom.

The young man nodded. "I couldn't come right out and mention it, sir. Laura seems to have fallen under the man's spell. She's convinced he can channel a way for her to converse with her deceased mother."

"How is it she came to be so set on this?" Ravenwood desired more information.

"I'm afraid I'm partially to blame for that," Sir Henry admitted. "She took my wife's death very hard, you see, and I felt that perhaps an older, more mature female influence might help her through her grief. I contacted Phyllis, Laura's mother's younger sister, and invited her to come visit us. She'd been abroad, and hadn't been able to come to the funeral, so she readily agreed." He paused and drew deeply on his cigarette. "Apparently, she'd previously become associated with this Prince Mubashir character on her trip to Europe. She brought him with her, and introduced him to Laura."

"Laura was so excited to have her aunt back in her life," Tom picked up the narrative. "That I think she bought into the possibility of the spirit world and somehow contacting her mother."

"Pure poppycock, if you ask me," Sir Henry exhaled a plume of smoke. "My apologies, Mr. Ravenwood. Tom told me that you're an expert in the field, and I meant no disrespect."

"No offense taken," Ravenwood shrugged. "I am in total agreement that there are many unscrupulous characters about." He turned to Tom. "You said that Laura was excited to have her aunt 'back in her life?' What did you mean by that?"

"Laura hadn't seen her since she was a little girl. Perhaps fifteen years or more."

"That's quite a gap."

"Phyllis was quite the epicurean," Sir Henry said. "The McArthur family is quite wealthy, and Elizabeth told me that Phyllis left as soon as she completed finishing school and embarked on a rather bohemian lifestyle, trotting around the globe. They hadn't seen her since Laura's fifth birthday. In fact, I had to hire a private detective to track the woman down. She was in London. With the Prince, no doubt."

"Interesting," Ravenwood mused aloud.

"We've got a surprise in store for him," Tom glanced eagerly at Sir Henry, who looked toward Ravenwood.

"Are you familiar with Professor Karl Fenninger?"

"Yes," the Stepson of Mystery replied. "He's regarded as the preeminent expert on psychic mediums and the fraudulent methods they sometimes use for nefarious purposes."

"Do you know him?" Sir Henry asked eagerly.

"Only by reputation."

"So you've never met?"Sir Henry asked.

Ravenwood shook his head.

Sir Henry nodded, tossed down the remainder of his sherry, and set the glass on the serving tray. "Well, knowing that Phyllis and Laura were planning on having the Prince perform one of his séances at the ball, Tom contacted Professor Fenninger and asked him to come here. It's our hope that he'll be able to expose that damn Levantine for the phony he is."

"There's a lot at stake, you see," Tom's face took on a troubled look and Sir Henry reached over and patted Tom's arm.

"This debutante's ball has been planned for quite some time," Sir Henry said. "Even before my late wife's death. As I mentioned, the McArthur family is quite wealthy. It was written in my wife's will that in the event of her death, the entire estate was to be turned over to Laura upon her twenty-first birthday."

"Which is tomorrow," Tom said.

"So you're fearful that this is the motive behind the Prince's obsequious behavior?" Ravenwood concluded.

Sir Henry nodded once more. "Not that I'm against Laura having control of the estate. It's her birthright." He brought the cigarette to his lips and inhaled on it, bringing the ash almost completely to the folded filter. His words were couched in smoke as he continued. "I am independently wealthy, so it's of little matter to me what she does with the fortune, but I shouldn't like to see her taken advantage of by some scoundrel."

"What about Phyllis?" Ravenwood arched an eyebrow. "As part of the family, doesn't she share in the estate?"

"Phyllis, as I said, has always been something of an embarrassment to the McArthur family. Elizabeth's father, Laura's grandfather, practically disowned his bohemian daughter when she was barely out of her teens, although she does live off an established trust fund. That was how I was able to track her down."

Ravenwood was about to ask another question when a clamor of angry voices in the outside hallway became audible. Sir Henry's brow wrinkled and he walked briskly toward the door, which burst open. Jarvis, the butler, stepped in and held the door. A group of five men followed through the opening, one of whom was Stagg, who had a look of rage plastered on his face. His arms were pinioned behind his back by two huge men. Another man walked in behind them holding a large revolver.

"What is the meaning of this?" Sir Henry demanded.

"Please forgive the intrusion, sir," Jarvis said. "But Chester and his associates found this man lurking on the grounds."

"I wasn't doing nothing of the sort," Stagg retorted. "These three jamokes came outta nowhere and jumped me."

"Shaddup, buster," the big man with the pistol warned. He was the largest of the three, having a chest the size of a wine barrel. The revolver hung comfortably in his grip.

"Please," Ravenwood held up a hand. "This is my manservant. And his name happens to be Horatio, not Buster."

The big man's jaw sagged a bit. He looked at Sir Henry.

"Chester, it appears your overzealousness has caused a regrettable mistake," Sir Henry stated the obvious. "Unhand the man immediately."

The two men holding Stagg's arms released him and he stumbled forward. After regaining his balance, he turned and glared at the big man.

"This one pointed a gun at my head," Stagg declared angrily.

"Hey, you was asking for it, sneaking around like that," Chester said.

"I wasn't sneaking nowhere," Stagg fired back. "You big lug."

"Horatio, please," Ravenwood stepped forward and placed a hand on Stagg's shoulder. "Remember that we are here as guests of Sir Henry and his staff." He then addressed Chester. "My apologies for this misunderstanding."

Sir Henry stepped forward administering a severe look at the big man.

"Chester, please apologize at once to Mr. Ravenwood and his man. The type of conduct you've exhibited is certainly untoward. And put away that bloody revolver."

The big man took off his hat and held it by his waist, trying to conceal the gun.

"I... I'm sorry," he muttered. There was a rough look to him. His hair was red and thinning out in several places. Ravenwood noticed a ridge of scar tissue over both of the man's eyebrows. That, and the crooked bulge of his nose indicated that Chester had been in many a physical altercation. "We was just trying to do our jobs, is all."

"Your jobs?" Ravenwood asked.

"That will suffice," Sir Henry said, gesturing for them to leave. He turned to Ravenwood. "Again, my apologies for the inconvenient intrusion."

Ravenwood nodded and told Stagg to wait in the hallway for him. Sir Henry closed the door and turned around with a smile.

"Nothing like a bit of excitement to make the day go by quicker, eh?"

"Quite," Ravenwood scratched his chin. "But tell me, who are those men?"

"They're my groundskeepers. They are a bit rough around the edges, but they manage to keep the estate in tip-top shape."

"Are all of your groundskeepers armed?"

Sir Henry's smile became self-effacing. "That is not normally the practice, but as of late, we've been plagued by the presence of a vagrant on the property."

"A vagrant?" Ravenwood repeated with a puzzled expression.

"Yes. I've only seen him from a distance, but I have no doubt he's up to no good. I was out hiking and saw him a week or so ago. I called out to him, to question what he was doing on private property, and the man ran." His forehead creased. "That seemed to indicate that his intentions were questionable. We found evidence that he'd been camping on the estate for a while. Thus, I thought it prudent to arm the men, in case the bugger had nefarious intentions." He clapped his hands together. "And now, I think it would be prudent for us to go freshen up before the evening meal. Do you agree?"

"That does sound like a good idea," Ravenwood said. "I'm looking forward to meeting Professor Fenninger. Will he be at the dinner?"

"I hope so. He has yet to arrive."

With that, Sir Henry opened the door. Ravenwood started to walk out, and then paused. "May I use your phone? I just remembered I needed to make a call."

"Why, certainly," Sir Henry called to Jarvis, who was standing next to Stagg. "Take Mr. Ravenwood and his manservant to the Green Room." He turned back to Ravenwood. "There's a tellie in there you can use."

The big butler nodded and held out his hand. "This way, sir."

Stagg glared at Ravenwood as he passed and muttered under his breath, "*Manservant.*"

Chester and his two cronies were standing by the front door watching the conversations. The big man turned and pointed at the large window. "Looks like there's a storm on the way."

Indeed, there is, Ravenwood thought.

"A vagrant?"

Ravenwood looked in the mirror as he expertly knotted the bowtie. He stepped aside and inspected the pristineness of his white tuxedo jacket next to his black trousers. Stagg swore and strode from the bathroom, holding his hands out in frustration. A sloppily knotted bowtie hung partially suspended from his collar.

"Why'd you go an order this monkey suit for me anyhow?" he grumbled. "I never could figure out how to tie one of these damn things."

Ravenwood motioned him forward. He undid the knot Stagg had made, which had left one portion of the tie dangling down his chest.

"It's just like tying one's shoe," Ravenwood said as he fashioned a new knot.

"Yeah, well, that still don't excuse the monkey suit. You're gonna owe me a big favor for this one, buster."

"Buster?" Ravenwood flashed a grin. "That was uncalled for, Horatio. I'm sure you felt a bit miffed when Sir Henry's groundskeeper addressed you with that appellation."

"That big lug," Stagg snorted. "If you wouldn't have insisted I leave my gun at home, I would've…"

Ravenwood made a tsking sound. "Remember, you're undercover. And a professional manservant should have no need for a firearm."

"Manservant. There you go again." Stagg sighed as Ravenwood finished the knot.

"There," he said. "Jarvis will be green with envy."

Stagg leaned over and glanced at himself in the mirror, then shrugged. He slipped on his black, butler's jacket and adjusted it over his shoulders. "Speaking of green, remember our little excursion into the Green Room?"

"I do." Ravenwood removed a shoulder holster from a compartment of his suitcase and slipped it on. Stagg's eyes widened as Ravenwood then removed his Luger pistol from another compartment and slipped it into the holster.

"Hey, how come you got your gun?"

Ravenwood slipped on his jacket and checked the fit in the mirror. The jacket had been specially made to allow for the shoulder holster. "I thought it prudent that one of us be armed, in case of trouble."

Stagg swore again. "Don't that beat all?"

Before Ravenwood could reply, there was a knock at the door. He turned and opened it. Tom Parker stood there, also dressed in a tuxedo.

"I hope I'm not disturbing you?"

"Not at all, Tom. Come in."

"I thought I'd tell you that Dr. Fenninger has arrived. I just finished showing him up to his room and briefing him on the situation."

Ravenwood nodded. "Did he offer any suggestions?"

"He thought it was a good plan, us allowing the séance to go forward." Tom's mouth drew into a tight line. "I'm so worried about Laura. She seems so taken with that turban wearing Svengali."

Ravenwood placed a hand on his shoulder and was about to speak when a loud explosion was heard from outside. They rushed to the window but could see little, save the steady rain and an occasional trace of lightning.

"What was that?" Stagg asked.

"I don't know," Ravenwood replied, "but perhaps we should investigate." He gestured toward the door.

They walked at a rapid pace through the hallway and saw Sir Henry and several other guests moving toward the stairway as well. Ravenwood slowed his pace and indicated that Stagg drop back as well.

"What were you about to tell me before Tom came in?" Ravenwood asked in a whisper. "About the Green Room?"

"When I finished telling Clancy to run a check on that Prince Mubashir guy," Stagg reported, "I waited out of habit and heard a little click before I hung up."

"So someone was listening on an extension?"

"That's sure what it sounded like. I was trying to figure out who?"

Ravenwood considered this. Sir Henry had suggested they use the phone in the Green Room, but this was done in the presence of the butler and the groundskeepers. Without knowing the locations of any house phone extensions, pinpointing who might have been listening, if someone was, was like speculating how long the rain would last. As they neared the front door Ravenwood quickened his step and got next to Sir Henry.

"Do you have any idea what that was?" he inquired.

Sir Henry shrugged. "The lightning, perhaps. We do have lightning rods installed at various points around the mansion."

Just then the front door opened and Chester stepped through, water dripping off of his hat, his clothing totally sodden. He held a large flashlight in his hand.

"Looks bad, sir," he told Sir Henry. "You'd better come quick."

Sir Henry snapped his fingers at Jarvis, who grabbed a pair of umbrellas. The big butler turned and handed one to Stagg. He then stepped out onto the porch, opened his umbrella, and waited for Sir Henry to step underneath it. They then followed Chester down the cobblestone pathway toward the roadway. Tom started to follow, but Ravenwood placed a hand on his shoulder and held him back.

"Perhaps it would be better for you to check on Laura," he suggested.

The groom-to-be nodded.

Stagg looked at the umbrella in his hand and frowned.

"Horatio," Ravenwood commanded slyly. "Do be mindful to handle that bumpershoot with the utmost care."

Stagg stepped out into the rain and flipped the umbrella open with a sharp jerking motion, holding it upward.

Ravenwood stepped underneath it and they proceeded down the sidewalk as well. The beam of the flashlight bounced perhaps thirty feet ahead of them.

A jagged line of lightning sliced the black velvet sky and a thunderous roar rolled over them a few seconds later. The rain continued to fall unceasingly. Chester led them along the road and then stopped. He shone the flashlight over the horizontal trunk of a very large tree that had fallen across the roadway.

"Damn," Sir Henry swore. "This is blocking the road. Chester, can you remove it?"

Another crackle of lightning flashed overhead, accompanied by the sound of thunder.

"We can't do it in this storm. That big Dolmer chainsaw takes two men to run it," Chester said. "I'm scared we'd get electrocuted."

Sir Henry frowned. "Very well, let's go back to the— hullo, what's this?" He pointed to the thick tree trunk. Chester shone the flashlight in that direction and the beam swept over a pair of legs that protruded from under a section of branches.

They all rushed over and Chester set the flashlight on the ground, grasped the legs, and pulled. The rest of the man's body slid into view. The side of his head had been crushed. Chester retrieved the flashlight and knelt next to the body.

"Looks like he's dead, Sir. The tree must've hit him when it fell."

"May I?" Ravenwood offered reaching for the light.

Chester glanced at Sir Henry, who gave a curt nod.

The big man handed Ravenwood the flashlight and he squatted down next to the supine figure. A pair of glazed-over, unblinking eyes starred vacuously and unflinching into the bright beam. His lips curled back, showing a row of even teeth, smeared with blood and looking like a bone exposed by a wound. The man appeared to be in his late forties. The side of his head that wasn't damages showed a fringe of short, gray hair. His clothes were ragged. Ravenwood gripped the man's right wrist and lifted it into the beam. After a few seconds, he set the arm down.

"He's dead, all right," he confirmed, getting to his feet and shining the flashlight over the fallen tree before handing it back to Chester. "No pulse."

"Hell, I coulda told you that," Chester retorted.

"Any idea who he was?" Ravenwood ignored the man's attitude.

"Why, it obvious, isn't it?" Sir Henry said. "Look at his clothes. He's that vagrant I was talking about. A bit of poetic justice, not that I would wish such an untimely end on any man."

"Quite," the Stepson of Mystery agreed.

Sir Henry turned toward Chester. "Get some of the men and put the body in the tool shed. We'll have to notify the authorities, but that can't be done until tomorrow."

"Tomorrow?" Ravenwood looked confused. "Isn't that a bit of an unseemly delay? Why not at least call them tonight?"

"Two reasons," Sir Henry said, pointing the tree. "If you'll notice, that tree took down the phone lines. I happened to be on the phone when the lightning strike occurred. The line went dead." The angle of the rain changed slightly, causing the drops to gather on the left side of his face. "And secondly, I shouldn't want that the accidental death of this wretched soul upset Laura's debutante ball. As you said, the man's dead and there's nothing to be done at this point except notify the authorities in a timely fashion."

"I see," Ravenwood held his hand up to catch so of the slanting rain. "By all means, the ball must go on."

"Righto," Sir Henry said. "May I suggest we all go back to the comfort of the house? I believe that dinner was about to be served."

Ravenwood was enjoying the sweet smell of Allison's perfume as he held her close while they danced to the band's rendition of "When They Begin the Beguine."

"These guys aren't half bad," he smiled. "Cole Porter would approve."

"Yeah, yeah, if you say so." She leaned close and whispered into his ear, "So tell me about the dead guy."

"Now why do you want to spoil such a nice moment between the two of us by bringing up such a sordid matter?"

"Are you kidding? This could be my big chance to get off the society page and turn in a real story."

Ravenwood liked the feel of her lush body pressed against his. "Sir Henry seems to think that the man was a vagrant who'd been frequenting the area."

She leaned back slightly and looked at him. "A bum? Is that all? Damn. I was hoping for some real intrigue, or something."

Ravenwood rubbed his right hand over the exposed skin of her back. She stiffened a bit and shot him a sharp look of disapproval.

"Now is that any way for my date to behave?" he said feigning a disappointed expression.

"Date? You know why I'm really here. Now are you holding out on me, or what?"

Ravenwood heaved a theatrical sigh and glanced at the opposite end of the capacious ballroom. The Prince had insisted that the band switch to the other end of the room so he could make the necessary adjustments for the séance. It was scheduled to begin shortly.

"Well, perhaps it would interest you to know that we'll be spending the night here."

"In your dreams," she chuckled. "No story's worth *that* much."

"I'm afraid it's a *fait accompli*, my dear. That explosion not only took out the telephone lines, but it also blocked the only egress from the manor until morning."

"What? We're trapped here?"

"You needn't make it sound so dire. I'm available to keep you warm in case the blankets aren't enough."

Allison frowned. "Like I said, buster, in your dreams maybe." She looked around and leaned closer. "But I'll keep the proposal in mind. In the meantime, what's your impression of this Prince fellow?"

Before Ravenwood could answer, he felt a tapping on his shoulder. He and Allison stopped dancing and turned toward Tom Parker, who stood there looking a bit self-conscious.

"Are you thinking of cutting in?" Ravenwood cocked an eyebrow.

Tom's face flushed. "Gosh, no, sir. I wouldn't dream of it." He quickly looked both ways and bent closer to whisper. "Dr. Fenninger asked to speak with you."

Ravenwood nodded and stepped away from Allison, giving her hand to Tom.

"And so he shall. Now do be a good fellow and finish this dance with my girl."

Tom glanced at Allison, who looked sumptuously radiant in a white gown that hugged her voluptuous figure.

"Come on, kid," Allison came into his arms. "Before the music ends."

Ravenwood walked across the floor to see the man he'd been briefly introduced to earlier. He had a rather thin build and wasn't very tall. His dark hair was slicked straight back from his forehead, and he wore a pair of gold-rimmed wire glasses that made his eyes appear smaller. He greeted Ravenwood with a fractional nod.

"I'm so glad you and I could talk before the séance," Fenninger said. "I wanted to get your impression of Prince Mubashir." His voice had a high, nasally sound to it.

"I think I'll reserve my opinion of him until after I see the séance."

Fenninger looked shocked. "Don't tell me that you believe in all that nonsense."

Ravenwood smiled whimsically. "All right. I won't tell you."

Fenninger's eyes widened behind the thick lenses, and then he forced out a laugh. "For a moment I thought you were being serious." He was clearly nervous. "You weren't, were you?"

"Hardly." Ravenwood noticed that the man's teeth were heavily stained with tobacco residue. "How are you going to proceed?"

Fenninger seemed to warm to the question. "Well, after this so-called séance and visitation, I'm going to confront him about Sir Arthur Conan Doyle's own sad foray into the world of spiritualism." He bumped up the glassed, which had slipped down on his nose. "You're familiar with that, I assume."

"I know that Doyle instructed his wife to charter an airplane for a séance to be held after his death."

"Exactly." Fenninger smiled again, showing his bad teeth. "A ridiculous sham, but Doyle was delusional. Obsessed with contacting his dead son and brother. Even the magician, Houdini, tried to dissuade Doyle from such absurdities, but to no avail. No, the best course is to let him have his show, do his tricks, and then attack his credibility."

Ravenwood was about to respond when Laura walked up to him.

"It seems your lady friend is dancing with my fiancé, Mr. Ravenwood." She transformed her pout into a bright smile. "So I think it's entirely appropriate for us to give them some competition."

Ravenwood returned the smile. "Of course. Professor, if you'll excuse us?"

Fenninger eyed Laura. "Certainly." As he turned away Ravenwood noticed that the tip of the man's tongue darted quickly over his lips. Ravenwood and Laura walked onto the dance floor. Another waltz was playing.

"Who is that awful little man?" Laura questioned.

He noticed her breath was redolent of the smell of alcohol.

"He's a friend of your step-father."

Laura frowned. 'That figures. It's my debutante ball, and I don't even have the say over who gets invited."

"Well, Sir Henry seems to have made every effort to make this a memorable occasion."

She leaned forward and placed her head on Ravenwood's shoulder as they swayed to the music.

"If only…" Her voice drifted off.

"You miss your mother a great deal, don't you?"

Laura looked up at him with glistening eyes. "I do. Terribly. She was… such a part of my life. It took her many years to get over the loss of my father."

Ravenwood said nothing.

"What did you think of Prince Mubashir?" she asked.

"Interesting fellow. How did you meet him?"

"Aunt Phyllis introduced us. She'd been living over in Europe, and that's where they met." Her face took on a cheerful expression. "When she introduced us, it was like the whole new world opened up for me. He told me things… Things only my mother would have known. That's how I know he really is what he says he is."

"Laura, please don't take this the wrong way, but I need to ask you, has the Prince ever asked you to finance any of these communications with the spirit world."

She stopped dancing and stared up at him, the cheerfulness vanishing from her face, replaced by a look of pain. "How can you ask me that?"

"I'm sorry, but there are a lot of people who might seek to take advantage of a young lady in your position."

"No. The answer to your question is emphatically no. He's never asked me for a dime. Just ask Aunt Phyllis."

"Did I hear my name mentioned?"

Ravenwood turned to see Laura's aunt approaching, holding a cocktail glass in each hand. She was wearing an elegant black evening gown, which was cut low enough to expose a very good view of her décolletage. Her smile held a faint trace of wickedness as she looked Ravenwood up and down, then said, "I was hoping for a dance, but the Prince is almost ready to start." She handed one of the glasses to Laura, who then took a quick little sip.

"Perhaps we could share a drink after the séance," Ravenwood suggested.

Phyllis plucked the olive out of her drink and leisurely placed it in her mouth.

"Perhaps. Come, Laura."

Sir Henry appeared beside them, his face red and his manner officious. He noticed the drink in his step daughter's hand.

"Laura, do you really think you should be imbibing so heavily?"

"Oh, loosen up, Henry," Phyllis chided. "She is going to be twenty-one tomorrow, isn't she?"

Sir Henry turned his attention to her. "I've had just about enough of you and your... bohemian shenanigans. First you bring this charlatan into Laura's life, and now you're priming her with alcohol."

Phyllis laughed and then took a sip of her drink. "Is Sir Fuddy-duddy upset?"

"I happen to be concerned about my daughter's welfare."

"I'm not your daughter," Laura said in a voice loud enough to attract the attention of those standing close by. A sudden silence hung in the ballroom. "And I won't have you calling the Prince a charlatan. He's not, and he's going to show us all."

Sir Henry stood there stoically. After several seconds of silence, he said, "Very well. Do as you wish, but I'll not be a party to it." With that, he turned and left the ballroom. Tom walked up and took Laura's hand. She immediately began crying and fell into his embrace.

Ravenwood felt a tap on his shoulder. He turned and saw Stagg standing there with a serving tray loaded with glasses.

"Can I get you something?" Stagg asked formally.

Ravenwood took him by the arm and walked him to the edge of the crowd.

"Have you noticed anything out of the ordinary?"

Stagg shook his head. "Nothing that convinces me that this whole trip's been nothing more than a wild goose chase."

The sound of three piercing gongs reverberated through the room, and everyone's eyes turned to the dark, velvet curtain that had been strung across the rear section of the ballroom. The Prince's assistant, now clad in a rather revealing green colored dress, replete with veils, stood holding a large hammer-like tool in one hand and gold-colored, circular gong in the other.

She spoke in a loud voice: "Prince Mubashir, the esteemed mystic of the desert, bids you to enter and see his next foray into the spirit world." She grasped the corner of the curtain and pulled it back. Everyone began meandering into the cloistered section of the ballroom.

As they entered, Ravenwood noticed a dark tent had been erected against the far wall. Several rows of chairs had been set up, with a semi-circular row closest to the tent. The Prince stood in front of the tent clad in a garish, purple robe and accompanying cape. A large, red jewel now decorated the front of his turban. The assistant took Laura by the arm and walked her to a chair in the front row. Her aunt took the seat next to her. Tom sat on the opposite side.

The Prince raised an eyebrow. "And where is your step-father, my dear?"

"He's not coming," Laura said.

The Prince glanced at Phyllis, who nodded.

"Very well then. We shall continue without him."

The assistant struck the gong again and the lights in the room were extinguished, except for a trio of candles that had been set on a table next to the tent.

"I have asked that all the lights, save for these three candles, be extinguished," the Prince explained. "We are about to invite the spirits to visit us, and they are afraid of bright lights."

Ravenwood stood near the back next to Stagg. Dr. Fenninger came up next to him.

The Prince made several pronouncements, and then took the hand of his beauteous assistant, escorting her to the tent. "At risk to her own well-being, my assistant, Fuchsia, will act as a channel from this world to the next. She will be placed in a state of trance in which the spirits use to transverse the bridge between our two worlds." He spoke with slow deliberation, pausing to make eye contact with members of the audience. "Presently, I will then call upon the spirit of Elizabeth McArthur to visit us in this very room."

"This guy musta made his living selling snake oil," Stagg whispered.

"Exactly," Fenninger said. "These are no more than parlor tricks."

A plump woman sitting in the row in front of them turned and shushed them.

Stagg frowned.

"I know there are disbelievers among you," the Prince continued, raising his arms high above his head. "But soon, they, too, will see the light. I must demand total silence and non-interference as this ritual is conducted. The safety of Fuchsia depends upon it. She is placing herself at great risk."

A murmur of assent reverberated through the crowd. The Prince took one more look around, his visage stone-faced, and then he flipped back the curtain of the tent exposing a tall wooden box with a glass front. "And now, she assumes the transitional position."

Fuchsia stepped into the box and stood still, her arms at her sides. Her body was totally visible through the glass. The Prince made a show of securing the door from the outside with a metallic bolt. He then waved his arms and muttered something indecipherable. He then closed the curtain and waved his arms again. He strode over to Laura and held out his hands. She took them and he lifted her to a standing position, leaning forward to whisper in her ear. He then went back to the tent and pulled back the curtain. Fuchsia's figure was still in the glass box, and she raised her arms. Suddenly, she disappeared. The Prince lifted his arms and started reciting a chant in Arabic. A strange humming sound began reverberating in the room, accompanied by another distortion, this one sounding almost like a woman's voice.

"The great moment has come," the Prince declared dramatically.

"Laaauuuraaaa," the disembodied voice called out. "Laaauuurrra."

Laura stiffened. "Mother? Mother, is that you?"

The Prince waved his arms again, and suddenly a woman's face, glowing white against the darkness, appeared in the glass case. The visage looked astoundingly like the portrait of Elizabeth McArthur.

"Lauuurrraaa," the face called out. "I've come back to be with you."

The words sounded strange, like high-pitched sketch of a human voice, only emanating from a vocal scale that was hardly human.

"Mother!" Laura stepped forward and reached out, but the Prince stepped in front of her. The glowing face in the glass box disappeared, and the sound transformed into a squealing wail.

Laura looked at the box and then collapsed in a twisting fall to the floor.

The light from flickering candles danced over the astonished faces in the room.

"Lights," the Prince said. "Someone turn on the lights."

As this was being done Ravenwood noticed the Prince replace the flap across the opening of the tent, and then stoop down next to the fallen girl. Tom ran to her side and knelt there as well. The lights came on and Ravenwood made his way to the front of the room. Laura's face looked pale, but she had regained consciousness.

"Is your assistant all right?" Ravenwood asked the Prince.

...and she raised her arms.

He stood bolt upright and went to the tent, pulling back the curtain. Fuchsia was still inside the glass box, standing as still as a statue.

"Why, she's still in a trance," Fenninger observed. "I don't believe that she is pretending."

The Prince reached over and picked up the gong, striking it four times. The woman inside the glass cage shuddered suddenly and opened her eyes. Ravenwood stepped over and pushed back the metallic bolt, opening the door. Fuchsia started to step out of the box, and then collapsed into Ravenwood's arms.

"What happened?" she asked.

"It seems the visitation did not go as well as planned," Ravenwood motioned to Stagg. "Horatio, get us two glasses of water for these ladies."

Stagg's face twitched slightly, but he turned and left the curtained-off section. Other people started filing out. Allison came up and stood looking down at Ravenwood.

"Always there for a lady in distress, eh?" she teased, her lips pulling into a wry smile.

A woman's scream echoed from the ballroom beyond the curtain. Ravenwood handed the recumbent Fuchsia to the Prince and ran through the opening. A young woman, one of Laura's friends, stood nearby, her hands held defensively in front of her. Sir Henry came running into the ballroom from the hallway.

"What happened?" he asked.

"I saw a face," the frightened girl said, pointing to the window. "A man was looking in at us."

Sir Henry's jaw tightened. He looked at Ravenwood.

"Perhaps the deceased vagrant had an associate," Ravenwood said.

"Yes," Sir Henry pulled open his smoking jacket and withdrew a Webley eight-shot revolver from his waistband. "And if he did, I'm going to find him."

Stagg came up to Ravenwood as Sir Henry strode toward the door, the gun held down by his side, yelling for Chester to join him in a search of the grounds.

"Looks like this little party's heating up pretty good," Stagg said.

"To quote Al Jolson," Ravenwood cautioned, "you ain't seen nothing yet."

Ravenwood was slipping on the black shirt as he heard the chimes of the grandfather clock in the lower foyer tolling twelve times. Seconds later the light tapping on the door to his room became audible. He glanced at Stagg, who sat in a chair next to the door.

"That should be Thomas," Ravenwood slipped the Luger into his beltline and motioned for Stagg to open the door.

Stagg sighed as he got up and pointed to Ravenwood's gun. "I sure would feel better if I was carrying one of them."

"I'll see if I can find one for you next time," the Stepson of Mystery promised.

"Ain't gonna be no next time," Stagg snapped. "Not if I can help it."

He opened the door and Tom slipped inside. He was also wearing dark clothing, as Ravenwood had instructed and carrying a canvas bag. He did a double take when he saw Stagg standing there similarly clad.

"You're going to have your butler accompany us?" Tom asked.

"Butler!" Stagg began to curse. "Listen, buster—"

"Thomas," Ravenwood interrupted, "I think it's high time you officially met Inspector Horatio Stagg of the New York City Police Department."

Tom's jaw dropped.

"How's Laura?" Ravenwood changed the subject.

"She was resting comfortably when I left her a few hours ago," Tom said. "Your lady friend, Miss Hayes, was staying in the room with her."

"Capital," Ravenwood pointied at the bag. "You brought the flashlights?"

Tom nodded.

"Then it's time for us to do a little midnight exploration."

As they headed quietly down the hallway, the Nameless One's voice silently crept inside Ravenwood's head.

There is much evil about, my son. Be careful.

I shall, Ravenwood telepathically replied. *The game's afoot.*

After descending the long stairway, the three of them made their way to the ballroom. Ravenwood shone the light over the door knob and gripped it. The knob didn't move. He knelt in front of it and removed a set of lock picks. After inserting one, he had the door open in a matter of seconds.

"Just where did you get them things?" Stagg whispered.

Ravenwood flashed a grin. "An old police detective gave them to me when he retired."

He pushed the door open and the three men slipped inside. They went immediately to the curtained off section where the Prince had conducted the séance. Ravenwood moved toward the still-standing tent and pulled back the flap.

"This is where he made that dame disappear," Stagg said. "You gonna tell me how he done that?"

"Like this," Ravenwood moved to the glass box and pulled open the door. He stepped inside and pulled back the black curtain that was hung on the rear section of the box. After pulling it, he pointed to the solid rear wall. He felt along the edge and found a small lever, which he then pushed. The door slid to the side, revealing a tented opening that went to the rear wall of the room.

"Unbelievable!" Tom gasped.

Ravenwood shone his light over the wall showing a stone fireplace. The hearth was completely empty and the curtain had been fastened over the upper ledge the framework. Ravenwood stepped closer.

"You mean she was standing right there the whole time?" Stagg said.

"Part of the time, anyway," Ravenwood elaborated. "Remember the first law of illusion is to make the audience think they're seeing one thing, when in fact, they're failing to notice another."

"But what about that floating face?" Stagg asked. "It didn't even look like her."

Ravenwood was busy inspecting the fireplace. He ran his fingers over the inside of the bricks and the damper, then looked at them.

"Either Jarvis, the butler is very meticulous in his cleaning duties," Ravenwood rubbed his thumb and forefinger together, "or this fireplace has not been used in quite some time."

"I don't believe it has," Tom concurred. "This whole room was being renovated for the party the last time Laura and I visited here."

"I have no doubt that it was," Ravenwood squatted down and shined the flashlight into the opening. He reached upward and pulled on an obscure lever. The rear wall of the fireplace shifted to one side.

"Well, I'll be damned," Stagg said. "One of them secret passages, just like in the movies."

The hearth area was large enough that Ravenwood had to merely had to hunch down as he stepped through the darkened opening and into a tunnel. The beam of light danced over the walls. A small room had been fashioned from brick and mortar. A table with a long, black cape draped over one side sat in the middle. A leather valise was next to it on the floor. Ravenwood picked it up and set it on the table.

"Let's see what Santa left," he smiled.

As he opened the valise something glowed inside.

"Turn your lights off," Ravenwood ordered.

The room went totally dark, except for the glowing from inside the valise. Suddenly a face leapt up and hung suspended in the air. Stagg muttered a gasp and Ravenwood flicked on his flashlight. The rubber mask dangled from his fingers. Ravenwood shut off his light and the glowing mask once again dominated the room.

Switching his flashlight back on, Ravenwood set the mask on the table. "It was apparently fashioned to look like the late Elizabeth McArthur, and coated with phosphorous."

"What's that?" Tom pointed the beam from his light illuminating a metal box-like object with a length of plastic tubing attached to its top. Two electrical cords ran from the box to an outlet in the wall.

Ravenwood's light followed the length of plastic tube and exposed two flat, rubberized pads.

"It appears to be one of those talk boxes. Those pads are held against the throat while a person is speaking causing a strange distortion to his, or in this case, her, words." He shone the light along the wall, following the second cord. "That wire is no doubt connected to some microphone in the ballroom wall. With those pads, the mask, and wearing that black cloak, the appearance of the late Elizabeth McArthur was easily accomplished."

"I'll be a monkey's uncle," declared a wide eyed Stagg. "I knew that floating head thing was a phony."

Ravenwood stepped out of the room. The passageway extended along the length of the wall, and then turned. "It appears to be relatively new construction." He cocked his head for the others to accompany him. They followed the tunnel to a right angle where the passageway continued. As they walked along two pinholes of light appeared on the wall perhaps fifty feet in front of them. Ravenwood halted. He heard something…voices in the darkness.

"Tom, any idea which room is located on the other side here?"

Tom shook his head. "It might be the library."

Ravenwood moved closer to the two dots of light, and then heard the murmur of voices, a man's and a woman's. Their words were too indistinct to be understood. He moved to the dots and saw the light was coming from twin holes in the wall of the adjacent room on the other side. He switched off his flashlight and leaned close to the holes. The back of a man's head was visible over the rear portion of a chair. The voices grew clearer. The male voice groaned in pleasure.

"Oh, you do that so well."

It was Sir Henry's voice.

"I've had a lot of practice lately," replied a female voice.

Ravenwood recognized that one as well: Laura's Aunt.

She stood up from in front of the chair. Phyllis was nude from the waste up and began readjusting the front of her gown over her bare breasts.

"I'll just be glad when this thing's over," she said.

"It will be soon enough," Sir Henry said. "Now, don't get dressed. Let me take you around the world."

Ravenwood motioned for Tom to take a look. The young man leaned close to the second hole and an expression of shock spread over his face.

"Oh, my God," he muttered.

Sir Henry's head jerked. "Did you hear something, love?"

"No," Phyllis replied. "What was it?"

"I'm not sure." Sir Henry stood and pulled up his trousers, his head rotating like a ball on a pivot. Through the hole, Ravenwood saw him striding toward the wall. Suddenly, the passageway became illuminated as a portion of the wall slid back and Sir Henry glared at them.

"I say, how did you get in here?"

Ravenwood walked past Sir Henry and stepped into the room. It wasn't the library, it was the Green Room.

"Nice place for a midnight rendezvous," he said casually looking at Phyllis.

Her face twisted into an ugly scowl. "Go to hell!"

Ravenwood turned to Sir Henry. "Interesting."

"Now, see here," Sir Henry tried to defend himself. "This isn't what it appears to be."

Both Tom and Stagg entered the room behind him.

"Just what is it, then, sir?" Tom questioned.

Sir Henry flashed a nervous smile. "Thomas, I…" He looked at Ravenwood. "You're a man of the world. You'll agree, a gentleman can hardly be expected to live the life of a eunuch, can he?"

Ravenwood remained silent.

"Sir Henry, how could you?" Disappointment covered Tom's face.

"Oh, grow up, you little worm," Phyllis countered, the scowl on her faced deepening. She glared at Sir Henry. "You and your big plans."

Suddenly the Nameless One's voice echoed inside Ravenwood's head: *My son, you must hurry. Lives are at stake.*

A woman's scream pierced in the night.

Ravenwood glanced toward the door and began running. Tom and Stagg followed. Bursting through the door, Ravenwood entered the hallway. The front door was open and the wind and rain whipped through.

A trio of figures, two men wrestling with a woman, struggled in the foyer. Ravenwood pulled out his Luger and rushed toward them, his flashlight beam illuminating their faces. One of the men was Professor Fenninger, another was Jarvis, and the woman was Allison. The big butler released the struggling woman and grabbed at his waist band, pulling out a pistol.

Ravenwood brought the Luger up and fired.

Jarvis jerked and grunted, staggering backward a few steps. Ravenwood fired again and this time the hulking butler fell face down. Professor Fenninger released Allison and raised his hands.

"Please, don't shoot," he pleaded.

As Ravenwood moved toward them, Allison regained her footing and delivered a hard, round-house punch to Fenninger's jaw. His knees sagged, but he remained on his feet long enough for Ravenwood to step closer and strike him in the face with a powerful left hook. This time he dropped to the floor.

"Are you all right?" Ravenwood asked her.

She nodded, running a hand through her hair. "They came into our room. They took Laura."

"Where?"

Allison pointed to the door. Outside a burst of lightning flashed the darkness.

"Come on," Ravenwood motioned for Stagg to grab the pistol that Jarvis had dropped. "There's not a moment to lose."

Without looking back, he ran through the door and into the night. A cold rain pelted his face and another burst of lightning wiggled over the velvet sky.

Oh, Nameless One, Ravenwood called out telepathically. *Can you show me the way?*

Sensing the reply, Ravenwood ran down the cobblestone roadway. As he neared the downed tree, the Nameless One told him to veer left. He crashed through some bushes and saw a pathway leading toward what he thought must be the high cliff overlooking the water. The drop had to be at least one hundred feet. Pushing through the unforgiving shrubbery, Ravenwood caught a glimpse of bodies ahead of him. Quickening his pace, he pushed through more of the clinging plants.

The group was a scant twenty-five feet away now: Chester, along with his two cronies, was carrying an unconscious Laura toward the cliff. Ravenwood estimated that in another few seconds they'd be there.

He raised his pistol and fired a shot over their heads and yelled for them to halt.

Chester stopped and his large head turned toward Ravenwood who became cognizant that Stagg and Tom were next to him now.

"Set the girl on the ground and raise your hands," Ravenwood commanded. He shone his flashlight into the big man's eyes.

"Okay, okay, don't shoot," Chester said. He and his lackeys set Laura on the ground. Ravenwood moved closer to them and told Tom to get Laura. As the young man moved forward, Ravenwood saw Chester's mouth twitch.

"Try anything and you're dead," the Stepson of Mystery warned.

Tom knelt and checked Laura, feeling for her pulse.

"She's alive," he reported. "But unconscious."

Ravenwood was ordering the sinister giant to slowly remove the revolver from his pants with his non-dominant hand when a flicker of a grin jerked the big man's face.

"What you smiling for, ya big lug?" Stagg asked. He pointed the gun he'd taken from Jarvis at Chester, who continued to smile.

Ravenwood was about to repeat his order when a voice growled from behind them: "I'll thank both of you to drop your weapons. Immediately."

It was Sir Henry.

Ravenwood felt the cold hardness of the Webley against his neck.

"I can hardly miss at this range, old boy," Sir Henry threatened.

"Gowan, will ya?" Phyllis said in a voice that was near hysteria. Her long, black hair was plastered to the side of her head and the dress clung to her body. "Shoot him and toss 'em all over the side and be done with it."

"Relax, darling," Sir Henry advised her. "Just a little longer and it'll all be over."

"That's what you said about hiring those three goons in the city," she argued, affecting her voice to imitate his British accent. "It'll merely look as if they were the victims of a robbery." She spat. "You've screwed this thing up from the beginning. The only thing you did right was hiring me to play Auntie Phyllis."

"Shut up," Sir Henry growled. He nudged Ravenwood with the barrel of the Webley again. "Now, do drop the Luger, old chum."

"I should have known you were in on this." Ravenwood slowly let the pistol slip from his fingers. "No one but you could have supervised the renovations to the old house so masterfully."

Sir Henry started to laugh, but he suddenly was knocked to the side.

The Nameless One is here, Ravenwood thought. He reached down to retrieve his weapon, but Chester was already gripping his gun. Suddenly another figure burst from the darkness, slamming into Chester and knocking the big man off balance just as he was drawing the long-barreled revolver.

Ravenwood's fingers found the Luger brought it up and fired. Chester's head jerked backward and he went down like a crumbling building. The figure who had slammed into him lashed out, striking one of the lackeys, who fell to the ground. Ravenwood shot the third lackey as that man began to pull out his weapon.

"I got Sir Henry covered," Stagg yelled. "And his girlfriend, too."

Ravenwood stepped forward and kicked away the guns from the fallen assailants. Tom was cradling Laura. The mysterious figure who had interceded stood up. Another burst of lightning illuminated the man, who appeared haggard and bearded, with long, unkempt hair down to his shoulders. He gazed down at Laura, who had regained consciousness.

She looked at the stranger.

"Who are you?" she asked.

The man said nothing and Ravenwood answered for him.

"Laura, this is your father."

The midmorning sun shone brightly on the drying vegetation and Ravenwood watched as Stagg, his chest puffing out in exaggerated fashion, related the story to the county sheriff. Several deputies were loading Sir Henry, his paramour, and the ersatz Professor Fenninger into a paddy wagon. The remaining groundskeeper lackey, the Prince, and Fuchsia all stood next to the doors in handcuffs awaiting their turn. The bodies of Chester, Jarvis, and the other scoundrels lay on the cobblestoned roadway covered by sheets.

Allison was next to Ravenwood furiously scribbling in her notebook, as Tom, Laura, and the man now known to be her real father stood nearby. The beautiful reporter had finally gotten her big story, and she was determined to make the most of it.

"So, it was all a plot to keep Laura from getting her inheritance," she stated still jotting down notes.

"Which takes effect today," Ravenwood added. "It's called hedging one's bets, on Sir Henry's part. After his hastily conceived plot to hire the three hoodlums in New York was thwarted, he fell back to the more elaborate scheme which had already been in the works for months. This one included the Prince, the reconstructed mansion, and the woman he'd hired to play your Aunt."

"I've been such a fool," Laura said.

"You were taken advantage of in your grief over losing your mother," Ravenwood excused the young woman. "A sad, but all too familiar story where con men, and women, are involved."

"When did you become suspicious?"

"Rather early on," he confessed. "But my conjectures were borne out completely when we investigated that downed tree blocking the road."

Allison stopped writing and stared at Ravenwood. "The one that forced us to… spend the night together at the mansion?" Her smile was telling.

Ravenwood smiled in return. "Exactly. The tree had obviously not been felled by the storm. Lightning usually strikes at the highest point, and the trunk had been partially sawn through."

"Stormy weather did them in then?"

"That and the impersonation of Dr. Fenninger. The man who was killed was purported to be a vagrant by Sir Henry. Although his clothes were ragged, his hair was well trimmed, and his fingernails had been meticulously manicured." Ravenwood shrugged self-effacingly. "It was obvious that the man was no beggar. In fact, he was the real Dr. Fenninger."

"My, but you're so observant," Allison gave Ravenwood a sly wink. Then she turned to their surprise savior. "Dr. McArthur. Just one more question, please. Why did it take you so long to come back to the United States? I mean, seventeen years…"

Clarence McArthur's eyes betrayed his sadness as he spoke. "It's one of my greatest regrets. I spent too much time exploring jungles, and thus missing the formative years of my daughter's life." A tear wound its way down his cheek and Laura reached out and squeezed his hand. "When I was in the Amazon I became separated from my guides. I was captured by an indigenous Indian tribe. Then I caught this virulent fever, and nearly died. It took me the better part of a year to recover, and when I did, my memory of who I was had vanished. The tribe was reclusive and kept moving deeper and deeper into the forest. They adopted me, so to speak, and accepted me as one of their own. I lived with them, learned their ways, and their language. Eventually, my memory began to come back. I thought it was a dream, until one day I found a locket that one of the Indians had kept. Inside were pictures of Elizabeth and Laura…" He stopped and began crying. His words became laced with sobs. "It was then I knew I had to get back to them... But I was penniless. It took me a long time to get back to New York."

"You're here now," Ravenwood said. "And you have what few men get in life: another chance to make things right."

Clarence McArthur reached out as squeezed Ravenwood's arm.

"Thank you for all you've done. Ravenwood. We can never repay you."

"That goes double for us," Tom said expressing his own gratitude.

Laura shook her head. "I still can't believe that Sir Henry perpetrated the whole thing. Arranging for that woman to impersonate my aunt, having the Prince claim to have psychic powers..."

"It all goes to show, Miss," Stagg said, strolling back toward them, "that there ain't no such thing as spirits. Right, Ravenwood?"

Ravenwood listened as the voice of the Nameless One echoed in his head once more: *Some things are best left unsaid, my son.*

"To quote the immortal Bard," Ravenwood concluded, "all's well, that ends well."

The End

ESSAY ON VOICES IN THE DARKNESS

Back in my youth, the one day a year that I was allowed to stay up late was New Year's Eve. This was a big deal for my cousin and me. My parents would host a party at our house, and my cousin and I would sequester ourselves in a back room and watch old movies on television. I know this sounds pretty mundane, and looking back I realize how boring it was, but one movie I saw stuck with me. It was called *You'll Find Out*, starring orchestra leader, Kay Kyser, as a musician playing a gig at a big house that turned out to be menaced by the likes of none other than Bela Lugosi, Peter Lorre, and Boris Karloff. Having been a big fan of the old, classic horror movies (*Frankenstein, Dracula, The Wolfman*, etc.), I quickly became engrossed in the movie, which we'd turned on mid-way through. I watched it until the end, and always wondered about the parts I'd missed. They haunted me for years, until I happened to catch the movie on a late, late show broadcast. Filling in the blanks was interesting, and the plot concept always fascinated me. The idea of a group of people who were trapped in an old mansion and in danger is a common mystery scenario, and Kyser and his friends played it for laughs. I felt that these plot elements, though, had the makings of a real dynamite story if they were played seriously.

The years passed and *You'll Find Out* got sort of pushed to the back of my memory, but I always hoped to one day write a story along those lines... One set in a remote mansion, replete with sinister villains and secret passages. When editor extraordinaire, Ron Fortier, mentioned that he needed a story about Ravenwood, the occult detective, I jumped at the chance. I've always been a fan of the old pulp heroes, and Ravenwood, the Stepson of Mystery, was among the best. Ron sent me the guidelines, and I read them over. Using a setting of the 1930s got me thinking about *The Maltese Falcon* and some of Dashiell Hammett's pulp work. Although the *Falcon* and the Continental Op stories were set in San Francisco, *The Thin Man*, my favorite of Hammett's novels, took place in New York City, where the Ravenwood stories were set. In writing my Ravenwood story, I tried to emulate Hammett's laconic style while still incorporating the elements of murder in the mansion. The result was "Voices in the Darkness," which I hope you will find as entertaining as one of those old pulp stories.

MICHAEL A. BLACK - is the author of thirty-six books and over one-hundred short stories and articles. His latest novel is *Legends of the West* and he is also writing the Mack Bolan Executioner series (*Stealth Assassins, Dying Art, Cold Fury*). He also writes westerns under the name A.W. Hart (*Gunslinger: Killer's Choice, Gunslinger: Killer's Brand, and Gunslinger: Killer's Ghost*).

KINCAID'S HOUSE OF ALTERED CATS
by Michael F. Housel

PROLOGUE

Rifle blasts cut through the nocturnal, Louisiana spring air, followed by a mighty, hissing roar.

"It's close by," Jerome exclaimed, directing his rifle over the thick brush. He was a mere twenty-two, frightened out of his wits and now regretting with every ounce of his being for having accepted the damn internship. "They're sticking to the dry spots, away from the swampland. Might make them easier to track." He paused, squinted. "Yep, I can see one now—beyond the small cypresses."

"Which one?" asked Pamela, a fair-haired beauty, one year his junior. "The first or second?"

"How should I know?" Jerome snapped. "One's as damn ugly as the other."

"One's smaller," she emphasized, "not as vicious…should be easier to lure."

"Lure?" Jerome chuckled. "You're still harping on that, are you? As if we could honestly hope to capture these things. Kincaid knows it's fruitless." He hoisted his weapon. "Why else would she have armed us?"

"A precautionary measure," Pamela explained, lowering her rifle to imply her disdain. "I say we reason with them, Jerome."

Their friend, Brian, a freckled face lad of barely nineteen surfaced from the side, covered in dirt and dust, jutting his rifle about like a sword. "I saw them a short distance from here…sniffing up a storm, circling back, it seems. I think they know we're on to them. Probably want us out of the way. Oh, and one of them had something in its mouth—an animal…a deer, I think."

"They're behaving as expected," Jerome said, "like lions and tigers, but more cunning…more dangerous." He looked at Pamela. "We can't play around. They'll do us in, then head for town."

Another horrible hiss filled the air, followed by thumping paws.

149

Treetops wavered, creaked and fell. The ground rumbled.

"Dear God," said Brian, trembling.

Pamela tried to stay calm, her eyes shifting from left to right. "They're only riled because they've been pent up for so long—and they know we're after them...mean them harm. Dr. Kincaid should have shown some compassion. Animals have feelings. It only goes to reason they'd react this way. I'd behave the same way if I were—"

From behind, the great cat leapt upon her, its claws slashing, its mighty head a blurring, bulbous torsion of white-and-black stripes. Her weapon sailed across the grass, and in an instant, the young lady's body snapped within the creature's prodigious jaws, eliciting a tempestuous splash of blood, guts and bone.

Jerome fired repeatedly at the beast, peppering its face, while Brian froze, his eyes bulging in disbelief.

"Brian—please," Jerome screamed, his ammo depleting. "Snap out of it. Back me up—damn it."

Brian broke from his stupor and raised his weapon. The beast's bloodied face slinked into view, one gleaming, emerald eye still standing, fixed with hate. Pamela's pale arm dangled from its crooked mouth, notching back along its wide, slithering tongue.

"It's the smaller one," Brian croaked. "Look...look what it's done." He glanced about. "The bigger one can't be far off."

"Shoot, Brian," Jerome pleaded, sweat seeping from his face. "For God's sake, shoot the damn thing."

The beast finished swallowing Pamela's appendage, licked its lips and arched its massive back, ready for attack. Quivering, the boy fired into its thick, furry husk, then blasted its neck.

The beast moaned and gurgled, stretching upon its rear legs, adapting an unwitting, bipedal pose, continuing to lurch forward as the freckled-faced boy fired again and again, until the specimen silenced, its emerald eye glazing over. The beast fell onto its side with a reverberating thud.

"I...I did it," Brian gasped. "I...I killed it, Jerome. Did you see? I...I... killed it."

"Don't rejoice just yet," Jerome cautioned, watching the thing's heaving chest. "Still has some life in it. Give it a moment..."

"No," Brian protested, "it's dead. There's no way that it could be—"

A throaty growl rose from the left.

The young men looked at each other. Jerome shook like a leaf and reloaded as fast as he could, his gaze bouncing about, uncertain how close the creature might be.

"Look out," Brian screamed, as the massive thing skidded forth: its head part yellow fur; the other, a patch of sickly, creamy flesh, with eyes as pale-blue as the morning sky, and from its thin, black lips dangled the bloody remnants of a deer. It eyed the young man with a spark of recognition, but then regarded the rifle. Its ears rose as it dropped the gnawed meat, its long back twisting, its fur fanning like prickly spikes.

Jerome fired and grazed the thing's ear. It reeled, its finger-like claws tearing up chunks of dirt.

Again, Jerome fired, but this time the beast shot upward and pounced down upon him. In an instant, the boy's head was ripped from his neck, his body falling like a sack of potatoes onto the grass.

The monster turned, its gem-like orbs now on Brian, its mouth curling back into a sinister smile, invoking a voraciousness that was both prehistoric and yet misguidedly modern.

Dumbstruck, Brian steadied his rifle, squinted with teary eyes and aimed, but far too late.

The beast bolted and clamped his torso within its jaws, crushing him with a whipping turn of its mighty neck, spitting the rifle from the side of its mouth, sucking the lad's shattered frame inward, relishing the gamut of his flesh, when then it abruptly paused.

A bald, muscular man dressed in khakis and sleeveless shirt slipped into view—a man the beast knew all too well, and it regarded him with trepidation, respect and above all, rage.

"Damn you," the man bellowed in a thick, Egyptian accent. From a plumb pouch tied to the side of his belt, he pulled a circular object. He shook it hard, before cracking it between his fingers, so that it beamed lines of luminous green.

He cocked his arm back. "You were never meant for this world—you malformed monstrosity. Back to the bowels of Hell with you!"

The boy's mangled remains fell from the beast's jaws. The creature bristled, though not to attack, but rather an urge to flee, for it sensed the danger the capsule contained.

With a contemptuous smirk, the Egyptian tossed the object before the great cat, where it sparked and smoked, churning fumes that spread from all angles. Within seconds, it encompassed the creature's hulking frame.

The creature snorted and choked, then whimpered like a kitten as the foul, gaseous formula saturated its body, forcing it down upon its stomach, its sinewy limbs stretching outward like rubbery vines.

The Egyptian regarded his handiwork, aware of the raven-haired woman who approached from behind, dressed in medical white, her expression cold and calculating.

"Are they dead, Ramses?" she asked.

"All three," he stated.

"No," she clarified. "The cats..."

"Yes," he confirmed. "The other was shot to death. I found its carcass on the way over." He unfastened a small gas mask from his belt and offered it.

"No thank you," she said. "I believe I'm finally growing immune to the fumes."

Ramses nodded and refastened the mask to his belt.

She clicked her tongue. "The locals would raise holy hell about this. You'll need to purge the evidence, Ramses—and I do mean all of it."

A bubbling ooze flattened the cat's husk, creating a pool of mush, its luster subsiding as it burnt into the grass and discolored the dirt.

"I'll do my best, but it won't be easy," he said. "It'll be dawn soon, and—"

"No excuses," she snapped. "Just do it."

"Of course, Dr. Kincaid," the Egyptian replied with a sigh.

She bowed her head. "I'm sorry I didn't place more stock in your warnings."

He shrugged. "What's done is done. However, vivisection and its variants work only as a preliminary means. The ancient ways are consistent...reliable."

"Sorcery," the doctor scoffed. "You know as well as I, it's only at best science disguised."

"Precisely," said Ramses. "I've been saying that all along. It's foolish...wrong...to distinguish. I also told you it was only a matter of time before this latest trial derailed due to your constant over-analysis. You never listen, though. In fact, I could have tracked those monsters on my own, kept the youngsters from harm, but what did you care? It almost makes me wonder if you—ah, no matter." He eyed her over. "At the very least, you should have armed yourself. In the name of blessed Bastet, I can't fathom how one of such high intellect can behave so impulsively."

"You've room to talk," the doctor replied with a wry grin. "As for the casualties, they're just part of the consequences...the name of the game, if you will."

Ramses shook his head. "Inquiries will be made. The interns' silence will draw suspicion...attention."

Kincaid yawned and turned. "That's the least of our concerns. Besides, it's not as if they'd stay forever. For now, it only matters that we pick up where we left off. And this time, Ramses, mistakes aren't an option."

"Of course, doctor. Time will surely charm our cause."

"Charm, indeed, Ramses," she agreed, sauntering away with smug defiance. "When at last things fall into place, it'll exceed even your forgone prophesies. Think of it, Ramses. The world will change, my faithful friend—and all for the cataclysmic better."

In a dark raincoat and grasping a large, black umbrella and bronze-trimmed luggage in his snug, leather gloves, Ravenwood spotted the distant, windowed glow of the grim, gray-bricked estate. Beads ricocheted from off his rugged, rain hat (a practical substitute for his favored Fedora), onto his broad shoulders: an inclement metaphor, he fancied, for impending danger, but perhaps more so, a symbolic cry for the purification he might grant the task he was assigned.

The umbrella's steel frame at least withstood the torrential wind, though acted as little more than an upside-down substitute for the dapper walking sticks he desired. Despite being out of his element, he would do his best to make do, but still wished he were back on the train. Trains, after all, had that wonderful knack of inducing restful reflection. He only hoped he had gained enough per his long journey…

He took a moment to lean against a sagging cypress, its base conveniently firm, and glanced down at the nailed piece of paper upon it, creased so that only half of the black-crayon text showed: LOST CAT… PLEASE HELP…WE MISS HER…

It broke his heart to see such a heartfelt plea, for in an indirect way it reminded him of his perished parents and the deep sorrow he still felt whenever he reminisced upon them. That sense of loss made him want to allot some time to the poor cat, though the odds of ever finding a lost pet were at best unpropitious, even for one of superior discernment as himself.

All the same, it was best he concentrated on the task at hand: interestingly enough, another matter of evident loss, of which the causes and effects were yet murky, though linked to a biochemist/zoologist of renowned and controversial standing.

Per the information his faithful servant, Sterling, had relayed, Dr. Katherine Kincaid was one who took pride in the unconventional. She also had a tendency of keeping her critics and the general curious at bay. Though she was not prone to receive visitors, let alone speak to anyone via phone (relying on her assistant to make infrequent, collect calls to university staff from town), Ravenwood's venerable standing at least proceeded itself. From what Sterling had been told, Kincaid seemed pleased that the legendary investigator would act as a liaison to her scholarly financiers, even if his visit's doleful cause regarded the whereabouts of "missing" interns. (She had, in fact, evaded initial, written requests on the matter from her benefactors until they managed to reach her via telegram and even then, a response came only after a substantial pause.)

At any rate, Sterling's account of the doctor made Ravenwood as equally anxious to meet her, though her reputed exercises left him skeptical and perhaps even a trifle uneasy.

By reputation, Kincaid's work catered to cats and their precarious relation to human genetics. Ravenwood was hard pressed to see the correlation, at least from a modern vantage, though he was aware, thanks to the tidbits offered by his live-in, Tibetan guru, the Nameless One, of the Middle-Eastern, Asian, Slavic and Serbian sects that yet exalted those of alleged, feline lineage. Perhaps, he thought, Kincaid's work played upon such fables from an empirical stance, but again, for what gain? Even her recent research papers, though layered with intricate data, averted any compelling confirmation. It was, therefore, Kincaid's weird elusiveness that ultimately sparked her peers' concern.

To worsen matters, Kincaid's insistence that her young recruits sign legal documents promising not to reveal the unique nature of her work, or else face severe, financial penalty, raised concerns further. Indeed, while Kincaid's abstruse demands had initially delighted her colleagues as frivolously unconventional, they now feared such might be further evidence of a veritable crackpot...

The rain worsened: the drops reminding him of tears, the wind wailing like a maddened mourner. Within this driving, forlorn mode, Ravenwood decided to forge onward, aware that his irritability would likely intensify by the time he reached the grim façade, but why delay the inevitable?

When he reached the door, he jostled his luggage and umbrella, setting his chin against its honeysuckle door: its subtle scent teasing his nostrils, the inebriating wood reminding him that most felines preferred this scent over nip. A brass lion-bust precipice, featuring an ominous, opened mouth and extended fangs, added to the theme. He was grateful that it shielded him as he fiddled with his items and even fancied the object would have made a stately companion piece to his penthouse's brass, tiger knocker. He then triggered his umbrella shut and keeping his luggage braced under the same arm, rapped several times with his free hand before he heard heels approach, followed by the swift sweep of a latch.

The door opened with an eager swoosh and a spill of inviting light, inside which Kincaid stood, smiling from ear to ear, more attractive than her stuffy, university photos could ever convey. Her attire was more fashionable than he would have expected, as well: a tight, short, white dress, raven hair fixed into a bun, red lipstick and a smart smear of rouge.

"Mr. Ravenwood, I presume," she said, scanning the drenched but dashing, young gent. "Oh, please, do come in. I'm Dr. Katherine Kincaid. I can't tell you what an honor it is to meet you. For several years, I've ruminated upon the eminent Stepson of Mystery, wondering if he was little more than a publicity stunt. In any event, if my colleagues say you're the real deal, then I suppose I've no reason to doubt them."

"I assure you," said Ravenwood with a blustery tone, "I am the real McCoy, both in flesh, blood and reputation." He rattled the rain off from his coat. "My, is it ever treacherous out there." He set his umbrella and luggage against the foyer's far wall, leaving them to drip copiously onto the tiled floor, though due to his annoyance, he offered no apology. "When I hailed a taxi from the train station, the driver informed me that passage to your estate was prohibited: some sort of monetary arrangement you struck with his employer." He yanked off his gloves and tossed them with his hat atop the luggage; then ruffled his wavy, brown hair. "I'm grateful that the man drove me halfway. I had to rely on my intrinsic sense of travel for the remainder." He laughed. "His walking directions would have left much to be desired, in any event."

"He shouldn't have afforded you that much," she replied with a grin. "Though in this instance, it's good he obliged. As you may know, I'm wary of visitors. Besides, the trails leading here are meandering at best, some even detrimental. It would be easy enough for anyone to get lost, even one of keen intuition. You should have seen the lad who delivered your telegram today. Vexation personified!"

"I was aware you were off the beaten track when I consented to the assignment," Ravenwood said, "though I must admit, this proved worse than anticipated. Though my intuition generally alerts me to pressing affairs, the interludes binding them can sometimes slip through. I was initially tempted to take one of my roadsters for the long haul, but I'm glad I went with my gut and paid heed to those national weather reports. No sense in placing unnecessary wear and tear on such intricate machinery when a train ticket and reliable gear will do."

She savored his eloquence and stepped back to observe his strapping frame: so impeccably distinguished even after the flustering trek, with his silvery tie and white vest straight and smooth, his high-shined, black boots devoid of any distracting speck. Yes, she was impressed, though perhaps not yet convinced he was who he claimed. She then caught his eyes' nondescript pigmentation, which may have been green, brown or blue at that instant. Per legend, such shifting ambiguity was Ravenwood's most noted attribute: an arguable trademark that helped bolster his eminent mystique.

"If I had been given more notice as to your arrival," she explained, "I could have accommodated you accordingly. Nonetheless, I humbly apologize for any inconvenience caused."

Ravenwood gave her a congenial squint. "I won't hold it against you, as long as my trip wasn't in vain."

She smiled and teased, "Well, I've been anticipating a rather large check from my supporters. I don't suppose you're here to deliver it."

Surely, she was joking, but what an awful way to jest. As such, Ravenwood felt compelled to scan her, but within her aura, he could only cull the here and now, laced with ample arrogance and perhaps a deep-stored trace of disrespect.

"Actually, Dr. Kincaid, I'm here regarding the whereabouts of your interns: Jerome Lieberman, Brian O'Malley and Pamela Scott. I was informed you were aware of the concern. Their families haven't heard from them in months, let alone their department heads. Simply put, there was no expeditious way to reach you—or them. With concerns mounting, and considering my unique, investigative know-how, as well as our known, eccentric comparisons, it was felt that I would be an apt intermediary. Before boarding the train, I decided to have Western Union wire you an estimate of my arrival, knowing how lengthy the trek would be from New York to Baton Rouge and beyond. I must confess, it was at best an after-thought, though based on your delayed response to the telegram your colleagues sent prior, I wondered if the gesture was for naught. I can't help but wonder now."

Kincaid turned pale. "I see…"

"Mail was sent to each student via your post-office box," Ravenwood continued, "all within the same time frame—all unanswered." He cleared his throat and winced. "Am I to assume the students are no longer under your tutelage?"

"No…no, they are not," she said, capping the comment with a raspy groan. "I've been working so hard these past months, you see, and have apparently overlooked a number of matters." She cracked an apologetic smile. "As for the interns, they simply moved on. I imagine they found work elsewhere and no doubt, with less rigorous demands. It's not surprising. Youngsters have no loyalty these days, no sense of commitment."

"All three quit at the same time?" asked Ravenwood.

"Yes," she said, her gaze hazing. "I didn't think much of it, really. I do recall Ramses mentioning that some mail had arrived in the aftermath, but again, I saw no reason for concern. I…I presumed they contacted whoever they saw fit regarding their decision. I must confess, I'm not known as the easiest person with whom to converse, let alone work, and so, why stir the pot, especially if I were to reach out later for replacements?"

One need not have been a psychic to know she was lying. "Ah, I see," said Ravenwood. "They abandoned ship when the requirements became too arduous. Still, that they've not contacted anyone since such time is peculiar, don't you think?"

"Perhaps," she said with a haughty shrug.

"You realize," said Ravenwood, "I must report this to the authorities. Both family and faculty have been assured that I would, in the event I failed to locate them."

"I suppose this was only inevitable," she said, shaking her head. "Perhaps if I possessed a maternal streak, a better communicative means, I could have intervened, but again, my work is paramount." Her tone then adapted a tempting pitch. "I think you'd be most impressed with my accomplishments, in any event. However, if you must tend the students' whereabouts, I understand. The local precinct is roughly a mile away, though I can't imagine anyone of authority on duty at this hour."

Ravenwood appreciated her ploy and for the moment, decided to play along.

"Accomplishments, you say?"

His expressed curiosity rejuvenated her, and she rubbed her hands. "Accomplishments, indeed, Mr. Ravenwood, and as of today, undocumented. Beyond my assistant, you'd be the first to see my handiwork."

"I dare say, doctor," Ravenwood chirped, "you have me hooked. It would only make sense to visit the precinct in the morning, and I see no reason to let such an enticing invitation slip. I assume you'll have no objections if I were to share the details of your work with those who sent me. Chances are, it would only usher more funding your way."

"I've no objections," she said and stepped toward a small, brass-fringed intercom on the side wall and tapped it: "Ramses…Ramses…would you please come to front entrance. Our visitor, Mr. Ravenwood, has arrived." She removed her finger and with a flutter of her lashes, glanced at him. "Typically, Ramses is the one to greet visitors, but I insisted that he concentrate on preparing dinner on this occasion, in anticipation of your arrival."

A deep, Middle-Eastern voice spewed from the box: "Yes, doctor…on my way."

"Ramses assists me on all of endeavors," she explained, "whether menial or high-order. In fact, he's proven invaluable about the estate. At any rate, perhaps we can dine and thereafter, I'll grant you a tour of the laboratories and their adjoining chambers…"

Without question, Kincaid knew considerable more of the interns' disappearance than she let on, but a reveal of the locale might offer substantial answers. Alas, the doctor's complex and scattered mental rhythm proved difficult to decipher. For now, he could only extend his performance and with fingers crossed, tackle whatever came his way.

Ravenwood scanned the dining area: spacious, cozy and faintly lit. For the most part, it matched his taste, with silverware of the finest casting and a silk tablecloth of Oriental import; but the golden walls were covered by bulky, brass-framed paintings, all featuring cats. From what he could discern, they were products of the Victorian era or at least emulations of such. Ravenwood thought them quaint, but unstinting for such an opulent milieu.

He was about to remark on the renderings, when Ramses, suited like a waiter, wheeled his cart into the room, and from there, slid several silver-domed serving trays off it, positioning each upon the table with a graceful bow.

"Thank you, Ramses," Kincaid said with an ebullient whiff. "I must confess, I'm ravished."

Ramses fingered the nub of the lid nearest her and lifted it. A burst of smoke spread from out, covering the contents. Ravenwood inhaled, though despite his aptitude for gourmet cuisine, failed to distinguish the dish.

"I trust you like delicacies," commented Kincaid. "They're Ramses' specialty."

"I like to try new things," said Ravenwood, as the small, brown hunk of meat came into view. "I also prefer to know what I'm eating." He caught the Egyptian's eye. "What might this cuisine be, Mr. Ramses?"

Ramses grinned, laying a shiny fork and knife upon it. "A combination of various meats, though poultry mostly, embellished by exotic spices."

"Egyptian, I presume, culled from your heritage," said Ravenwood, though he had engaged in enough such customs over the years (new, old, obscure and bizarre) to know otherwise.

"Far from it," Ramses toothily confessed, clamping a tender slither between the utensils and placing it upon Kincaid's plate. "This is my own concoction. I, like the dear doctor, relish experimentation."

Ramses was as hard to read as Kincaid and not only due to the evident, enigmatic barrier that he erected. He certainly appeared Egyptian and no doubt was, based on both facial features and annunciation, but then the worldly criminologist had once met a gent from Naples who passed for one from Dublin, right down to the red hair and accompanying diction. In any event, despite Ramses' apparent lineage, the detective inferred he likely hailed from everywhere and nowhere, having gained varied and unusual habits along the way, which would at least make any specific, claimed, cultural connection suspect.

"Oh, yes, Ramses certainly does love to indulge," Kincaid laughed, "which, I suppose, makes him my ideal accomplice."

"Accomplice?" Ravenwood stated, as Ramses slid a generous slither before the detective. "An unusual label…"

"I was being figurative, of course," she explained. "When one works outside the norm, one can't help but perceive one's actions as, to put it mildly, criminal: that is, the boldest experiments are often greeted with disdain by the scientific community. Many innovations are even misconceived as borderline evil. Thank goodness there are those like you, Mr. Ravenwood, who are open-minded enough to investigate any given circumstance or theory, no matter how seemingly singular, and acknowledge the possible, if not probable, validity."

Ravenwood carved the meat and rolled a morsel onto his tongue, hoping to determine its content, but to no avail. He swallowed hard and smiled. "Tasty."

"Thank you," said Ramses, but no sooner frowned. "Oh, dear, it appears I forgot the gravy. Please, do excuse me." He bowed. "I'll return momentarily."

However, as he opened the door, several felines bolted in: two white, two black and one gray, scurrying about in desperate confusion, meowing to the point of shrieking, zigzagging under the table and cutting between Ravenwood and Kincaid's legs.

"For heaven's sake, Ramses," the doctor admonished. "I told you to keep them caged."

As Ramses darted for them, Ravenwood smirked and stated, "Well, at least you needn't worry about mice. Nevertheless, there's no need to gather them on my part. I've no aversions to animals: house cats, in particular. There are times when I actually prefer the wee, four-legged critters to people, though due to an incident from my youth, the larger ones do tend to make me tense." He pointed to the paintings. "I see, you have an affinity for the cute, domestic kind. I also noticed the honeysuckle wood: a worthy, if not stylish supplement for your occupants, though I've been led to believe that such works best when trimmed: filed to a fine dust, that is."

Kincaid smiled, pretending she was undistracted by Ramses' pursuit. "I've come to find that some forms of shaved or liquefied, Lonicera tatarica—as it's known among botanists—can have unpleasant effects on felines. I feel it's better to present the substance in more structured, albeit expensive formats, in the way of doors and related trimmings, with the evident inducement subdued, yet prevailing. Of course, it all comes down to the manufacturer. Some have been more skilled than others in meeting my zealous specifications."

"You certainly know your stuff," Ravenwood commended. "I'm sure your pets appreciate the conscientiousness."

Grumbling, Ramses corralled three of the cats from off the floor and out of the room, and then pranced back inside to snatch the remaining two. The gray one squirmed about his arms, attempting to break free, at one point looking at Kincaid with eyes large and fervid, but the doctor averted its gaze.

"It's that precise generosity which led me to make Felis catus, and their various offshoots, the core of my work," she continued. "I could have chosen rodents, reptiles or simians for practicality's sake. However, I've always believed cats to be inordinately regal. They also harbor a physical propensity that could benefit us as a species."

"In the way of human genetics, you mean," said Ravenwood. He cut another piece of meat, though more for show than consumption. "Tell me, what is it exactly that you're pursuing? Your research presents various implications, but you've never defined your ultimate intent."

"I'm sure your pets appreciate your conscientiousness."

She hesitated, letting the candlelight caress her fair features. Despite Ramses' presence, she was lonely, he could tell. Perhaps she yearned for someone of her own ilk, someone like him, who could better indulge in her lofty speculations and whims.

She reached over and poured some wine, then took a sensual sip as she admired his face. "It's sufficient to say, Mr. Ravenwood, I'm fond of mergers. I believe that, in one way or another, all things correlate, whether by fate or forced design, but sometimes they require that essential push to become, let's say, more intimate. I'm under the impression you're of the same mindset…correct?"

Before he could reply, Ramses re-entered with renewed vim, fingering a shiny gravy boat. "Sorry for the delay, my good people. Here you are…"

"He does make the best gravy in all the land," said Kincaid.

Ramses dipped the boat and spread a thin splotch onto her slither and then glided it over to Ravenwood's.

"All the result of tenacious experimentation," the Egyptian bragged. "Indeed, if one tries enough times over, the most extraordinary things can—and will—culminate."

Ravenwood and Kincaid traveled the long, shadowy hall, where more cat paintings adorned the walls. They passed the kitchen, where Ramses now toiled and from where discontented meowing could be heard.

"Your laboratory is nearby?" Ravenwood asked, growing anxious.

"On the basement level," she said, moving with a playful grace that he found more trying than complimentary. "Come…I'll show you."

They ambled through a curving pass, to another honeysuckle door. With a wink, she opened it, beckoning him to follow with a coy flap of her fingers.

They walked down the plank-like stairs, the descending expanse murky due to its dull, gray bricks. However, by the time they reached the concrete floor, Ravenwood found the surroundings smooth and sparkling, with the white-washed walls invoking a sanitized aura: more institutionalized than the typical basement would project.

She pointed and led him to the right. "Here we are—around the bend."

They entered a long, rectangular area, which contained several large, steel sinks and two, unappetizing, paint-chipped, medical beds with long, dangling straps. One bed was half tucked and lopsided from a dented leg; the other sported disheveled sheets and a trickle of what looked like dried blood upon its compressed pillow.

Against the opposite wall stood a long, white cabinet, atop which were varying beakers, Bunsen burners and capped test tubes, all housed within wooden braces, a number containing luminous liquids of green, yellow and red.

In front of these were queues of clasps, scalpels, syringes, stethoscopes, ominous canisters and several gas masks. Higher up were three-tiered, boxed shelves, which held clustered, wired models of cat and human anatomy: hands, feet, tails, vertebrae and skulls, some represented in pure bone form, while others featured clinging portions of fake muscle and flesh.

There were also compartments jammed with books, which intrigued Ravenwood, since he was an avid collector and author in his own right. In this instance, most of the spines referenced stuffy, surgical topics, though some were, in fact, subjects he had written upon at one point or another: ancient and lost civilizations; myths and rituals; potions and elixirs. There were also several offerings on Victorian artwork and Greek/Roman sculpture, fringed by ghoulish fiction, including Mary Shelley's "Frankenstein"; H.P. Lovecraft's elusive "Herbert West"; as well as H.G. Wells' "The Food of the Gods" and "The Island of Dr. Moreau".

He wondered if the fiction was included for carefree purposes or practical intent. After all, based on the many odd incongruities he had encountered through the years, he had come to realize that the line between fact and fiction often proved indivisible.

Kincaid folded her arms and asked, "So, what do you think, Mr. Ravenwood?"

He raised an eyebrow. "I, uh, must say, it's quite impressive…expansive, as well." He pointed at the models. "You seem to have both species covered." He then turned to the disheveled beds. "And it appears you've been tinkering. I couldn't help but notice the stain. Was it alive or dead at the time?"

"Oh, dear," she said with a huff. "The bed is generally kept in another chamber. Ramses wheeled it in here, intending to sterilize it, but you're right, I have been tinkering, though on nothing conscious, I assure you. For the most part, the beds act as temporary fixtures for the various appendages we dissect: makeshift, work stations, if you will, whereupon we can spread the parts, then if required, wheel them about for convenience."

"Interesting," said Ravenwood.

She smiled and strolled to the cabinet and grabbed a capped tube of green liquid. "Some of the compounds are simple in construction," she explained, "but unique in the way their finer properties interact." She shook the luminous contents. "They're not the sort of thing one can find at the local pharmacy, let alone those institutions of alleged higher learning." She held the tube to the light, allowing the substance to shimmer. "Indeed, the scholarly elite would frown upon such a concoction by its mere luster." She laughed and with a swift thrust, held the tube out to him. "Please…"

Ravenwood took it and studied its ambiguous allure. "It's beautiful, but I must confess, I'm at a loss."

"I wouldn't expect you to identify it, Mr. Ravenwood. As I implied, it's specialized, unless one knows something of ancient alchemy, and even then, the odds wouldn't favor a categorization."

"I see," said Ravenwood. "So, what is it, then? What's its purpose?"

"It holds recuperative agents," she stated with pride. "It heals flesh… mends it. For what it's worth, there's an antithesis version of the same luster that dissolves flesh, as well as muscle and bone. One must be careful not to mistake one for the other, though the eroding formula takes a long and precarious duration to ferment. It's specifically labeled to prevent error."

"Good gracious," said Ravenwood, returning the tube to her. "If you don't mind, I'd rather not take a chance. So, you apply such to your experiments?"

"Of course," she said, placing the tube back into its fixture, "I use the mending agent for vivisection and organ mergers. It works most effectively, if I'm prudent about the dosages."

"And how did you come about this amazing technique?" he asked.

"Through Ramses," she stated. "I learned of him and his methodology through surreptitious sources. He hails from a recherché tribe: portrayed as fragmented and nomadic in historical references, if mentioned at all. His sect bears no distinct label, though is known among esoteric groups for its expertise in medicinal mixtures, among other eclectic practices. Ramses' techniques could be considered a lost art, though in my estimation, such is only ever effective when applied through twentieth-century know-how. In other words, it would be mere witch-doctor impracticality, if not for current, scientific procedure."

Ravenwood rubbed his brow. "And you say you have examples of your success."

"I've several in progress," she said. "Allow me…"

She walked passed the sinks, to yet another honeysuckle door, entwined with locks and bolts, a few of which she unclipped and then led him into a brightly lit chamber.

Ravenwood was startled to see two rows of six, lean, hairless bodies hoisted from the ceiling: thin chains connected to the tips of their delicate appendages, which were yanked with pronounced rigidity.

Ravenwood first presumed the specimens a kind of giant swine, each about five feet in length and abnormally slender about their middles, but as he moved closer and took keen note of their craniums, as well as the structure of their closed eyes, he realized that they were feline.

"Though they look dead," Kincaid told him, "I injected them with certain compounds that keep them at least quasi cognitive. They would gain full cognition if prodded with further fluids."

Ravenwood found the sight repugnant, particularly the craggy, stitched incisions along their abdomens.

"Am I to presume," he murmured, "that these specimens are recent?"

"About three months old," she answered. "I suppose that would make them recent by my criterion. Please understand, under normal circumstances, they would have perished, decayed away, and yet I'm proud to say, here they remain."

Ravenwood grazed the side of one. Its touch felt lukewarm and sticky, much the way rubber feels when left out too long in the sun. As far as consciousness was concerned, the thing's chemical saturation had numbed any inkling, which for the sake of compassion was fortuitous, but beneath the surface, he still sensed a subdued element of anguish and woe.

"So, you've created mutations," he inferred, "hybrids."

She grinned, as if he approved. "They were once feral cats that Ramses trapped," she explained. "I couldn't bring myself to use domesticated ones any longer, though I must admit that some of those he captured could have been just that. It appears a cluster of the backward locals once tended to them, and as such, we've been awarded an ample supply. At any rate, these remaining members comprise my current stock, sustained for preliminary purposes. When need be, I'll inject them with variations of Ramses' samples: all in modified form so as to ensure the contents don't corrode the syringes. It's astonishing how such will take to delicate content and yet destroy studier forms. Though as I've learned from Ramses, it all comes down to what one can find, if one knows what to extract from one's surroundings…and as he claims, what to bless. Of course, scientific balancing is always the logical path to success."

Ravenwood was both exasperated and enraged, but maintained a serene façade. "The substances extend size, I see."

"Yes," she confirmed. "With the right dosage, I can maximize the framework. I also surgically enhance the internal and external traits, amending the development. It's just part of my meticulous style, not unlike any sculptor would perform, though I hadn't manipulated specimens this small before." Devilish delight beamed in her eyes. "Prior to this, I was in the habit of using larger cats: cougars and then their jungle cousins, which I had smuggled from Africa, India and the like. Quite an expensive undertaking and no small feat, I must say, considering my location, but the efforts were worth it, at least at first. Later, the results became dangerous and disappointing."

She stepped away from the quasi-cadavers and motioned him toward the adjacent chamber. "The initial experiments were housed in here."

Ravenwood followed her into a large realm that contained a set of conjoined, black-barred cages. The doors were bent and snapped from their hinges, placed against the side bars without apparent intent of repair.

"The first were leopards," she said, "which perished about a week after their preparatory injections. A set of panthers followed, which lasted a trifle longer, but it wasn't until the final pair—a lion and tigress—that the outcome became, to say the least, impressive and then harrowing. I anticipated the beasts would be aggressive—encouraged their ferocity to some extent, since I innately abhor diffidence—but I had no notion how far their aggression would go. They became more riled and demanding with their increased size. There was never enough food, never enough attention or understanding to keep them in check. They were, for all intents and purposes, unconscionable demons. What can I say? For all my ceaseless diligence, I failed miserably."

"From the look of things," said Ravenwood, "they got loose."

"Yes," she said with a quiver, "they escaped from the house and were put down a short distance from here. I already had an arsenal prepared, and those occupying the house were instructed by Ramses on procedure. You wouldn't know it by the look of things, thanks to my assistant's handyman skills, but the damage was significant. It's amazing, though, that the creatures made it upstairs, let alone through the front door. Nonetheless, the upheaval hit its summit when my staff was..." She hesitated, realizing she had said too much, but like the symbolic rain that fell, Ravenwood intuitively understood that on a subconscious level, she desired the outpouring, even if guilt did not accompany it.

"The interns," he inferred with somber conviction. "Your hybrids killed them."

She was reluctant to confirm, but after a long, superficial pause, from which he assumed she anticipated sympathy, she confessed. "I guess there's no point in hiding it now. It was most upsetting, but what could I do? Ramses dissolved the various remains. There are discolored spots that still mark where he purged the evidence, though to complicate matters, the soil emits a persistent stench. Fortunately, up to this point, no one has been the wiser."

The revelation was more troubling than Ravenwood had surmised. He wondered how his obstinate rival, Police Inspector Horatio Stagg (or for that matter, any committed, NYPD member) might have reacted.

"You must realize," said Ravenwood, "now that I know the truth, I can't let this lie. I'm sorry, Dr. Kincaid. Truly I am, but…"

Her eyes widened, appalled by his suggestion. "So, you still plan to go to the authorities? I thought you'd understand—appreciate—the complexity of my situation. You must realize that if my work was revealed—"

"I do realize," Ravenwood contended, "which is why I can't turn a blind eye. If it's any consolation, your research won't be in vain. Others will assess it, and from there—"

"Don't humor me, Ravenwood," she snapped. "No one will resume my work, because no one will know of it. It'll be tossed away without so much as a second glance—as will I."

How could he argue? On the other hand, maybe it was better to continue the charade. If she, or for that matter, Ramses, had committed atrocities in the name of so-called science, it was imperative that he, as the case's investigator, compile as much evidence as possible.

"Perhaps," Ravenwood said after a pretentious pause, "I've been hasty. You must admit, the magnitude of the situation is rather jarring, even for one of my broad-based expertise, and as for the missing interns…I dare say, such will be difficult to mask. Even if I were not to report the matter, others would certainly investigate in my wake, but for now, I suppose all we can do is stall and make the best of what time we have."

She nodded, her eyes gleaming of gratitude. "I knew you'd see it my way." She clapped and skipped as might a little girl. "Perhaps we can come up with a feasible alibi. In the long run, it'll be worth it. You'll see. I'm not exaggerating when I tell you I'm on the verge of something stupendous. Cats do possess the most indomitable traits. I've studied them for years and in ways that have exceeded the norm. They've granted me insight on levels that few humans could ever imagine. They hold physical and psychological advantages over humans, as well. A genetic splicing would benefit both species. Considering the rising strife in the world, the human race is already doomed. The right type of modification would be its saving grace."

"Cat people?" Ravenwood muttered, covering his disdain. "Sounds intriguing, but is it practical?"

"What I've created," she declared, "or more precisely refashioned, has thus far remained predominately feline. That's where I've stumbled. I've since taken matters to a more sensible level, and within the past few months, I've made outstanding strides. Before long—" She stopped and then rephrased, "Given time, I do believe that even the most myopic of my peers will have no choice but to acknowledge the value of my efforts."

Ravenwood rubbed his jaw and nodded. "I see…yes…I see, but if I'm to consent to this, especially in light of the students' deaths, I must insist on knowing all aspects of your work. Considering the circumstances, I don't think that's much to ask."

Kincaid smiled in a way that implied more than Ravenwood desired. "Not at all," she said. "I'm more than willing and able…if you get my meaning."

He forced a grin.

"It's getting late," she said. "We'll continue our discussion in the morning."

"Sounds reasonable," he consented and followed her from the chamber. "I do have one other concern, if I may."

She paused before the hanging cats. "Go on, Mr. Ravenwood…"

"Tonight's meal… It wouldn't have been by chance…"

She laughed. "Few things are as they seem around here, Mr. Ravenwood, but if Ramses said it was poultry, well then…"

Ravenwood commented no further on the matter, not even to the chef, who was pleased to escort the investigator to his quarters. Ravenwood did, however, mention what Kincaid had revealed of the interns (after all, she had not instructed otherwise), but Ramses took the revelation in stride, his mental shield remaining formidable, at least until they came to Ravenwood's room, whereupon the "accomplice" lowered his defenses enough to smile.

"I placed your luggage near your bed, your garments and umbrella in the closet," he stated and opened the door. "The sheets are clean and I do believe the accommodations adequate. Miss Scott kept her room tidier than the boys, though I was sure to sweep out any obvious residue from each of their quarters. Still this is the best of the three…"

Ramses reached in and flicked on the switch, then gestured for Ravenwood to enter.

The room was softly illuminated and fringed by further honeysuckle. There were several more cat paintings on the walls, including one above the crimson-cloaked bed, depicting a quartet of joyful kittens yanking yarn: charmingly detailed, but a tad girlish for his taste. There was also a window opposite the closet, outside which Ravenwood detected a looming cypress.

"This should more than suffice," Ravenwood said. "Thank you, Ramses."

"My pleasure, sir," the Egyptian replied, grinning to the point where Ravenwood wondered if he expected a tip. "Incidentally, the bathroom is to the left, and Dr. Kincaid's bedroom is at the end of the hall, across from mine. She'll arrive at her quarters momentarily, so rest assured, neither of us will be out of range, if you should require our attention."

Ravenwood was uncertain how he should take the comment. "That's comforting to know, Ramses. Thank you."

Ramses' grin continued to widen. "She likes you, Mr. Ravenwood, though I'm sure you can tell."

Ravenwood scratched his head. "And I do like her," he lied.

"She's been lonely for quite some time," the Egyptian went on, his smile retracting.

Ravenwood, of course, already knew as much, but said, "You obviously live here. Really, how lonely could she be?"

"It's more than a matter of another body present, Mr. Ravenwood," Ramses explained, his expression turning somber. "My tastes…my interests…lie elsewhere." He brushed his brow suggestively. "I was also the recipient of several, impairing wounds over the years, which restrict me in certain, physical ways, though perhaps the less said about that, the better." He again brushed his brow, though this time without the implied vivacity. "In any event, good night, Mr. Ravenwood." He stepped back and bowed. "Pleasant dreams."

Ravenwood smiled and closed the door. He then waited a moment before cracking it and watched as Ramses entered the room at the hall's end. The Egyptian returned with a large, honeysuckle chair and placed it alongside the threshold. Into it, he then plopped and gave a conspicuous, sideways glance at Ravenwood's room.

Ravenwood clicked the door shut and muttered, "So, you don't fancy me wandering about, eh? Why am I not surprised? Nevertheless, you certainly saw me peek…were probably even anticipating it. Perhaps I'm being tested. Well, whatever this tit-for-tat is, it appears I've no choice but to play along."

He glided over to the window, but as he placed his fingertips near the pane, he noticed it was nailed shut. How convenient. Was this done on his behalf, or for whoever occupied the room? How confined, indeed, were those unfortunate interns?

He glided back to the bed and tossed his luggage atop it, unclasped the latches and slipped his fingertips against its inner, back edge, until a panel snapped loose.

A small, silver blade capped by a roundish, blunt handle rolled into his hand, and with this, he strolled back to the window. With the handle pressed against his palm and forcing the blade into the wood, he ejected each nail.

"Will wonders never cease," he joked and pulled the window upward in such a way to prevent any sound. He then stuck out his hand and regarded the clearing sky. A good sign. An umbrella, coat and such would only hamper him now. The quicker he accumulated the necessary back-up, the sooner the situation could be put to rest. And if there was anything he had learned from his many sojourns, it was never to hesitate when inscrutable motives were at play, not to mention pseudo science and examples of sleight-of-hand. He was still unconvinced, after all, that what Kincaid told him was true, even if he was certain she and her partner believed it to be so.

He yanked off his vest and tie, while adjusting the shoulder holster and Luger under his shirt, assessing the branches, as well as the drop below. "Easy as pie," he chimed.

He returned to his luggage and reached under his obligatory attire, pressing again until another panel popped from the opposite end. From out a series of grooved compartments, he snatched a small, steel spoon and four, topped, glass vials. There was also a small palm-sized camera enclosed, which he had commissioned renowned inventor Harold "Doc" Edgerton to fashion: designed for snapping images fast and clear (and with fingers crossed and prayers aligned) maybe even inter-dimensional phenomena if the opportunity were ever to arise. Yes, it always wise to go with instinct (the ideal way to choose one's tools) when it came to prospective matters of the arcane.

He then took his clothes and along with the sheets and a pillow, molded them to resemble a nestled body. From there, he packed his front pockets (unobtrusive in their tailoring, yet deep and flexible), turned off the light and with great agility, made his daring descent…

He landed near the tree's massive, muddy base and from there, launched across the grass, scurrying under the hazy, violet-ruffled sky, scanning the surroundings, listening to all related sounds, when suddenly—

"Hello," a girlish voice said.

Ravenwood extracted his weapon, bristling in self-contempt that he had not sensed her approach, but his intuition at least assured him that, if for only the immediate vicinity, she was alone.

With caution, he then turned and was consoled to see a pretty, young lady, standing within the swirling mist. She appeared to be shy of twenty, about five-foot-two, with white, short-cropped hair. Her almond-shaped eyes looked blue at initial glance, but he soon realized one was slightly off—green—not unlike the eulogized thespian, Sally Chesney-Waite, whom he once had the pleasure of meeting. The young lady's lips were a natural pink, and she was, despite the weather's soggy aftermath, barefoot. To add to her eccentric semblance, her short, white dress matched her porcelain pallor, to the point that she may have passed for nude.

"What are you doing?" she asked.

"Going for a stroll," he improvised and with brisk adroitness, tucked his Luger back inside. "Sure glad the rain let up, even if it is still a tad messy." He pointed to the estate. "I'm a visitor of Dr. Kincaid. You know her?"

The young lady nodded.

"My name's Ravenwood…and you are?"

"Lily," she said. "My name's Lily."

"Lily," he repeated. "That's a lovely name."

"I suppose."

"You work for Dr. Kincaid?"

"I live here…help her whenever I can…Mr. Ramses, too."

"I see," said Ravenwood. "It's too damp out here to be dressed as you are. Shouldn't you be inside, where it's dry and warm?"

"Shouldn't you?" she said.

He fought back a laugh and continued his improvisation. "Would you like to stroll with me?"

She shrugged. "Sure. Where to?"

"Oh, just around," he answered, though then decided, why not test the waters? "Actually, I'm curious about some of the grass in this area. I've been told it's discolored...has a peculiar scent about it. Do you know of such?"

She rolled her eyes. "Maybe...but I'm not allowed to travel that far without Mr. Ramses' permission."

Ravenwood walked over to her and noticed that her conflicting eye color was more pronounced than he had thought: the sheen deeper and more marble-like than a mere mortal (even one of cinematic fame and fortune) might project. He nonetheless feigned indifference to such, since she appeared unconcerned with his own varying gaze, which he presumed, if only due to his piquing curiosity, was likely shifting at full capacity.

He leaned forwarded and whispered, "I won't tell if you won't tell."

She giggled, though louder than he preferred.

"Let's keep it down, dear," he said. "We don't want to wake the neighbors, now do we?"

She shook her head. "Really, I don't mind taking you, if like you say, you won't tell."

"I promise," Ravenwood assured her and raised his crossed fingers.

Though he could have relied solely on his intuitive skills, he believed she might prove a useful source of information. However, as they sauntered, her naivety became ever more apparent. She also wiggled her nose in a most peculiar way, eliciting curt, sniffing sounds, which implied it was her sense of scent that led the way. How extraordinary, he thought, not unlike a—

"There's one," she blurted, "near the brush." She took a deep breath. "I can even smell it."

Ravenwood also caught the scent, mixed as it was with an overriding wetness: ancient, pungent, yet as distinct as a disinterred corpse.

They approached the spot, which was oily beige and glowing.

Ravenwood knelt, wasting no time to dig through the rainy residue with his blade. He then scooped a decent sample into a vial.

"Why are you doing that?" she asked. "Is it for Katherine?"

Ravenwood pocketed the vial. "Katherine? Oh, uh, yes…yes, it is. Dr. Kincaid and I intend to study it."

"The color was brighter before," she remarked in an off-the-cuff way, "greener."

He stood, his focus first falling upon her emerald orb, before shifting to the blue. "When it comes to certain things in this world," he said, though perhaps more to himself than her, "the prettiest pigments sometimes vary, or so I've come to experience."

She stared at him, her eyes gleaming of what may been awareness and yet her expression, as well as the flow of her mind, remained unwavering.

He sighed, turned, aiming his little camera toward the stain and clicked in rapid procession. "Perhaps we can move on to the next," he said, already lured by the smell.

"Yes, let's," she agreed with a jubilant skip.

They marched onward and soon came upon the second, glowing splotch, plus another located several feet from it. Ravenwood wasted no time to gather his samples and as he did so, asked, "So, how long have you been with the doctor?"

"I'm not sure…not very long, I think."

"Well, how did you come to stay with her?"

"I don't remember." Lily paused and rolled her eyes. "Maybe I was born here."

Her innocence then lost its charm, though he figured it might still hold significance in some underlying way. It may have even been how she had eluded his detection. "Have you ever been to school…held a job?"

"I don't think so." She pouted. "I don't remember."

He grumbled and clicked his camera several more times, but upon swiveling, also snapped her image.

She had no idea what he had done and regarded him with the same dull glaze.

He shook his head, looked about and inhaled. "I don't suspect there are any other areas to check. Perhaps we should turn 'round."

"If you want," she consented and with that, they headed back to the estate…

Along the way, he took keener note of her, particularly her slender frame. This was not for any salacious cause, but due more to her radiant

"Well, how did you come to stay with her?"

aura and graceful gait. She could have passed for a model or actress, if not for her pronounced childishness, but then, who said intellect was a prerequisite for glamour? With the proper training, she could become another Chesney-Waite; maybe another Marlene Dietrich.

"You mentioned that you help the doctor," he said. "You do chores for her?"

"Sometimes I help Mr. Ramses around the kitchen," she said. "Sometimes I help him feed the cats. He lets me play with them, if I do. They like me a lot. With Katherine, though...with Katherine, it's different. I help her in other ways."

"Do tell," said Ravenwood, appreciative of her articulation.

"She examines me," Lily explained. "It's to make sure I'm okay. She checks my heart...my reflexes. It never takes long, unless she puts me under. That's different. That takes longer, though I can't really tell since the gas puts me to sleep. Sometimes when I wake up, I have stitches, but that hasn't happened in a while."

The account sounded more macabre than caring. He considered the interns: what they may have seen, participated in before their deaths.

He pulled out his wallet. "I'd like to show you something, Lily." He yanked three photos, each culled from a recent, college source, and handed them to her. "Do you recognize these people?"

She regarded the young men, but conveyed no discernible reaction. However, when she came upon the young lady, her gait slowed and her eyes widened.

"You know her?" Ravenwood asked. "She also worked with Dr. Kincaid... Katherine."

Lily studied the image a bit longer, but then shook her head and handed the photos back to him. "Sorry...no."

He was unconvinced, but considering her muddled mindset, it was impossible to gauge her. Nonetheless, as they picked up pace, he studied her further and became struck again by his disconcerting, if not outlandish suspicion.

There was, indeed, something peculiar yet uncannily familiar about her bodily sweep, in the way she swayed her arms and hips, how she bounced off the balls of her feet. Here was a woman with no evident long-term memory, a woman with rare, varying eye color, experimented on by one who favored felines, who believed their attributes could benefit human physiology. Could it be...?

"Here we are," she said, prancing toward the house. "You going inside?"

"Yes," said Ravenwood as he moved toward the cypress. "And you?"

"Don't know." She smiled, tiptoeing around the mud, her feet glazed by a conspicuous, but delicate dew. She pointed upward. "I could follow, if you'd like."

He was taken aback.

"I saw you climb down," she said. "You were quick. I wonder if you can climb up as fast." Her eyes twinkled. "Say, would you like to race?"

"Don't be foolish, young lady," Ravenwood replied, but there was something in the way her eyes glistened that enthralled him. It was a kind of devil-may-care wonderment, the sort of impulse that had made him throw caution to the wind on so many occasions past, though perhaps for far better intent. "Well, all right, but under one condition…"

"Yes?" she said.

"We'll chat again. You'll be around, I assume."

"I'm always here," she said. "Besides, Katherine doesn't want me to leave…at least not yet. She told me so."

"Understood," said Ravenwood and scanned the branches.

Lily did the same and then met his gaze. This time, a stronger link formed between them, as if some symbiotic conduit had been propelled. He liked the sensation and had to admit, regardless of her inordinate daftness, it felt good.

He smiled. "Ready?"

"Ready," she replied.

With this, they sprinted, their nails clasping the ridged bark. He rose with an empowered determination, if only to prove his virility, while on the opposite side, she excelled, a shimmering streak, never moving beyond him, but seeming to match his fluid ascent with graceful purpose, much as in a dance.

Remarkable, thought Ravenwood. How was it that one of such slight and diminutive frame could exude such momentous dexterity?

With a deep huff, he came to the window and bolted inward, somersaulting onto the floor, but with such nimble finesse as not to graze its frame. He bounced up, smiling, and peered out as Lily looked in, her face full of exuberance and respect. Had she let him win? Her expression seemed to say so, but then she stiffened, as if startled, and with a quiver, glanced downward.

"What's wrong?" he asked.

Without a peep, she sprang away, prompting him to dart to the ledge. He caught her lithe form as it touched the ground and then scooted from view, but in her wake, a brooding shape entered—Ramses.

With intimidating flair, he braced his rifle upon his shoulder, smiled and waved.

"Well, I'll be..." Ravenwood grumbled, embarrassed that he had not sensed the man's presence sooner, though Lily had proven a most consuming distraction.

Then, if only to startle him further, he heard from behind, "Hello, Mr. Ravenwood." It was Kincaid. "Quite an entrance you made."

Ravenwood grasped his Luger and spun around. Kincaid stared at him, arms folded, her expression undaunted.

She nodded at the bed's unraveled clothes and pillow. Alongside them, the remainder of his luggage was strewn.

"Who sent you, Ravenwood?" she asked. "Who sent you...really?"

"Your financiers...the concerned parents," he said. "Who else?"

Paranoia inundated her eyes. "Ramses knew you were insincere—detected it from the start. He's highly trained in such matters, you should know. His intuition is impeccable, probably superior to your own. I'm glad I took his advice to heart this time. He suggested we give you a little test, continue to layer on the charm, see how far it would go."

"You're mad," Ravenwood charged, "both of you. You belong behind bars—no, make that padded rooms. I'm still not sure what happened, but you'll pay dearly for those young people's lives. And by the way, who's the young lady? Another unwitting soul you had the unwarranted urge to malign?"

Kincaid stepped toward the night stand, where a gas mask was placed. She slipped it on and reached into an inconspicuous hip pocket. In her palm, she revealed a crusty capsule.

"Stop right there," Ravenwood warned, extending his weapon, though more out of show than intent. Surely the object could propose no threat, and even it did, he was inside an open-window room. On the other hand, maybe it was foolish to be so remiss. If only her thoughts were clearer, not so wracked by delusion, he could better determine...

From behind the mask, her eyes jiggled with sinister glee. She then dropped the sphere, letting it skid across the floor, where it slowed to a halt, cracked open and emitted a buzzing burst of pernicious cherry-red, its plumes rising fast.

"Damn you," Ravenwood gagged and then in a harsh, brutal flash, his cognition crashed...

In little time, Ravenwood found himself tumbling in a deep trance, his mind taking him where he might better analyze his circumstance. For all he knew, the commencement of his plunge might have consumed hours or mere minutes. Perhaps it promised a premonition or an extrapolation based on the details he had accumulated. However, the angle did not matter if insight was achieved. Dreams and their instructive meanings were important to Ravenwood, but the current context would have been so much better, if the Nameless One graced the way...

"I am here, my son," the auspicious, loinclothed guru replied on cue, with a voice that echoed throughout time, his round, celestial face appearing before Ravenwood like a sun or moon, though marked by a long, wintery beard and meditative stare. The face floated ever nearer, bobbing from out the dark regions of Ravenwood's consciousness, or was it rather the Nameless One's comforting, candlelit chamber inside luxurious Sussex Towers?

"You are safe within your thoughts," the guru said, "safe within this forming fabrication. It is from this source that you will find—and forge—a temporary reality. Here explanations will be revealed. You will see what could be, what is and what may never be—and from it, learn."

Considering his timorous state, Ravenwood did realize the beaming vision might have been pure, desperate whimsy. Still, with nowhere else to go, he placed unconditional faith in the transmission, letting the curtains of his unconscious unfurl...

A long, entrance hall appeared, at initial glance resembling the banquet variation. There were cat paintings on the walls, imprints of what he had already seen; and much to his delight, the sophisticated Sterling stood by his side, dressed in his butler's best. The valet gave a nod and pointed to a distant, honeysuckle door.

"I've stolen dear Sterling's image," said the Nameless One, his voice reverberating past the replica's lips, "since his courtly presence, for whatever sentimental prompt, bestows you a sense of stability, but I will remain your guide through his cordial guise: two providing partners rolled into one."

"I don't know, sire," Ravenwood said, surveying Sterling's semblance. "Illusions like this can be so confusing."

"Only when they don't fulfill their purpose," the Nameless One said. "Come now..."

The replica led Ravenwood to the door, their heels clicking with pomposity, elevating the phantasmagorical stream.

"It may have been more convenient to start on the other side," said the replica, with a proper British accent now installed, "but the mind requires progression, a logical path from which to move when discovery is pursued." The fake Sterling clamped the doorknob and gave it a curt turn. "At this point, it's best to let the scenario unfold as any terrestrial path would. Your mind will adjust to it better."

The door swung open and in a burst of chandelier light, Ravenwood saw stately dressed men and women sitting at long, honeysuckle tables, their faces smudged as if in spasmodic development. Before them, silver goblets and brass bowls were placed, the latter brimming of colorful seasonings. Upon the wide, silvery plates, steaming hunks of Ramses' mysterious meat were spread, though some of it looked rarer and ruddier than what Ravenwood had devoured, thus increasing his curious, sagacious bent

As was no surprise, the expanse was covered with further cat images, though not paintings, but rather stony reliefs that protruded from the matching walls, featuring crude, carved sketches of humanoid bodies, capped by feline heads. Shown hovering above these entities were variations of the ankh-grasping, Egyptian goddess, Bastet, modified by long, bared fangs and attire so snug (or rather, so faintly etched) it was, for all intents and purposes, nonexistent...

In an excitable burst, Ramses entered from a side door, garbed once more as a waiter, swerving his cart about as he resupplied his silver-domed delicacies.

In a tight, black dress, Kincaid presided along the opposite wall. Her eyes shifted to Ravenwood, though displayed no acknowledgement, for he realized she was but a fixture in the unfolding play.

"Dream or not," Ravenwood remarked, "there's something most foreboding about this place."

"An astute observation, Master Ravenwood," confirmed Sterling's reflection, "but it could be just part of the deflecting decor, due to our experience with a particular cat of much larger scope." (The Nameless One referenced that fateful day when Ravenwood's father had saved the wise man from a tiger, which then prompted the shaman's lifelong allegiance to the son.) The replica then smiled and with a click of the fingers declared, "My, take a look, would you? It does appear our guest of honor has arrived."

Ravenwood spotted Lily's silky white hair bobbing forth, heading to the front of the lip-smacking crowd. When she came into fuller view, she looked a tad more mature than before, though perhaps it was due to her attire: a lovely, white, evening gown, adorned by a pearl necklace that sparkled from the overhead light, but even this was eclipsed by the gleam of her dueling, gemmed eyes.

"She looks older," Ravenwood remarked, "evolved."

"Yes," the replica said, "though I believe we may be idealizing her for the sake of this instructive trip."

"Makes little difference," Ravenwood said. "For better or worse, I rather fancy her this way: more woman than girl, that is."

The blurry faced participants turned to Lily, who she greeted with a magnanimous bow. They murmured (or was it, purred?) and then dipped their faces back into their plates, voraciously consuming their food, behaving for all intents and purposes like animals and in that regard, as much like insolent children, disrespecting a parent.

"Such self-indulgent things," Ravenwood said. "Most disrespectful..." He paused, feeling a trifle queasy. "I wonder... If those portions are even to a small degree feline and those who feast upon such are much the same, does that make them, well...cannibalistic?"

"You're on to something, sir," the replica concurred. "Perhaps it's a way to accentuate what they already are, a kind of bestial boost or ritualistic communion, if you will."

Ramses, meanwhile, had moved against the wall opposite Kincaid, loitering beneath a relief that featured several bipedal deities gathered behind a table that resembled the ones he had served. The faces within the relief were directed down at ambiguous flesh, around which small, cracked balls were featured, eliciting ascending squiggles. A prophesy... an inadvertent reflection, perhaps. Either way, it vexed Ravenwood.

Ramses glanced at Kincaid, who curled a contented smile, but the Egyptian did not reciprocate. Interesting...

"I wonder," said Ravenwood, "if what he sees pleases him."

The guests continued to purr and slurp for an interminable duration, then wiped their mouths and licked their lips, and for a fleeting moment even lifted their heads. Their faces were then clear, as symmetrical and comely as Lily's, but as with her guise, something anomalous brewed inside: something so riled, vile and unnatural that Ravenwood felt it scream for release.

"This prophesy is forced," Ravenwood deduced. "How would anyone reproduce something so impalpable, especially after so many centuries?" He looked at Kincaid, who offered an approving glint. "She cares little about the lineage. To her vantage, this outcome is satisfactory." He then looked at Ramses. "But he wants to get it right, at least based on what he thinks is right, but if cryptic carvings are all that either has…"

"Try and try again, Master Ravenwood," the simulation said. "Sooner or later, an experiment is bound to hit the mark, or so that's our henchman's hope. Though fate may have brought these birds of a feather together, they behave as would political parties: each on the claimed, same side, but with different notions on how to attain their goals."

The guests then clawed across their tables, grabbing doughy capsules by the handful (or was it the pawful?), slamming them down, cracking them open like nuts. Fumes rose, and the participants shifted about their seats, purring in unison, combining bestiality with an air of superiority. And with this shameless pomposity, they grew all the larger, longer, the thickness of their manes wavier, wilder.

They also began to cling to one another, ripping one another's garments, nipping one another's skin…lapping one another's blood.

"How horrid," Ravenwood said, preferring the ghastly vision to end.

Lily then rose, so prim and ethereal in her stance. Disgusted by the revelry, Ravenwood was glad that she might become the focus. He watched her arms spread, as a queen would do when addressing her subjects, but once more, the highbrow rabble paid her no mind, far too immersed in their maddening orgy to care.

Her sweet face drooped, and she backed away, like some high-hope thespian booed off the stage. She was not meant for this gaudy composite, Ravenwood realized. She was, in truth, an entity like himself, tottering between two worlds, though with her, there was no grasp of command. He felt a need to comfort her and may have even done so, if not for what then transpired.

With mighty grunts and roars, the guests tipped over the tables; plates and utensils soaring and clanging, bodies bumping and grinding atop the spreading mess.

Teary-eyed, Lily fled the Bosch-ian spree, and with her dramatic departure, the lights dimmed.

Kincaid and Ramses melted into the shadows, while the entities rolled forth in a great, dark wave. Ravenwood darted beyond the mob, while Sterling's guise glided into it, breaking like a puff of smoke, but his voice— or rather that of the Nameless One—prevailed.

"The tide shifts," the sage said. "You flowed inward; now you must flow outward…"

As the obstreperous beasts rushed toward him, Ravenwood shot toward the door, which by the time he reached it was no more. He fell into the hall, where the paintings now exuded Victorian-mimicked arrangements of Ramses' carved impressions: tall, regal cat people twisting and chomping, each lewd cluster presided by a hovering, pseudo Bastet.

The images adapted further detail as he continued his flight, featuring defenseless humans laid upon alters, arms plucked, hearts torn…

Ravenwood continued to yet another porous door, but this time when he slid through it, he entered the outside world.

The air was hot and oppressive, the sky an eerie red, the buildings tall and looming; and because of their modern relegation, they oozed of prophetic threat; the street, a river of blood, peppered with human torsos and heads.

The monsters sloshed after him with a vigor he could not match, leaving him to collapse near a gushing alley, his body immersed in the disseminating carnage.

The dapper but stoic Ramses stepped from out the grisly gloom, a visage born as if from brick and trash.

"This is the way it must be," he proclaimed, his palm nestling his infectious spheres, "the purge quick…merciless…brewed with alchemical impetus…just as prophesy ordained."

He dropped the balls, which erupted upon touching the blood. Surges of color curled and swirled, filling Ravenwood's nostrils, as the beasts piled atop him in one horrific swoop. His thoughts creased and crackled, but due to his pensive resilience, his pain drained, and soon the demonic vision ceased.

"Be patient, my son," the Nameless One said, his voice a faraway whisper within the enveloping dark. "You now know the symbolic path before you and possess the fortitude to see it through… Your presence acts as the proverbial monkey wrench…the wedge that will stop this nightmarish machine from reaching fruition…"

The Nameless One's words inspired and consoled Ravenwood, and he yearned to open his eyes, but alas, when at last he did, he was no less restrained…

"So, he's come to."

Ravenwood recognized Kincaid's chilly timbre.

"Breaking from his trance it appears," Ramses responded, "though his irises look odd… violet phasing to grayish blue, but then I suppose such changing hues are his main gimmick." He slapped Ravenwood's cheek. "Snap out of it, ol' chap. Time to pay the piper."

Ravenwood's wrists, ankles and waist were roped in complicated, zigzagging fashion to a chair, the wood's soothing scent pleasant enough to mock him through the numbing tightness.

"Figures," he groaned. "Seems I have a penchant for tie-ups."

Indeed, this was not the first time he had found himself in such a shackled predicament, but it seemed more debilitating this time out, restricting his ability to nudge even his fingers. To add further insult to injury, his arched wallet instilled a persistent, stabbing pain into his buttocks, as if it had been extracted, only then to have been shoved back in without care. Also, his disheveled, open shirt implied the absence of his holster and of course, he realized his gun would have been seized no sooner than he had blacked out.

Through his groggy, limited view, he discerned the surroundings were new: white-tiled and sparkling, though tinged with an indelible, fleshy aroma. The latter also reeked of chemicals, which upon further inhalation accentuated his unsteady focus, hindering any convenient attempt to re-summon the Nameless One.

For a moment, he considered praying to Shiva to administer some quick justice, though the odds of that the god would interfere in that easy a way were slim to none. On the other hand, the detective mused, his Yoga mastery might numb the brunt of his discomfort, but then was it not better to stay as alert as possible in light of the impending doom?

Kincaid cleared her throat. "I'm still miffed that you didn't succumb to my advances. I truly believed we could have merged…and in more ways than one. Coming to my room could have commenced a long line of experimentation, but it appears Ramses was right. You chose the window route. It was just a matter of how you'd tackle it and how fast he could make his way downstairs to let Lily out. I'm confident, though, that despite your nosey needs, you still hold an amorous inclination. All playboys do, including the self-proclaimed, psychic sorts, I'm sure. I'm at least grateful you favor our dear Lily, which for the direction we're headed, more than meets our purposes."

She stepped nearer, her black dress tight and cruel upon her high-heeled frame, much more imposing that it had been in his dream. "You see, Mr. Ravenwood, you're not the only one to spur a con. I've been conducting one for a good number of years, dishing out just enough bloody blather to keep my work secure until the big moment arrived. And here we are…"

"Splendid," Ravenwood groaned. "A veritable wish come true…"

She ignored the remark and took a long, contemplative pause. "I asked before, and I'll ask again," she said, her body stiffening with distrust. "Who sent you? There are those who'd love to stop the natural course of things. Ramses told me of their spiteful ilk…how they tend to emerge whenever one least expects it. Are you part of their judgmental clique? Is that how this little visitation came to be?"

"I already told you who sent me," Ravenwood explained.

She glowered at him. "Ramses found an interesting card in your wallet." She sneered. "Tell me…who's this Horatio Stagg?"

"Stagg works for the NYPD," Ravenwood said, exasperated. "I help him on cases. If you know of me, you'd know of him through the papers."

"Yes," she said, "which only confirms your authoritative link. Oh, how convenient with the timing of the interns' disappearance…an ideal excuse to pry your way in. Clever, Mr. Ravenwood…very clever."

"Oh, please," Ravenwood scoffed. "This is ridiculous. You're trying to connect dots that aren't there."

She ticked her tongue and began to pace, as if searching for a rebuttal that was hopeless to gain, and in so doing, granted Ravenwood a better vantage of the décor.

It was a kitchen, but as much a laboratory, with large, metallic stoves and long shelves covering the walls, inside which compact, glass-paneled cookers were queued and plugged, accompanied by jars of presumed seasonings that would likely enhance Ramses' questionable flesh. Nearby counters braced brass clasps and bowls of brownish dough, some kneaded and some half rolled. The leathery consistency was unidentifiable to Ravenwood, some of it flanked by cupped samples: cracked just enough to reveal their glowing interiors.

Not far from such were cabinets constructed of translucent, icy-green panels, inside which dangled felines like those downstairs, most missing limbs, their bellies flayed, their gummy viscera protruding from out moist, crimson cavities.

Against the far wall, live, woeful-eyed cats—in fact, the very ones that had rushed into the dining room—regarded him from their smelly, sand-duned, wired cages, resigned to their fates, except for the gray one, which braced his chubby paws against the mesh, signaling an urge for release.

Kincaid curled her finger, prompting Lily to slink into view. Whether by choice or demand, the young lady wore a sheer, white slip, which augmented the surrealistic tone.

"Here she is," the doctor said, her face aglow. She stroked the girl's hair, making Lily bend and purr. "I'm not at all surprised you're smitten. Lilly is an indisputable beauty and to date, my one, rousing success."

"Our success," Ramses corrected and twirled Ravenwood's Luger with playful panache before ramming it into a familiar, shoulder holster. For what it was worth, it complemented his camouflaged coveralls, which Ravenwood postulated the goon wore on all occasions of intimidation. Indeed, these folks knew how to dress their parts.

"Of course, Ramses…our success," Kincaid complied. "The dear girl wouldn't have taken shape if not for your exotic unguents, but then, I'm the one who sculpted her, the one who gave her preternatural enchantment."

"Preternatural," Ravenwood laughed. "Well, she's unique, all right. I'll give the dear girl that much." His eyes met Lily's, and his heart brimmed of sorrow. She had no idea what she was; let alone the bizarre direction of her fate. Perhaps it was all for the best she remained naïve. "Too bad she's a mere novelty."

"A novelty," Kincaid said, considering the term. "Perhaps, Mr. Ravenwood, but as you're undoubtedly aware, most novelties tend to have huge impacts on the masses. Personally, I consider Lily a prototype: a complex blueprint upon which others of her kind will progress and grow."

"And this is to help the human race in exactly what way?" Ravenwood asked, still confused by the doctor's ultimate intent. "As the saying goes, if something ain't broke…"

"But it is," Kincaid seethed. "It's been broken since humans have set foot upon this earth. Ramses and his people have long yearned to remedy the matter." She turned to her partner and smiled. "Isn't that right, Ramses?"

Ramses beamed. "Indeed, doctor. Our crusade has endured for centuries. We've implemented whatever corrections we could whenever possible, but the process has been tedious. We've joined forces with others, but mercenary factions are never reliable, and there are those in the know who simply dismiss our goals as misguided magic, with no real chance for change. Still, we've persisted with our pursuit of the old ways—and the day when the winds might shift to our advantage, always acknowledging and respecting those who once ruled. Under them, we hope to serve again."

"So, your toils are based on legends," said Ravenwood, "something that may have never even existed, or if it had, perhaps it's not even aligned with your perception. How could you hope to recreate something that existed so many centuries past?" He shook his head. "Think of it. You serve nothing more than a murky fantasy: a dream more off-the-cuff than scientifically, let alone spiritually assured."

"Those of the modern mindset never understand," Ramses answered. "Besides, the western world has reigned far too long. That alone justifies an alteration. All that my people have ever asked is for the chance to reinstate what once rightfully ruled. Now, I—and Dr. Kincaid—will be the catalysts of that glorious return."

"Hate to break it to you," said Ravenwood, "but few folks will comply. In fact, I'm certain most would rebel against it, just like they're doing now in Europe. Dictatorial reigns never remain the rage."

"In this instance," Kincaid rebutted, "it appears they've no choice." She tugged a strand of Lily's hair and pointed to Ravenwood. "Do you like our man of mystery, my dear? Does he entice you?"

Lilly placed her cheek upon Kincaid's shoulder, while digesting Ravenwood's princely scowl. "Oh, yes, I do," she whispered. "He's such a nice man…and so very attractive."

Kincaid chuckled, as did Ramses, but within their revelry, Lily moved away, slinking toward Ravenwood. With this, her handlers hushed and with quavering anticipation, watched.

Ravenwood matched Lily's stare as she edged nearer. He was an effective mesmerist when need be and abetted by his eyes' ever-changing pigmentation, had reached remarkable success with his subjects. Perhaps he could rekindle the technique, and if Lilly was susceptible, perhaps even strong enough, she might help him get loose. Even a partial loosening of an arm or a leg might be enough to do the trick …

"So, it begins," Ramses whispered.

"Yes," Kincaid murmured. "It does appear…"

Lily stopped a few inches before him and donning a smooth, focused countenance, hunkered down, reaching out with eerie slowness until her fingers grazed his cheek, her eyes still probing his, but then she pulled back.

With a forceful roll of his warm, ruddy brown eyes, he lured her back in, reminding her that he was, indeed, a nice man and would be even nicer, if her sharp nails might fall upon his wrist, and…

She purred, edged closer, growing intrigued by his variegating command, her contented breath reaching his brow, her fingers notching downward. However, just as Ravenwood sensed success, Kincaid interrupted the fostering flow by adding, "Yes, she's performing as hoped. There's no doubt she's ready."

The hypnotic surge faded, leaving Lily to shut her eyes and sway her head.

"Then I should proceed as planned," said Ramses, looking about with pretentious pity. "In a way, it seems a shame to destroy all this." He glanced at Ravenwood, contempt dripping from the cruel lines of his face. "If he truly came here for the interns, others—whoever they may be—will come for him. We've no choice but to start anew."

"We have what we want," Kincaid argued. "It only matters that Lily fulfills her task. When she's impregnated, we'll tend to her and the inevitable litter elsewhere. You'll take the necessary steps to change our identities, of course, and then we'll devise the means to garner new funds. We'll be as right as the purifying rain."

Ravenwood cringed. Litter? What in the world was all this? He then recalled the creatures of his dream. Were they who he thought them to be? Could things get any stranger?

Lilly twisted her neck, swiveled her hips, looking both cautious yet ardent.

"That's right," said Kincaid, encouraging her onward. "Get in the mood, dear. Remember what you practiced with Mr. Ramses, but this time it will be for real. It will go to the point where your instincts take over. Let Mr. Ravenwood appreciate your strength...savor his pain." She shot Ravenwood an impertinent glance. "You know this man wants you, in a way that Mr. Ramses could never—that every ounce of this man desires your conquest of him...welcomes it unconditionally." She strolled to Lily's side, leaned her lips against her ear, then grasped her wrist and stroked her fingertips. "Even if he says or acts otherwise, he has no choice but to comply. Destiny, my dear, will dictate the terms."

Lilly shifted her gaze back to Ravenwood, studying his iris' rich, fiery sheen, though not yet daring to peer beyond.

Kincaid backed away and gestured Ramses to follow, leaving Lily to lick her lips and twitch her nose in a most suggestive way. Kincaid and Ramses then slipped out, pulling the door shut, latching it.

An uneasy silence ensued before Lily purred, "You do like me, don't you? I mean...*really* like me." Her lips spread thin and wide, her pearly incisors exposed. "And I...I like you...*really* like you. This is going to be so wonderful...so magical...just like Katherine promised...just like Mr. Ramses said."

If there was only some way to draw her back into his stare, Ravenwood thought, but her demeanor seemed sidetracked now, too inebriated to

She purred, edged closer…

break. He could only hope that she might yet see fit in the throes of passion to release him. But even then, would he have enough time to make his move? What if the dreadful duo was watching from some inconspicuous hole, set to intervene if things went awry? In fact, now that he focused, he could see a couple circular lenses to either side of the door, ideal for peeking. Indeed, with the opportunity at hand...

"Yes, I do like you, Lily, very much so." He lowered his voice to an almost inaudible whisper. "I'd like to show you how much, if you'd only help get me loose. Perhaps just a little tug or two about my wrists. I can muster the rest. Would you do that for me, Lily...if you *really* like me, as you say?"

She nodded, as if to relay her understanding, but then curled her hand behind his shirt, grazing the webbed scar he had earned from a bike accident in Paris. She seemed to take it in stride, perhaps perceiving it as simply another result of Kincaid's medical tinkering.

She then stroked his neck and slid her fingers onto his chest, where she then placed her palm. She shook her head and pouted. "Katherine said you might trick me...that you're a liar who came here to fool us." She purred more deeply, pushing the chair backward. "Is that true?"

"I'm not a liar," he assured her. "I came on behalf of the students. I showed you their pictures, remember?"

She shrugged her indifference.

Ravenwood groaned in frustration. "Listen, to me, Lily. It only matters that we're together. That's what Katherine wants...Mr. Ramses, as well... and here we are, but if I'm restrained, there's not much we accomplish. I'm certain that whatever you practiced with Mr. Ramses was nowhere near this restrictive."

She cocked her head, considering the matter. In the meantime, he whiffed her rising scent: a pheromone spurt, spiked by something old and yet unlike anything he recognized, permeating with underlying ferocity.

"Katherine might be testing you," he continued, hoping to sound more conniving. "I'm sure she'll critique your performance, and if our, uh, consummation isn't conducted properly, my hunch is she'll be none too pleased, but if that's what you want, Lily..."

She stiffened. "No," Lily asserted. "I want to do this right." She leaned closer, her breath beating harder against his skin, as she slid her cheek against his until their lips met.

If he had not known any better, if that horrid reverie had not influenced his thoughts, perhaps he may have gone along for the reckless ride. The best he could do now was imagine a distracting counterpart and thought of the many ladies with whom he had been intimate over the years. This exercise helped; however, when she tried to slip her tongue between his teeth, his amorous imagining faltered, but at least inspired him to rock his weight upon the chair, thus making it wobble and therefore, start to weaken.

Lily lifted both head and hand in one passionate swoop, as if practicing some bizarre ballet tactic, and then drove her index finger into his upper chest, slicing it with her nail. He grimaced, fighting off the sting, returning his eyes, now bright and hazel, to hers, concentrating on the green, then the blue and back again, all the while jockeying his seat.

"This feels nice," she hissed, "so very nice."

Ravenwood smiled, consuming her odd equanimity, the rocking intensifying.

She again raised her finger, which spiraled of his blood; and then with a sensual flip of her neck, she licked it away.

"It's good to taste," she said, smacking her lips. "Mr. Ramses told me that if we taste each other, we share a part of each other. He said it sets the pace, like in a ritual…like in magic…very old magic."

Magic. She seemed to trust in it. If only she knew the content of his reverie. Nonetheless, he decided to let her believe. He would continue the game; maintain his fake glee, his willing stance.

"Ramses told me you tasted the flesh last night," she cooed, her eyes glistening of dewy wonderment. "He said it was a warm-up for your system, but it wasn't the real thing…not *really*…not like me." She placed her hand upon her bosom, cutting through her slip, into her skin, where the faint hint of a scar lingered. "I bet I tastes better than Ramses' meat." She pulled his face near. "Go on, Mr. Ravenwood…taste."

KKKRRRAAACCCKKK!!!

The chair hit the floor, its pieces scattering. Ravenwood pushed her off him and rose straight and strong, shaking the splintered appendages from his limbs and with staunch agility shook his bonds loose.

Lily looked stunned, then full of rage. Her mouth unhinged, exposing the full length of her fangs, and from her throat came a long, drawled shriek.

From beneath the little, glass portal, left of the door, Kincaid's eye enlarged. "Stay calm, Lily," she insisted. "Don't let him distract you. There was always a chance this might happen. Remember how you performed with Mr. Ramses. This is just another part of the process…another part of the plan, my dear."

Lily bowed her head, arched her back, her ears protruding from out her silky strands.

"Listen to Katherine," Ramses urged from the opposite portal, his eye just as fervid. "Follow through. Remember the steps. Do it, Lily. Do it…"

Ravenwood was too tense to predict what might come next and decided to push her out of the way. He believed he was strong enough, angry enough, to rattle the door, snap its lock and hinges, and from there, he would tackle Ramses, then subdue Kincaid.

However, as he charged, so did Lily, springing high, her fingers spread, her legs flailing.

The caged cats stirred, meowing to the point of howling, scurrying about their diminutive prisons, the gray one pressing ever harder against the screen.

Ravenwood managed to skid beyond Lily's lurching reach, but within a few, mere stomps, she had latched onto his shoulder and dragged him down. They rolled onto the floor, over and over, until she squirmed her way atop and regarded him with keen, cruel severity.

For a moment, she glanced at the door, perhaps hoping for another encouraging command, and in so doing, dropped her guard, allowing Ravenwood to roll her over and harness her beneath him, her wrists and ankles clamped beneath his.

"Don't allow him the upper hand," Kincaid cried. "Take control. Seduce him. Enchant him. Do whatever you can, Lily. Trust me, he'll succumb."

"It's no use, Lily," Ravenwood told her. "I don't want to hurt you, but if you leave me no choice…" He searched her feverish eyes. "These people are using you. What future could they possibly give you? Do you want to be hauled away to some faraway laboratory, prodded and probed day after day? That'll happen, you know. And what happens when there are more of you? I bet those two will turn them against you. And what then? You'd be of no use to anyone anymore—a wasted novelty, no more or less."

Her calm countenance seemed to convey that he had reached her, but then a peculiar scent rose. Ravenwood glanced at the door and saw green smoke seeping from a small compartment below.

"This will help you, Lily," Ramses bellowed, a devilish grate to his voice. "I've kept a few capsules ready. The contents are flowing through the little compartment I made, all set to let the magic spread. It'll make you stronger, Lily, him weaker. You can do what you wish with him, then. And if you finish the task, I assure you, Lily, no harm will come to you. We'll take care of you, as we always have. I promise."

"What have you done?" Kincaid scolded him, her voice muffled, but tense. "You've inserted too much. This will ruin everything."

"The experiment was already botched," Ramses shot back. "This may be the only way to remedy it. Let Bastet shine through. Let the human side dwindle. It's what we should have done from the start."

With the gas expanding, escape became essential, and so Ravenwood leapt off Lily and dashed again for the door, but unfortunately, this was where the substance proved densest. Ravenwood threw himself against it repeatedly, while yanking at its knob, and though the hinges seemed to loosen, he then began to choke.

He waddled back, grasping his throat and blinking his eyes, tripping past the panic-stricken cats, ramming into one of the icy green compartments. The eviscerated felines danced within like puppets. He turned from the grotesque sight, only then to encounter another.

It was poor Lily, standing at least a foot taller, her garments snapping off her body, her skin sprouting thick, white fur. Her fingers and toes grew long, yellow claws, and her ears ascended high above her spectral crown.

With big, mournful eyes, she reached out to him, her nose flattening like an inverted triangle, her nostrils curling, her mouth stretching back, her lips darkening.

"Hold on, now, Lily," Ravenwood reasoned, swatting against the mist.

Disoriented, she rolled her head, turning around to reveal a tendril-like tail, which whipped as if keeping time, extending notch by notch, until she stumbled toward the cages and fell to her knees.

"Grab your rifle," Kincaid ordered Ramses, "and give me that Luger. There's no point in continuing, now. We'll put an end to this, retrieve what we can."

"You said there would be no mistakes this time," Ramses berated. "So much for your promises, doctor. The chamber's flooded, anyway. We open the door, and the smoke will fill our lungs. It's better to let the process run its course."

Lily trembled; seeming to understand his words, and from this came an intense, desperate rage. With a swift click of her claws, she snapped the little cages open, allowing the cats to sprint out, the gray one leading the way, but to where?

Ravenwood, meanwhile, amplified his concentration, resuming his attempt to loosen the door. However, Lily then leapt up and with the regal finesse of a lioness, charged the structure, knocking him out of the way as she bludgeoned it with such force that the surrounding foundation vibrated and shook.

With a guttural growl, she then jaunted back and repeated the gesture, inflicting more damage with each strike. The door splintered and began to wobble. Ravenwood heard the compartment at the bottom snap loose, clanging across the floor from the opposite side.

Ravenwood breathed a sigh of relief, and though his throat tingled in a most alarming way, he still felt limber and strong. The cats latched onto his empowerment, scooting about his legs, as Lily made one last, unsparing thrust

The hinges finally popped. The door fell, the toxic wealth of the room rolling beyond the threshold. Ravenwood careened toward the opening, the cats following suit.

Though Kincaid reached forth, Ramses yanked Ravenwood's Luger from his holster and fired it repeatedly, but Ravenwood averted the bullets, barreling into his foe, knocking him to the side. Ravenwood then landed a solid jui-jitsu chop to the back of Egyptian's neck, hurling him into the green-fogged floor, the Luger flying from his hand.

Ramses shook his head, his neck creaking, but forced himself up, just as Ravenwood dived for the weapon.

They clashed midstream, exchanging blows, forcing the Luger farther from reach, Ramses using an unorthodox, combat technique unknown to the investigator, but the detective was deft enough to regain leverage, which may have then led to a his victory if not for Kincaid's curdling shriek.

From the doorway, Lily emerged, now towering over the seven-foot mark, hunkering over Kincaid with oval eyes as big as locomotive lamps: the green and blue flickering like frantic, demonic signals through the hazed hall.

Within the unremitting gas, her body wafted with rubbery looseness, her face insinuating, if only for a moment, the comely countenance that had once enchanted him, the one of an aspiring actress or model, the one of royalty prohibited to reign, but no sooner had it surfaced, the beast again ruled.

Inspired by this frightful sight, he envisioned a cityscape behind her, though not the modern version of his reverie This was something older, undocumented, with crimson sky and sizzling, barren sand and disjointed, abstract chucks of wall, etched with more images of bipedal cats, running, leaping, slaying their victims upon long, ominous tables. What was new was old again, and vice versa, though neither realm ever deserved to exist.

Ramses leapt past Ravenwood, falling at the doctor's side, where he regarded the bizarre giantess with a look of utter dread.

"The two sides are colliding," Ramses said. "I warned you of this. It had to be one over the other. You should never have installed so much of the girl. I only wish I had purged what was left of her. The feline traits should have dominated, no matter what the semblance. I said it time and again…"

"What girl?" Ravenwood asked, as the hallucinogenic strands left his mind.

Lily had grown more puzzled and confused as the words drilled into her gargantuan head. She stomped and squealed.

"It was Pamela," the doctor bawled, quaking with the bragging need for confession. "She was dead…no more than a mangled mess, but Ramses salvaged what he could…shared those remains with me. We had another specimen, as well—completely white, but without the general anomalies associated with such types—and when the body had become large enough through chemical alteration, Pamela's parts were implanted…assimilated. The process moved ideally. After a time, Lily learned to walk upright, even speak. She named herself…came to trust us. No human child could have equaled the progression, and unlike a kitten or human infant, she remained alert—innocent, yes, but always willing to learn. There was no indication that she would be like the others. We had every reason to believe she'd be the prototype for—"

"A renewed race," Ramses said, his face rippled with scorn, "but we were wrong yet again—or at least the doctor was. This…this thing is another miscalculation…another damned monstrosity bound for the bowels of Hell."

Lily unleashed a long, yowling meow.

"Your stupid, archaic potions are to blame," Kincaid chastised. "You knew she was vulnerable and yet you had to oversaturate her. And to think how close we were. She would have found her way. She just needed more time. Damn you, Ramses."

Ravenwood spotted his Luger not far from the door's unhinged compartment. He moved fast, snatched it up and tucked it into his pants. His attention then turned to a door farther down the hall, lured by the sound of the cats scratching at its frame. He ran to it and let the frantic felines through, prepared to follow, when Lily beckoned.

"Noooooooooo…" Her moan seized his senses, her confusion and anguish filtering through his soul. He watched her flashing eyes as she stepped past her fickle parents, her long, clawed fingers fanning, her lanky frame stumbling like some oversized toddler.

Her mouth slipped into an eager, slack-jaw grin, as if believing he would be pleased to see her. The poor thing had no idea what she had turned into, and Ravenwood's contempt for her creators could not have been greater.

With pity, he told the poor creature to "Stay...stay now, Lily. Don't come any closer. Calm yourself. Rest, my dear."

She cocked her head and purred, though it sounded more like an erratic gurgle and ignoring his plea, continued to step. He could now sense her nagging loss of innocence, as well as her inexorable drive to slash, hunt... kill.

"Stay, Lilly." He pointed his Luger. "Stay..."

In desperation, Ramses bounced up and from out his pocket, pulled several more crusty capsules.

"What are you doing, you fool?" Kincaid shouted. "Enough of your insipid hocus-pocus."

The Egyptian tossed them anyway.

"They'll subdue the residue," he explained, "dispel the transforming properties. We'll breathe easier. Give it a moment. You'll see." The spheres' steam seeped from behind the creature, spewing smoke of foul red, orange and blue.

Lilly turned, her tail swiping at the intermingling colors, baffled and intrigued by their tumultuous mating. She then growled and groaned, her lanky limbs shaking.

"See what you've done," Kincaid screamed. "You've worsened it."

Ravenwood watched awestruck as Lily's limbs, claws and ears continued to grow. Her cheeks puffed outward, with whip-like whiskers snapping forth. Her tail appeared more demonic than feline, ridged and sharp, swatting ever faster, as Kincaid cowered and Ramses raised his fists, though more in reflex than practicality.

Ravenwood was tempted to fire upon her, but his moral disposition snuffed the urge. He instead slipped into the next chamber, which was lit by dusty, shade-less bulbs, where musty furnishings and more feline portraits hung. The cats scratched at their final door, screaming for escape, one pushing atop the other, until the gray one gained the forefront.

Ravenwood flung the door open, and watched the critters scatter across the grass. A moist, foreboding air smacked his sweat-beaded face. He stepped out, taking a moment to catch his breath and then circled around the front...

His eyes fell upon the menacing lion bust, its gaping countenance daring him to make his next move, but he was too dazed by the billowing chemicals to think. A rumbling boom then struck from within, knocking the eerie sculpture to the ground, while thick, colorful, whipping plumes danced across the roof.

Yes, thought Ravenwood, this was the prophetic beginning of the end. As he well knew from experience (as well as from the Nameless One's many instructive chats), destruction was an apt cap to many an unsettling scenario; that this pit of Hell adapted such a volcanic comeuppance was only expected. It also reeked of a symbolic cleansing: an ancient evil long desired and projected, but like so many attempts to make mad lore real, it was never meant to flourish.

From the side, he heard yelling, followed by another thundering blast. Kincaid then stumbled into view, shoeless and holding her stomach, blood dripping from her lips.

With a defeated grunt, she fell to her knees, cranked her neck upward and looked upon the detective.

"Ramses...he...he rigged the entire estate," she gurgled, "in case we ever needed to cover our tracks. It was his intent to...to dissolve everything through a chain reaction after you...after you and Lily mated. It's...it's happening fast now...the chemicals quickening the process. Lily...that sick, demented creature...is still in there. She's...she's after him." She shook her head in despair. "But why...why should I care? The fool brought it upon himself. He deserves this outcome, and I...I just want to get away from here." With weakened arms, she reached up. "Please..."

Ravenwood walked over to her, though he held no pity. Her mind spewed only insincerity: the type that was flat and blunt, filled with a slow-burn conceit that was aimed at those only who wished her good will. Indeed, her temperament may have favored cats, but as Ravenwood learned from her subconscious flow, she chose them per sadistic default. Everyone—and every thing—was her enemy, for no other reason than that it seemed right. Katherine Kincaid was not just deranged. She was evil.

In disgust, he grabbed her arm and with one, swift sweep, flung her over his shoulder and marched away from the collapsing estate.

Another explosion hit, then another. Bright spurts, mixed with flashes of green, red, and blue mushroomed upward, generating an unsettling stench. Then from out the melting bricks, Lily's titanic head rose, her bulging, oval eyes refracting the many, turbulent hues, and in her mouth, a dark, muscular arm dangled.

Ramses then appeared out of the wreckage, zooming around her like a frightened mouse, yelling and jumping over the shifting rumble, his back streaming of multi-colored flame, blood blasting from his bitten shoulder.

He spotted Ravenwood, which made him scream all the louder, and then he stumbled, falling flat upon his face, the gaseous plumes spreading over him like lightning, merging with the complementing chemicals, fanning the bittersweet scent of rising ash, dissolving his clothes, his flesh, pulling him (or so Ravenwood fancied, with an air of ironic satisfaction) into the censorious bowels of Hell.

As she watched him die, Lily swatted a portion of disintegrating wall away, as more explosions let loose, the smoke and nauseating aroma growing higher and wider.

She pranced about from the balls of her enormous feet, chomping upon the appendage, making it flap at both ends, the fingers emulating a feeble farewell.

Logic urged Ravenwood to flee, but there was something in the way Lily's eyes settled upon him that made him stay. What did she want? Forgiveness? Pity? No, he decided, it was something more basic, more primal than that.

Her vengeful eyes fell upon the woman he carried. Yes, he knew what fate had in store. Should he intervene? Did he care enough to do so?

The doctor squirmed and slid down his back. Ravenwood turned, deciding it only right to lift her, when Lily bolted with unbridled fury toward them. It was too late. Destiny had, indeed, dictated the terms.

Ravenwood jumped backward and kept moving, watching the great cat-thing slurp the remnants of Ramses' arm as it approached the crouched woman.

In the throes of these final moments, Ravenwood believed he understood: It all came down to Lily's innocence or rather its loss. It spewed of springtime grass; butterflies; a ball of yarn; a child's laugh…an elation so grand, so unfettered that there was no feasible reason for these people to have stolen it, and yet they did.

Lily's jaws widened, cranking inch by inch, as Kincaid's head rose. That was all Ravenwood needed to see or know…

A short while thereafter, between the distant cypresses, he witnessed the rainbow sea roll, splashing hard, burning the grass and weed, eliminating all that dared to exist within its vehement reach.

Ravenwood bowed his head, closed his eyes. He would rest—a calm, empirical rest—though for only as long as he could replenish his mettle. His mission, after all, was not over yet…

EPILOGUE

He awoke feeling rested enough to wander the Louisiana outskirts, tending to mundane tasks, like checking his Luger's bullets and his wallet for funds (thank goodness Ramses had not left him bare). He was also glad to find his train ticket home and gave the interns' portraits one last, mournful glance, lingering the most on Miss Scott. He then used his torn shirt to swathe his lacerated chest, after yanking a halfway decent one from some trash he had passed...

He still had his camera and samples, thank Shiva, all intact and ready for analysis. It was odd Ramses had not taken them, but then, Ravenwood supposed, they were intended to dissolve, along with all aspects of his person, upon the estate's rigged destruction. In any event, he was pleased with what he had, and indeed, chemical and photographic evidence would act as worthy supplements for the account, even if such failed to cover all bases...

On this basis, he decided to stroll back to the estate, or rather what was left of it. He figured he could still gather some buffering details, of which he could also share with the Nameless One, whether through another swift, intangible swap or face to face; and later present the lump sum to Sterling for their paranormal files, in the event something comparable should ever arise.

However, by the time he returned to the fetid fringes, a decent crowd had already gathered, consisting mainly of police, some of whom wandered about the cloudy, discolored foundation, while others ensured that no commoner entered: each man a perplexed, ersatz Stagg, pinching his nose to dispel the lingering miasma, meaning well, but ingenuous to the cause.

On the outer cusp, several locals stood, and among them Ravenwood decided to mingle...

"...An explosion—that's what it was," a craggy, old gent said to a pot-bellied teen in overhauls, both waving their hands before their faces. "Think it was some sort of medical facility. Heaps of strange stuff going on there or so folks say. I suppose it was only a matter of time before—kapow."

A bleary lady of dowdy dress scooted over to them, her voice drawn and raspy. "They shouldn't keep such places so close to where people live. I'm surprised no one was killed."

"How do ya know no one wasn't?" the old gent said. "Who could survive somethin' like that?"

"That's right," said the pot-bellied boy. "Just look at it—scorched all the grass and trees 'round here. Ain't nothin' left of that big, ol' house. Had to be somethin' mighty fierce to do that."

Ravenwood nodded as he passed them, his eyes a disconsolate, dark blue. He was now accustomed to the stench, but coughed to fit in, wandering back toward the inspectors and patrollers, listening further to their misguided theories and implausible speculations. Perhaps it was good they were at a loss. A substantial, acidic discharge would be the most acceptable justification and would work to explain the missing participants, including the interns, though it irked Ravenwood that he should embrace such "facts". On the other hand, considering the astounding nature of the truth (and that it would certainly be discounted as a lie), for the "record", what alternative was there?

When he was satisfied with the information he had collected (or rather the lack thereof), he decided to trudge to the station, but as he trekked the winding pass, something caught his eye: the posted cypress he had encountered on his way to the estate.

Standing before it was a solid man in hunting gear, cradling a bundled, golden-haired girl of about six or seven.

"We have to find her, Daddy," the girl sobbed, pointing to the crayoned image. "We have to..."

"We've been trying for a long time now, dear, each and every morn," the man said. "Things aren't looking very promising, Katie."

"But if we could go a little farther, Daddy..."

"This is as far as we go, dear. They say there was a bad accident yonder. The area might be tainted. We should go home." He pecked her cheek and pressed her close. "We'll get another kitty soon, I promise. Lord knows there are lots of them in these parts. I spotted a fine looking gray one not too far away. Maybe we can find him...coax him along. You can name him, too, if you want..."

The man set her down, took her hand, and into the distance they traveled, leaving Ravenwood to ruminate their exchange.

As he neared the tree, a fated breeze rustled the paper, adjusting its creased allocation: LOST CAT...PLEASE HELP...WE MISS HER...SHE IS WHITE...HAS ONE GREEN EYE...ONE BLUE...HER NAME IS LILY...

Ravenwood studied the crude, rain-speckled outline of the whiskered face, its quirky, little smile, its eyes colored accordingly with a stare that was innocent and curious, enigmatic and unwavering. He knew that face well: the heir-apparent Bastet, never meant to flourish.

With heavy heart, he forced himself onward, considering the correlation between lost animals, lost people, lost legends. Indeed, when they fell from view, the odds never favored their return. Pity, he thought, such was not the case this time…

The End

HOW MY CAT HELPED CREATE A RAVENWOOD MYSTERY

I miss my cat, Cody. She was all white, with one green eye, one blue. She departed our dimension in Spring 2017, the result of physical complications, but I still feel her presence. She was that special to me and my wife, Donna.

I use the pronoun "she" in default for Cody, for our beloved pet was a hermaphrodite, adopted under the claim of being male, but we later came to learn that our family's latest addition also possessed female traits. After an exploratory surgery and an accompanying alteration, Cody became more girl than boy. Her appearance and behavior were female, at least to our eyes.

Since I was having a tough time dealing with Cody's passing, my father suggested that I incorporate her into a story for therapeutic intent. I toyed with some ideas, but nothing felt quite right, until Ron Fortier suggested that my interest in the supernatural might be put to positive use in a story based on Frederick C. Davis' Ravenwood: Stepson of Mystery.

I familiarized myself with the character and discovered that Ravenwood was a kind of Carl Kolchak of his time, a pre X-Filer, with a decent dash of Marvel's Dr. Strange and DC's Dr. Fate woven into his mystique. In this regard, he also held a kinship with my creation, Michael Mansford, the Persona. Neat...

It then became a matter of whom, or what, to engage Ravenwood. Since my beloved cat lingered on my mind, I decided to fashion something to include her. I also had a desire to inject some traditional, creature elements into the story, which might cover mystical, psychological and scientific motifs.

As such, "Kincaid's House of Altered Cats" takes more than a few cues from Val Lewton's 1942 "Cat People" and its bold, Paul Schrader 1982 remake, where the macabre sensuality is presented with much broader strokes: a technique I decided to use for my own rendering, though with some constraint.

There's also an "Island of Dr. Moreau" element in the tale, as well as one of its popular, cinematic knockoffs, "Terror is a Man" (aka, "Blood Creature", which became the basis for Independent International Picture's

"Blood Island" franchise). In addition, there is a heaping of "Konga", "Re-Animator" and "Sssssss" woven into the tapestry, which I am confident horror fans will recognize and appreciate.

I also added some magic to the plot, to counter its science fiction. In this respect, Kincaid's sibylline partner, Ramses (a nod to H.G. Lewis' "Blood Feast" antagonist) stands in contrast to Kincaid's methodical, monster maker. Nevertheless, it was important that when push came to shove, the villains craved the same, abhorrent result: a cat-people conquest!

To me, the story's colorful hodgepodge, anchored by a hybrid grappling with internal and external changes, makes it extra pulpy, but at its core, the account is still one of a lost pet and in that respect, a lost life and lost innocence.

I cannot claim that my Ravenwood contribution has made me feel any better for losing Cody. Perhaps, if only due to the story's finale and epilogue, I've come to miss her all the more. At least my weird tale stands in defiance of my lament, and with that maybe, just maybe, I have given Ravenwood readers something to enjoy. I do hope that is the case and trust even more so that dear Cody is looking down, purring her approval.

MICHAEL F. HOUSEL - resides in Trenton, NJ with his wife, Donna. He has written two novels for Airship 27 Productions: "The Persona, Vol 1: Enter—the Persona!" and its sequel, "The Persona, Vol 2: Green-Fleshed Fiends". Airship 27 has also published his novella, "The Hyde Seed": a boxing tale of strange and combative duality.

One can visit his musings on horror, science fiction and fantasy at … https://bizarrechats.blogspot.com/.